In this tempestuous new series, rebellious hearts prove hard to tame—but can England's most dangerous rake be captured by a wild Irish rose?

They call him Lord Ash, for his desires burn hot and leave devastation in their wake. But Gabriel Finch, Marquess of Ashborough, knows the fortune he's made at the card table won't be enough to save his family estate. For that he needs a bride with a sterling reputation to distract from his tarnished past, a woman who'll be proof against the fires of his dark passion. Fate deals him the perfect lady. So why can't Gabriel keep his eyes from wandering to her outspoken, infuriatingly independent Irish cousin?

Camellia Burke came to London as her aunt's companion, and she's brought a secret with her: she's written a scandalous novel. Now, her publisher demands that she make her fictional villain more realistic. Who better than the notorious Lord Ash as a model? Duty bound to prevent her cousin from making a disastrous match, Cami never meant to gamble her own heart away. But when she's called home, Ash follows. And though they're surrounded by the flames of rebellion, the sparks between them may be the most dangerous of all….

Also by Susanna Craig

The Runaway Desires Series:
To Kiss a Thief
To Tempt an Heiress
To Seduce a Stranger

The Companion's Secret

A Rogues & Rebels Novel

Susanna Craig

LYRICAL PRESS
Kensington Publishing Corp.
www.kensingtonbooks.com

LYRICAL PRESS BOOKS are published by

Kensington Publishing Corp.
119 West 40th Street
New York, NY 10018

Copyright © 2018 by Susan Kroeg

First Electronic Edition: April 2018
eISBN-13: 978-1-5161-0400-0
eISBN-10: 1-5161-0400-5

First Print Edition: April 2018
ISBN-13: 978-1-5161-0401-7
ISBN-10: 1-5161-0401-3

Printed in the United States of America

To Amy,
for listening, suggesting,
and most of all, believing—
from the very beginning

Acknowledgments

Many great people helped to make this book, and the Rogues & Rebels series, possible: Jill Marsal; Esi Sogah and the team at Kensington; my colleagues, students, and friends; my husband and daughter; and especially you, dear reader. Thank you.

Chapter 1

London, May 1798

Gabriel Finch, Marquess of Ashborough, played by his own rules—one of which was never to hold his cards during a game. A fan of cards amplified the movements of a man's hand: his nervousness, excitement, shock. Besides, staring at them had never yet forced the pips into a different configuration.

In response to the dealer's silent call, Gabriel squared the small stack lying on the table in front of him before turning over the topmost card. The gesture was quiet, efficient. Only reckless men proclaimed loudly when they had been beaten. Or when they won.

Like the fools at the far table, who had been making raucous demands all evening—of their dealer, the servants, the painted ladies employed to distract the cardplayers. Years of practice had proved insufficient to tune them out. Now, one man's voice pierced the miasma of smoke and sweaty desperation that hung over the gamblers like fog.

"You know I'm good for it," the familiar voice wheedled. "Or will be. Why, right this moment I could raise a mortgage on Stoke that would be worth ten times that pot."

Gabriel pushed away from the table and stood.

A footman hustled to his side, gathering his winnings, while the dealer praised his luck, subtly goading him to continue. The owners of this particular establishment used every trick in the book to encourage patrons to play longer than was wise. Good food, though not so rich that a man would feel drowsy. Plentiful drink, though not so much that a man would realize he was drunk. Painted windows and plush furnishings masked light and noise from the street, making it impossible to tell how many hours had passed. But there were always clues, if one knew where to look. Six-hour candles had dwindled to stubs. It must be nearly dawn.

Across the room, play continued. With a nod to the others at his table, who protested his departure with a mixture of groans, self-deprecating laughs, and sighs of relief, he took the bundle the servant handed him and was gone, his pocket bulging with scraps of paper—banknotes, vowels, and, if he was not mistaken, the deed to a square of land in some backwater shire.

The night had been a profitable one by any measure, but its most important gain had been intangible. Just a few words. *A mortgage on Stoke.* Interesting, very interesting. Would anyone take that bet?

Gabriel had been gambling too long to imagine the answer was anything but yes.

Damp air filled his lungs when he stepped into the dim, quiet street. As he had suspected, the hour was late—rather, early—enough that the girls who called to him from beneath the arcades of Covent Garden offered nothing more than moldering fruit. He paused to drop a handful of coins into the outstretched palm of a waif who in another week would surely be offering herself in place of the desiccated orange she pressed into his hand in return.

With a roguish smile, he tossed the fruit into the air, caught it, handed it back to the half-starved, wide-eyed girl, and resumed walking. A gamble, yes.

Why, he was tempted to lay a little wager himself.

When he reached his rooms in St. James's, his manservant, Arthur Remington, opened the door and held out his hand for his master's greatcoat. Instead of shedding the garment, Gabriel reached into his breast pocket and withdrew the wad of notes. Warily, Remington took the lot, looking as if he expected the papers to reek of brimstone. Perhaps they did. Gabriel had grown inured to that particular scent.

As Gabriel moved toward his study door, Remington spoke. "You'll find Mr. Fox inside, my lord." A smirk of satisfaction edged the man's voice.

Of late, Christopher Fox had been urging Gabriel toward pursuits that involved sunlight and fresh air and other things he generally avoided. His friend's well-meant interference had kept him from sliding headfirst into hell years ago, and for that he was mostly grateful. But nothing would keep him safe forever.

Gabriel's final destination was assured.

"Ah. Coffee, then, Remy," he called grimly over his shoulder. "A vat of it."

"Very good, my lord." This time, the smirk reached Remy's eyes.

Dressed for riding, Fox stood with his back to the door, perusing the bookcase. "Isn't it time you settled down and gave up these larks, Ash?" he asked without turning.

"Oh, Foxy. Only you would call my gaming and wenching 'larks.'" Gabriel's skill at the tables—and elsewhere, for that matter—was the stuff of legend.

"What's this?" Fox plucked a book from the shelf and turned with a flourish. "A guide to the peerage? Surprised to find you in possession of such a thing, Ash."

Snatching the battered volume from his friend's grasp, Gabriel settled into the buttery-soft leather of the chair closest to the window. "Is it so strange that from time to time a man would wish to recall the history of his family?"

"You?" Fox tilted his head and his gray eyes narrowed with interest. "Yes."

Gabriel dropped his gaze to the book, whose broken spine had flopped open on his knee, evidence that certain passages had received a great deal of study. Intersecting lines crossed the paper, resembling less a family tree than a scrub or a stump. He felt conspicuous on the page, which contained not only his name, but also the date of his mother's death—or his own birth, if one would have it so. The final entry was the date he had assumed the marquessate, the date of his father's untimely relinquishment of it. At the top of the page the name of the family seat was set off from the rest by italic type: *Stoke Abbey, Shrops.*

Many would insist that an estate and its people could suffer no graver misfortune than the infamous Lord Ash's inheritance of it. Gabriel was inclined to agree. But would those naysayers change their tune if they too had chanced to overhear a few words exchanged at a neighboring card table?

For all his sins, at least Gabriel had never attempted to gamble his legacy away.

"I happened to catch my cousin Julian in the act of laying a rather extraordinary bet," he said, "against the value of his future inheritance."

"But your uncle's estate is said to be mortgaged to the hilt already." Fox took up the chair opposite.

"Not my uncle's estate." With one fingertip, he traced the line that joined his father's name to his only brother's equally short branch of the family tree. "Mine. It seems he has been gallivanting around town styling himself as my heir presumptive."

Remington chose that moment to appear with a tray and placed it on the table between them. Beside the silver coffeepot and two cups in saucers lay the papers Gabriel had brought home, now smoothed and neatly stacked.

"Only one way I know of to prevent it, Ash," Fox said as he accepted a steaming cup from Remy.

"Oh, and how's that?"

"Why...*marry.*" For some time now, Fox had been hinting that a woman of impeccable birth could help restore Gabriel to the bright and airy sociability of the ton after a lifetime spent in the more comfortable darkness of the demimonde. With an expression caught between coaxing and condemnation, he added, "Rumor has it you've a way with the ladies."

This, Gabriel could hardly deny. From somewhere, he mustered a laugh. "With *women*, old friend," he amended. "Never ladies."

Reluctant amusement danced in Fox's eyes. "Well, I wouldn't think too much on a bit of bragging at the tables. Julian Finch is little more than a foolish puppy—"

"Once, I would have agreed with you. But the man I saw last night...?" Gabriel shook his head, recalling the note of desperation in his cousin's voice.

To Gabriel, Stoke Abbey was the most haunted dwelling place in England, a status that had nothing at all to do with the ghosts of long-departed monks and nuns. Since his childhood, he had spent no time there. But he had never truly abandoned it. Did he mean to do so in the end?

Perhaps Fox had the right of it. Perhaps it was time to think less of his past and more of his posterity.

Marriage to a lady of spotless reputation would—well, not *repair* Gabriel's standing as a gentleman, for that implied it had some prior existence, but *establish* it. A proper bride, a place in society, and an heir apparent in due course...his uncle would choke on the news. Ten years ago, it would have been insufficient punishment for all the man had done to him. Now, however, he saw an elegant simplicity in taking such an ordinary form of revenge.

There was only one problem. No decent young woman or her family would willingly form an alliance with him, despite his wealth and title. Fox knew it. And so did his uncle and cousin. In fact, they had obviously been counting on it.

Absently, he laid aside the book and picked up the pile of notes instead. Pausing over one particular piece of paper, he rubbed its edge between thumb and forefinger. Julian was not the only fool who had played too deep last night. "Tell me, Foxy," Gabriel said after a long moment, "what do you know of the Earl of Merrick?"

"A true gentleman, by all accounts. They say he's a force to be reckoned with in the Lords, though too Whiggish in his votes for my father's taste." Fox snatched the guide to the peerage from the arm of Gabriel's chair and flipped through its pages. "Here you go," he said, turning and proffering the open book. "The Trenton family. Of Derbyshire."

Gabriel accepted the book but did not look at the page Fox indicated. "As it happens, I'm somewhat acquainted with Merrick's...situation. Substantial properties in Wales and Northumberland, in addition to the Derbyshire estate. All entailed. One son, Lord Trenton, who was sent down from Cambridge last autumn and has since run up debts all over town."

"Some of them to you, my lord," Remington interjected as he poured Gabriel's coffee. "If all those little scraps of paper you bring home are to be believed."

Gabriel raised his eyes to his servant. "Collect the rest for me, will you, Remy?" Once more he handed over the bundle of papers, this time in exchange for the cup.

"You want a tally of the young man's debts?" Remington asked, not a trace of surprise in his voice.

Of indeterminate age and uncertain origins, Arthur Remington was not the typical gentleman's gentleman. Gabriel had a vague notion that Remy had spent some time in the army, for he could spit-polish boots to a mirror shine but had no patience for the intricacies of a well-tied cravat. Whatever his history, it had supplied the man with a host of far more useful skills, one of which was the ability to wrest information from even the most unwilling.

"Not a tally," Gabriel said. "The debts themselves." In a matter of days, Merrick's son—why, the earl himself—would be his to command.

One grizzled eyebrow arched, but the man gave a crisp bow. "Yes, sir."

"Merrick also has a daughter, has he not?" Gabriel asked almost before Remington had shut the door behind him.

"Er...ye-es." Hesitation rippled Fox's voice. "Pretty girl. Had her come-out last spring. Expected to make a brilliant match, until—"

"Until her brother gambled away her dowry," Gabriel finished for him.

Fox eyed him uncertainly. "What are you about, Ash?"

One last gamble. "Were you not just suggesting I marry? I'm arranging a...well, let us call it an introduction to Lady Felicity Trenton."

Fox's brows dove downward, shadowing his eyes. "Surely even you are aware there are more conventional ways to meet proper young ladies."

As a general rule, Gabriel cared very little for either convention or proper young ladies. Sometimes, however, a tiger might be forced to change his stripes. "In the face of certain social realities, a man must on occasion resort to cleverness to get what he wants…er, needs." The Earl of Merrick was a respected member of the peerage. So respected that, had his son not driven the family to the brink of ruin, he would never have permitted Gabriel even to speak his daughter's name. "When Merrick learns I hold all his son's debts," Gabriel said, "he will be glad enough to accept whatever terms of repayment I offer."

"And Lady Felicity's hand is to be your price." Fox chewed each word and, by his sour expression, apparently found them difficult to digest.

Closing the guide with a snap, Gabriel traced the deckled edges of the paper with the tips of his fingers, as if neatening a stack of playing cards, a gesture his adversaries at the table had come to recognize as the sign that their loss was about to become Lord Ash's gain.

"For the price I'm paying, I'll expect rather more than her hand."

Those words were met with a scowl of disapproval. "I can only pray that Lady Felicity will discover you've the heart of a gentleman after all."

Gabriel, who possessed no such organ, doubted it.

Fox was right about one thing, though. Lady Felicity Trenton was probably a fresh-faced innocent, a sacrificial lamb to be led quite literally to the altar. Hell, he was counting on it.

A wiser woman would not have him.

* * * *

Although there had been no knock of warning, Camellia Burke managed to slide her papers beneath her blotter as the door to her bedchamber swung open, the protest of one squeaky hinge alerting her to an intruder. And to think she had imagined that a position as her aunt's companion would afford her more privacy than she'd had at home with her family in Dublin.

"Oh, there you are, miss," exclaimed Betsy, the upstairs maid, sounding relieved to have found her, although Cami could not imagine where else the girl might have looked. "Her ladyship wants you in the drawing room right away."

"The drawing room?" She paused in the act of cleaning her pen. "Did she say why?" The Countess of Merrick was at home to callers today, a circumstance which generally earned Cami a reprieve from her duties.

"No, miss. But whatever it is, it's got her ladyship out of sorts. Won't you come, miss?" Betsy urged.

Cami corked her ink bottle before rising from her chair and following the maid through the door. Aunt Merrick had proved surprisingly generous with writing supplies, but one could never be too careful.

In the drawing room, Lady Merrick sat in the middle of a brocade settee, flanked on one side by her fat pug and on the other by her daughter, Felicity.

"Camellia. At last," Lady Merrick murmured reprovingly. She did not like to be kept waiting. Felicity gave a welcoming, if nervous, smile.

Cami approached, curtsied, and, at her aunt's nod of acknowledgment, perched on the edge of one of the elegantly uncomfortable chairs facing her.

"We have a visitor."

A caller hardly seemed cause for consternation, and no cause at all for summoning Cami. Unless... "Someone of my acquaintance, ma'am?"

Aunt Merrick pressed her lips together and shook her head. "No. A gentleman. Of sorts." The dog lifted his head from her lap and studied his mistress, as if his curiosity too had been piqued. "Lord Ash—that is, the Marquess of Ashborough."

Lord Ash? Her aunt was a notorious stickler for rank. What could be the cause of this unaccustomed familiarity—familiarity that bordered on insolence? Was the marquess still a boy? Or old and infirm?

"Merrick has given him permission to call upon Felicity." The quirk of her lips might have been pleasure or displeasure. Perhaps a mixture of both. She clearly disapproved of this Lord Ashborough, but not enough to refuse the possibility that her daughter might one day be a marchioness.

"And beggars, it seems, are not to be choosers," Felicity added sotto voce.

Cami darted her gaze to her cousin, whose cheeks looked unnaturally pink. She was half-persuaded the color must have been put there by the contents of a rouge pot. At those last, quiet words, however, it leeched from Felicity's cheeks, leaving her pale.

Felicity's beauty had never failed to earn her admirers. Last year, in her first season, it had even afforded her the power of refusal, as Aunt Merrick often found occasion to remind anyone who would listen. Felicity had been encouraged by her mama to decline two offers under the perfectly reasonable assumption that better ones would be made in future. This spring, however, shadowed by her brother's looming debts and her consequent loss of dowry, Felicity's loveliness had seemed in danger of proving an insufficient lure.

But of course, a man might require something other than a fortune from his bride.

"Lord Ash is accompanied by his friend, Mr. Fox. A younger son of the Earl of Wickersham, I'm told."

Felicity offered a quick nod of confirmation. "And you are never shy around strangers, Cousin Camellia."

"Felicity suggested your conversation might be a welcome addition to their visit."

More an order than an offer, and Cami knew better than to refuse, although it meant squandering her precious personal time on pointless chatter. Fighting the temptation to allow her shoulders to sag, she straightened her spectacles instead. "If you wish it, Aunt."

If she had not known better, she might have suspected her cousin of matchmaking. The younger son of an earl would be quite a catch for a lady's companion. But Cami had more important things to do than dangle her bait in the water, waiting for some man to snatch at the lure. She would have to rise an hour earlier tomorrow to make up the writing time she lost today.

Before another word could be spoken, Wafford, the butler, tapped at the door. As it swung inward on silent hinges to admit the visitors, Felicity's blue eyes flooded with dread and her face grew paler still. Instinctively, she reached up to pinch her cheeks and restore the color to them.

With the protective reflexes of an eldest sister, Cami leaned forward and caught her fingers before they could inflict any more damage. When she heard booted steps on the carpet behind her, she gave Felicity's hand a squeeze of encouragement and rose to leave the chair closest to her cousin for the marquess. Felicity clung to her a moment longer than expected, making Cami stumble. If strong fingers had not caught her elbow, she would have pitched headfirst into her aunt's lap.

The pug growled out a warning, and Cami jerked upright. The stranger's touch fell away before she could decide it was unwelcome. A sideways glance gave her an impression of brown hair, brown eyes. Neither a spotted youth nor an octogenarian. Rather, a man her own age, perhaps thirty. One with the sharp, almost cruel features she had come to associate with the English nobility.

She dipped into a hurried, clumsy curtsy. "I thank you, sir—er, Lord Ash," she corrected, then remembered herself. "Borough."

The belated addition did not escape his notice. Thin lips curved in what countless women no doubt fancied a warm, amiable smile, though it did not reach his eyes. "I am glad to have been of service, ma'am." His bow of acknowledgment was perfectly correct, yet somehow it managed to convey something else, something more. Something that made Cami flush in spite of herself.

"Merrick's niece, Miss Burke." Annoyance made her aunt's introduction blunt. "And of course this is my daughter, Lady Felicity Trenton."

Both gentlemen made their bows of greeting to her cousin while Cami walked stiffly to the farthest chair.

"May I present Mr. Christopher Fox," Lord Ashborough said.

"Lady Merrick, Lady Felicity," Mr. Fox said with another bow. "Miss Burke."

At a nod from her mother, Felicity gestured for Lord Ashborough to take the seat Cami had vacated and attempted to engage him in conversation. Without waiting to be invited, Mr. Fox chose the chair nearest Cami. He was not quite as tall as his friend, with sandy-brown hair and pale eyes.

"It is a pleasure to meet you, Mr. Fox."

"And you, Miss Burke," he said, pulling his gaze from Felicity. Although his appreciation of her cousin was as undisguised as any man's, it was far less practiced; at least, he was well mannered enough not to display disappointment that his lot had fallen to the companion. As a means of assessing a man's character, it was not much to go on, but Cami decided in his favor nonetheless.

Before she could speak again, however, her thoughts were interrupted by a snippet of the others' conversation.

"Lady Montlake's ball?" Her cousin sounded as if the event was quite unfamiliar to her, although Cami recalled having received the card a week or more ago. "I don't know...."

"Oh? I understood from your father that you planned to attend."

The merest hint of reproach edged Lord Ashborough's velvety baritone. Lady Merrick spoke sharply, with a scowl for her daughter. "Of course we do. We will account it a pleasure to see you there, my lord."

"Ah, wonderful. Then I insist on being allowed to claim a set, Lady Felicity." Lord Ashborough's voice dropped lower still, the tone of a lover coaxing a promise.

Felicity swallowed visibly, as if words of refusal had risen in her throat but dared not be spoken. Poor girl. "I—I would be honored, your lordship," she forced herself to say.

The contrarian in Cami wondered *why* beggars must be expected to forgo the dignity of choice. And why women were so often required to beg.

"A beautiful day, is it not?" Mr. Fox ventured.

Realizing she had been caught eavesdropping, Cami turned squarely toward him. She had been dragged here for her conversation, so converse she would. And if Aunt Merrick did not like the tenor of her questions, so be it. *Someone* had to ask them.

"How long have you known Lord Ashborough, Mr. Fox?" She felt uncomfortably aware of the man of whom she spoke, although he had not looked in her direction since she had sat down.

Mr. Fox warmed immediately to her choice of subject. "Oh, always, it seems. We met at school." The wistful note in his voice called up an image of a boy beloved by all, bestowing the favor of his friendship on the less fortunate. But his next words whisked Cami's mental picture away. "Ash was so terribly alone. So terribly miserable." He gave a slow shake of his head. "I had my elder brothers to look after me, and so I—well, I took it upon myself to look after Ash."

Even with the imagination of an artist, Cami was unequal to the task of envisioning a young Lord Ashborough shunned by his peers and a boyish Mr. Fox as his champion. "Have you sisters too, Mr. Fox?" she managed to ask. "Or only a surfeit of brothers?"

A wrinkle of uncertainty creased his brow at her turn of phrase, but his gray eyes sparked with good humor. "One sister, Miss Burke. Two brothers. All older than I, all married—and all quite eager to offer their opinions as a consequence. Especially the eldest," he added, "although my sister Victoria gives him a run for it. And you?"

"Three sisters, Mr. Fox, and two brothers. All younger. And I am quite sure, were they here, they would tell you I am the very model of a managing, opinionated eldest sister," she added, nudging her spectacles up to the bridge of her nose to underscore the point.

Mr. Fox smiled and glanced toward her cousin. "You are fortunate in Lady Felicity's company, then, or else you would miss them more than you already must. Are they all still in—in Ireland, then?"

She nodded. Despite her aunt's repeated…*recommendation,* she'd made no effort to disguise the telling lilt in her voice. "In Dublin, yes. My father is a solicitor there." Another detail Lady Merrick would have preferred her to hide; the notion of having a brother-in-law who worked for his living seemed to distress her.

Mr. Fox nodded sagely, no hint of the familiar disdain in his expression. "I think sometimes that my father might have preferred I take up the law. It seems a surer route to public distinction."

She found herself softening toward the man. She had not fully considered that even an earl's son might have to train to some profession, if he had not the good fortune to be the eldest. "My brother seems to imagine it has a bit of glamor in it," she acknowledged with a wry smile. And if it did not, then Paris—who was both too handsome and too clever for his own good—was determined to supply some.

"More so than the Church, certainly."

The Church? "An honorable profession—provided one has a vocation," she managed to say, struggling to imagine the circumstances under which this warmhearted, would-be clergyman willingly spent time with the kind of man who imagined a bride could be bought like a side of beef.

"Oh, indeed. I would not enter orders lightly, ma'am. I assure you, I understand the duties of a clergyman. I don't mind the thought of getting my hands dirty to save a few souls." Whether consciously or unconsciously, his eyes darted toward his friend. Did that explain the connection between them? Did he imagine Lord Ash had a soul worth saving?

Despite her hesitation about his choice of friends, she believed he was sincere in his calling. "But you are not yet ordained." One glance at his clothing revealed as much. Not the somber, dark garb of a clergyman, though more subdued than Lord Ash's expensively embroidered waistcoat.

"No. I have as yet had no cause. I have the promise of my family's living, of course. But—"

"The incumbent is proving regrettably long lived?" she supplied wryly.

This time, Mr. Fox laughed out loud, undeniably amused by her frank way of speaking. "I suppose one might put it that way, Miss Burke."

Out of the corner of her eye, she saw Lord Ashborough turn toward the sounds of their merriment. "I feel I must warn you, Miss Burke. Fox is unused to such attention. You will have him in love with you before you know it."

Something unfamiliar and unsettling gleamed in the marquess' eyes as he leveled his gaze on his friend. *Jealousy.* He was patently unaccustomed to being anything other than the center of attention.

"I say, Ash, that's not—" blustered Mr. Fox. His slight frown of disappointment made Cami think of her youngest brother's expression whenever the older boys had refused to play by the rules of whatever game had been chosen.

But Lord Ashborough ignored him and shifted his attention to her. "Are you enjoying your time in London, Miss Burke?"

He spoke as if she were here on holiday, and although it was not quite as irritating as the strangers who admonished her to be grateful to her aunt for her generosity, she bristled nonetheless.

"But of course she is," her aunt assured him before Cami could tame her tongue into a suitable reply. "Who in her position would not? She might still be in Ireland!"

Memories flashed across Cami's mind like tiny, devastating lightning strikes: The letter from Mama's brother relating the grim news of their father's death. Papa shooing the younger children from the room. Mama's angry, tearless sobs. The new Lord Merrick's hope that the past could now be put behind them. And an unexpected olive branch: a place for one of his nieces should she be willing to come to England.

Impatient to be where literary fame was made and broken, Cami had been quick to accept the offer.

Perhaps too quick.

"Och, aye," she tossed back in the closest thing to a brogue her furious tongue could manage. "'Tis certain I'd never be after meetin' an English lord on Grafton Street."

At the sight of her mother's disapproving frown, Felicity swallowed her hiccup of laughter. Mr. Fox developed a sudden interest in the pattern of the Turkish carpet beneath his feet.

Only Lord Ashborough met Cami's gaze. She caught flickers of gold and green in his dark eyes. Hazel. Not brown. And sleepy though they might seem, those eyes missed nothing. His languid smile and penetrating gaze sent a strange little pulse of uncertainty through her chest.

She felt uncomfortably transparent, as if that one glance had uncovered all her secrets.

Not that she had many secrets to hide.

Just the one, really.

Lord Ashborough bowed his head once more, and glints of copper shown in his brown hair as it swept forward to obscure his expression, though not before she caught a glimmer of amusement and, perhaps, approval there. "The pleasure, Miss Burke, is all mine."

The snap of Lady Merrick's fan prevented Cami's reply. Although she could still hear the echo of her foolish words in her burning ears, everyone else seemed determined to behave as if she had not spoken them.

"I wonder whether it will be fine again tomorrow?" Mr. Fox asked conversationally, returning to safer ground, the color in his cheeks the only indication of his dismay at her behavior.

But Cami could not shake the feeling that she had played right into Lord Ashborough's hand—and that alarmed her. When the others had returned to their conversation, she said, "Mr. Fox, may I ask you a question?"

He shifted slightly in his chair. "A gentleman may never refuse a lady, Miss Burke."

Although her claim to such a distinction was dubious, she pressed forward. "You said you befriended Lord Ashborough when he was alone and miserable. What had happened to make him so?"

Mr. Fox paled and his darting gray glance took in both Felicity and his friend. "Do you mean to say you do not know?"

She bit her lip and shook her head. "Please, Mr. Fox. If he is not an appropriate acquaintance for my cousin to cultivate, surely you—as a man of God—must see that it's only fitting to reveal what you know." The plea was driven by concern—concern mixed with an unaccustomed degree of plain curiosity.

Without denying the truth of her claim, Mr. Fox nonetheless hesitated. "The boys at school gave Ash a wide berth, Miss Burke. Most people still do." He lifted his chin warningly, but his voice was so low she had to lean forward to hear him. "You see, when he was just ten years old, he killed his father."

Chapter 2

Gabriel could tell by the expression on Miss Burke's face just what Fox must have said to her.

He did not blame his friend for revealing that horrible truth about his past. Fox was unfailingly honest, and he would never have had it any other way.

Besides, everyone already knew what he had done.

No, if there was blame to be cast, it ought to fall squarely on Lady Merrick's shoulders—she who must have known what lay at the root of his ruined reputation and said nothing to warn her niece. Perhaps not even her daughter, though the girl looked nothing short of terrified of him.

Then again, Lady Merrick was still quite young. Just past forty, he guessed. Fair and lovely, like her daughter, she herself might have been the object of his attention under different circumstances. She would not have been the first neglected wife with whom he had amused himself during the Season. Perhaps the countess really did not know what he had done. Perhaps the decade or more of scandal surrounding him had at long last created a cloud that obscured his original sin—though nothing could blot it out entirely, to be sure.

Abruptly, he rose from his chair. "You will excuse me, Lady Felicity. Fox and I are in danger of overstaying our welcome. We should go."

She murmured an obligatory protest that sounded to him more like a sigh of relief. "So soon?"

What in God's name was he doing here? Was he really the sort of man who destroyed the blush of some innocent blossom for his own base needs?

But of course, the answer was yes. He had been destroying the guiltless since the hour of his birth, after all.

So he smiled into her wide, worried eyes and asked, "If the weather stays fair, Lady Felicity, would you be disposed to join me for a stroll in the park tomorrow at four?"

As was proper, she glanced at her mother. "Felicity will be only too happy to go, my lord," the countess confirmed. Merrick had assured him that both his wife and daughter would happily accede to his wishes, whatever they were. But then, as if to spite that promise, Lady Merrick added, "Miss Burke will accompany her." Underscoring his mistress' lazy-sounding drawl, her pug lifted his head from her lap and yawned until his tongue curled and his mouth stretched in a wide grin.

The very last thing Gabriel needed was a clumsy spinster peering at him disapprovingly over her spectacles while he attempted to win over Lady Felicity. Not that his victory was in doubt. But Merrick had asked him, "as a gentleman," to take a few days to court the girl before making her an offer, to make her feel as if she were something more than a pawn, as if she had some choice in the matter. The novelty of the request, of the notion that anyone might imagine him to be a gentleman, had caught Gabriel off his guard, and he had assented to Merrick's request without thinking the matter through.

Now, given what she had just been told, would he have to win over Miss Burke as well?

The woman in question leaped to her feet and preceded the men to the door, her light step and lithe figure insufficiently disguised by the sort of ugly, ill-fitting dress that lady's companions—or rather, the ladies who employed them—seemed to favor. In the hallway, she lifted their hats one by one from the table where some other servant had laid them.

"Will you be joining us tomorrow, Mr. Fox?" she asked, not meeting Gabriel's eye.

"If you wish it, ma'am."

"My wishes are never consulted on such matters," she replied with a shake of her head. Heavy raven locks threatened to spill from the pins that only just managed to contain them. With her black hair and bright eyes, she was really quite striking, albeit in a thoroughly un-English way.

"Perhaps they should be," Gabriel said. As he reached for his hat, his gloved fingertips brushed her bare ones where they held the brim. Lady Felicity would have flinched at the contact. Miss Burke did not.

With a tip of his head, Gabriel turned to accompany Fox out the door. On the threshold he glanced over his shoulder, but Miss Burke's gaze had not followed them. She was speaking quietly to a footman, who handed over some piece of correspondence—not on a tray, as would have been proper, but surreptitiously, as if the note contained something she would not want others to see.

"Lady Felicity does not disappoint, I trust?" Fox asked when they reached the bottom of the steps.

"She is precisely what I expected her to be."

A perfect specimen of English womanhood. Replete with china doll charms—golden ringlets, rather vacant blue eyes. And young. Very young. She would be biddable, he had been assured. A virtuous Sophie to his jaded, world-weary Emile.

But young, biddable ladies had never been Gabriel's style.

"You, on the other hand, must have thoroughly shocked her," Fox scolded. "I must say, your society manners could use a bit of polish. Your behavior toward her cousin, for instance. Why, one supposes Miss Burke is little more than a poor relation."

A poor relation. Overlooked, in other words. Disregarded.

Vulnerable.

"Her position in the household no doubt entirely dependent upon her aunt's sufferance." Fox's rebuke was gaining momentum. "And you all but called her a flirt—!"

Gabriel lifted one brow, assessing the tone as much as the words themselves. It was in Fox's nature to play the knight to a damsel in distress. But if her conduct in the drawing room was any guide, Miss Burke seemed to have more in common with the dragon in that tale. So was Fox defending her, or himself?

Although his behavior could hardly be described as flirtatious, the simple fact remained that Fox usually tended toward a rather wooden demeanor around young women. Not, of course, that Miss Burke was precisely *young.*

"You will walk with us tomorrow, I hope?" Gabriel asked, echoing her invitation. "The lady in question seemed to desire it." He needed a way to distract and divert Miss Burke. Fox would do admirably. When he did not immediately reply, Gabriel pushed further. "What say you, Foxy? Shall you court the dark Irish cousin whilst I woo the fair English one?"

Fox blushed—*blushed!*—and shook his head. "Miss Burke is rather too sharp for a dull fellow such as myself." He walked a few steps, then added, without a hint of slyness, "I should think her more suited to someone like you."

An hour past, Gabriel would have laughed and said that a woman of a certain age who hid behind frumpy dresses and wire-rimmed spectacles was beneath his notice. But he could hardly deny that she had caught his attention. In his mind's eye, he saw Merrick's footman slipping that illicit piece of correspondence into her hands.

What else was she trying to hide?

Fox made a show of digging his watch from his waistcoat and starting in surprise at the information revealed on its face. "Goodness, look at the time. I must get home and change. I'm for Victoria's tonight."

So Fox hoped to avoid further discussion of what had just transpired? His reluctance suited Gabriel just fine. "Ah, another of Lady Dalrymple's interminable dinner parties," he drawled. "Do thank her for sparing me an invitation."

It was a joke, of course. No one ever invited Gabriel anywhere.

With a rather guilty nod, Fox took his leave. Gabriel watched him walk in the direction of South Audley Street, though his mind was still elsewhere.

One encounter with Miss Burke's sharp green eyes and even sharper Irish tongue had shown him a glimpse of a worthy adversary, and worthy adversaries were in short supply these days. He had grown rather weary of besting unworthy ones.

At this very moment, she was probably cautioning her cousin against him, relaying what Fox had confessed, making his life difficult. But every opponent he had ever faced had a weakness, and tomorrow's walk in the park would give him a chance to learn hers.

He would find a way to reveal the companion's secret and turn it to his advantage.

* * * *

"You asked me to keep an eye on the post, miss." Curiosity was etched into the second footman's face.

"Thank you, Tom." Cami had given him almost the last coin in her purse to keep him from revealing what he knew, but now she wondered if keeping her secret would prove too much for him at last. She reached for the letter he was holding, hoping her fingers would not tremble and betray her nervousness. As she touched the pressed paper, she saw the red seal but refused to glance at the direction for fear she would see a hand she knew—Papa's, or perhaps her sister's.

The young footman nodded his acknowledgment and returned to his post, but not before offering a cautious smile and words of encouragement. "Good luck, miss."

Not trusting her voice, Cami smiled weakly back, then hurried up the stairs to her bedchamber, clutching the letter against her breast.

Her name had *not* been written by a familiar hand. And she could tell from the postmark that the letter had been mailed within the city. She knew very well who must have sent it and the inevitable rejection it must contain. Still, she hesitated to open it, staring at the letter on her palm as if sheer dint of will could revise its contents.

"What foolishness," she scolded herself after a moment. Settling atop her bed, one leg tucked beneath her, she turned the letter over, slid a fingernail beneath the wax seal, and lifted it. No point in delaying the inevitable.

As she unfolded the paper, her eyes were arrested by the letter's opening words:

> *Dear Miss Burke,*
> *I have read* The Wild Irish Rose *with great pleasure—*

"Great pleasure" did not *sound* like a rejection. Surely a man as busy as Mr. Dawkins would not take time to express the great pleasure he had felt in tossing her beloved manuscript onto the rubbish heap...would he?

> *—and believe others will do the same, the more so given*
> *its timely—and, if you will permit me, rather extraordinary—*
> *subject matter.*

"Extraordinary subject matter"? A euphemism, she supposed, for a woman's foray into the world of politics. But as women's opinions in such matters were so little valued otherwise, how else was Cami to speak if not through the pages of fiction? She returned her eyes to the letter.

> *However, as this novel purports to be a work of realism and*
> *not of the Gothic school, I must draw your attention to one flaw.*
> *I fear that a London audience will find your English villain*
> *wholly unbelievable, a caricature drawn out of Irish prejudice.*

Annoyance pricked along her spine. *Caricature?* Ha! That only meant she had succeeded in holding up a mirror before one Englishman's eyes. Now, if only she could force them all to recognize their reflection.

> *A man, even an Englishman, is rarely as unrelievedly bad*
> *as your Granville. Though it may seem to go against the moral*
> *of your tale, I assure you his failings will be more powerfully*
> *felt if he has been shown also to have some strengths. A faithful*

portrait must be drawn with light and shadow.

If you are willing to undertake these revisions, we are prepared to review the manuscript again, with an eye to purchasing it outright for publication. This is, as I am sure you are aware, quite a generous offer for an untried author.

Please indicate your intentions by return post.

Yours, &c.

Benjamin Dawkins, Jun.

The letter slipped from her trembling fingers and drifted down to the coverlet. Despite his reservations, Mr. Dawkins was willing to take the time and trouble to read her book again. He hoped to purchase it, to publish it! He would not say that if he did not have some confidence in its potential to succeed.

Unexpected tears sprang to her eyes, fogging her spectacles. All the sacrifices—rising early, scribbling frantically by the light of a candle before even the housemaids were awake; exchanging the green of Dublin for the grime of London; even leaving her family, wondering if she would ever see them again—would be worth it.

If she could find a way to render the despicable Lord Granville more believable, or at least more palatable, she would be an author.

But just how on earth was she going to manage *that?*

Without a knock of warning, the door to her room swung open. Cami hastily folded the letter and thrust it into the drawer of her bedside table.

Felicity wandered in and flopped onto the bed, not waiting to be invited. "Oh, Cousin Camellia," she sighed, a tremor in her voice, "Mama says I must marry Lord Ash."

Cami sat more upright. "Marry him?" Although the news was not entirely unexpected—in the Earl of Merrick's circle, unmarried gentlemen visited unmarried young ladies with a single goal in mind, after all—the speed with which the decision had been made alarmed her. She had never even heard the man's name mentioned before today.

"Papa has reached a—an understanding with him, it seems. Something about Stephen's debts."

Just yesterday, Uncle Merrick had lit out for Derbyshire with his wayward son in tow, muttering something about teaching him the meaning of "rustication." Did the arrangement with Lord Ash also have something to do with their sudden departure?

"Are you to have no say in the matter?"

A thin smile, followed by an almost imperceptible shake of her perfect blond ringlets. "You know Papa is too gentle to force me to do anything against my will. But Mama says if I accept Lord Ash, we are saved," Felicity said. "If I refuse him, we will be ruined. If he asks me, how can I say no?"

Heat flared in Cami's chest and spread through her body, warming even the tips of her ears. When the first flush of shock passed, it left her chilled. She struggled to find words of consolation. "Perhaps it will not be an intolerable match. He is rather…that is, he's very…" Arrogant? Sardonic? No, those would never do. She needed a description Felicity might actually want to hear. Finally, she settled on "…handsome."

Felicity's pert nose wrinkled. "Do you think so? But he's…why, he must be even older than you, Cousin. And he's so…dark."

Felicity could be forgiven for thinking of thirty as old, she supposed. But *dark?* The writer in Cami wanted to press for more specific adjectives, words that would leap off the page and belong only to Lord Ash. Hair the color of burnished mahogany wainscot that disguised a secret passageway, eyes the precise shade of the forest floor in early autumn. And a voice…but here Cami had to concede that *dark* suited the timbre of his deep voice—a fitting pitch for the dark, troubled soul to which it belonged, if Mr. Fox's story was to be believed.

"King says Lord Ash's reputation is quite as charred and sooty as his name," her cousin continued. "He is said to be a—a *rake*." The last word was little more than a scandalized whisper. Cami knew she ought to chide Felicity for repeating servants' gossip, but she could not bring herself to do it. Not with his friend's revelation still ringing in her own ears.

Despair at her cousin's predicament mingled uneasily with the elation Mr. Dawkins's letter had brought, leaving Cami feeling something she could never remember having felt before: light-headed. And at a distinct loss for words. Should she repeat what Mr. Fox had said? But if Felicity's fate was already sealed, what would be gained by frightening her cousin further?

Felicity spoke for her. "Is it…is it true, do you suppose, Cousin?"

Cami started. Well, Mr. Fox *had* spoken as if everyone else already knew what he had told her. Why, that meant even Uncle Merrick must have heard what Lord Ash was said to have done and was nevertheless willing to sacrifice his daughter to atone for his son's improvidence.

Anger rose like bile in her throat. "Is what true, dear?" she managed to ask.

Felicity's smile was still weak, but hopeful. "That reformed rakes make the best husbands. You know…like in the novels."

Biting back an automatic denial—along with a stern recommendation that her cousin read better books—Cami reached out to pat her cousin's icy fingers where they lay on the coverlet. "If it is, then you will be the happiest of brides, for even Lord Ash could not fail to be improved by a girl as sweet and gentle as you."

Felicity's laugh sounded surprisingly jaded. "If you were a man, Cousin, people would call you silver tongued. Mama says it must be your Irish blood."

Cami twisted her answering grimace into something approximating a smile. She was quite familiar with the qualities—the failings, rather—her aunt attributed to her Irish blood. This despite the fact that so little of it actually ran in her veins, her mother being entirely English and her father half so.

But Cami never denied being Irish. She was not ashamed of her origins, and no Englishwoman—*or man*, she added, thinking of Lord Ash's mocking expression—could make her so.

"Still," said Felicity, pushing to her feet, "I hope you're right. He makes me so terribly nervous. Oh, I *am* glad you'll be joining us tomorrow."

Tomorrow? Ah, yes. The stroll in the park. She had forgotten in the rush of excitement about the letter.

Papa had cautioned her against taking the post as her aunt's companion, insisting that there was bound to be more to the task than managing correspondence and reading bad novels aloud. But she had never imagined her role would extend to chaperoning a sweet but sometimes heedless girl of almost nineteen.

She would do it, of course. She had always felt a strong sense of duty to family—even the branch of her family of whose existence she had learned just a few months ago. It was not why she had come to London, but if Felicity's parents were too weak to stand up for their daughter, then she would have to be strong.

Lord Ash might have cowed her aunt and uncle into accepting his suit, but he had not reckoned on Camellia Burke.

"You have nothing to fear," she assured her cousin.

Besides, it's May. It will likely rain.

When Felicity left, Cami felt suddenly restless. Leaping from the bed, she made her way to the window. Far below, Brook Street was mostly empty. A nurse pushed a pram in the direction of the park, while the three older Bates children toddled behind her in a ragged line. A few houses up, a carriage waited to take Lady Mercer calling. And directly below, so close to the front of the house that he almost escaped her eye, the Marquess of Ashborough still leaned against the area railing.

At the far edge of her vision, nearly out of sight, she saw Mr. Fox striding up the street. Such a kind gentleman deserved a better friend than an outcast from society. A rake.

A *murderer.*

Her mind caught at the word. Lord Ash did not *look* like a murderer.

Not that she knew what a murderer looked like. She certainly could not recall having seen one before. At least, not to her knowledge. She knew from her father's stories that criminals could be quite deceptively charming. And the phrase "deceptively charming" fit Lord Ash all too well, she feared.

But he had been a boy when the alleged crime had occurred. Perhaps there was more to the story than Mr. Fox had related. There must be, else Lord Ashborough would not be—well, Lord Ashborough.

She was not so naïve as to believe that children were incapable of committing crimes, even heinous ones. But she suspected they usually had provocation—ill treatment, misguidance, desperate need. She did not hold with the popular notion that some children were simply born bad. Had his father been cruel? Or had it been a tragic accident?

Whatever the circumstances surrounding the terrible event in his childhood, she knew that if he had been born just a few miles to the east—in St. Giles, say, rather than Mayfair—he would have been hanged for what he had done, deliberate or not. Instead, he had paid an entirely different price. To have that sword dangling over one's head, always... Cami shook her head. No wonder a shadow clung to the man, even on this sunny day. What a terrible story it was.

Against the rough nap of the attic's curtains, her fingertips tingled. In the right hands, what a story it could be. Hurrying to her bedside table, Cami jerked open the drawer, snatched up her letter, and read it again.

Might Mr. Dawkins be right? She was not in the habit of considering men as terribly complex creatures. They rarely took the trouble to disguise their motives or their desires. But she supposed it was possible that her portrayal of the villain in *The Wild Irish Rose* left something to be desired. When she began the book, she had known no English noblemen on which to base Lord Granville. Now, however, she could draw from life....

She flew to her desk, snatched up a pencil, and began a rough sketch of Lord Ash's face. Thinking back over their exchange in the drawing room, she tried to capture his mien, the way a rake and a murderer dressed and walked and spoke. The way he called forth an ingénue's blush. The way he...

Good heavens—Felicity! Here she was mapping out a shocking work of fiction when a truly scandalous story was unfolding right in front of her. And if Lord Ash was a suitable model for the villain of her novel, then Felicity might pose for an equally convincing portrait of Róisín, its credulous heroine.

But if Cami spoke in her cousin's defense, what good would it do? After all, Aunt and Uncle Merrick had already given their consent to the man's courtship of their daughter, despite his reputation. *If only there were a way to protect Felicity and still acquire the information, the experience, I need to make Lord Ashborough's story my own....*

Then she remembered that walk in the park. Tomorrow, she would have an opportunity to begin a thorough character study of the man. If she was clever, she could use the information she gathered to convince her aunt and uncle to sever all connection to a man of Lord Ash's ilk. She would find a way to use his courtship of Felicity to expose the depths of the man's depravity.

And if it also happened to benefit her book, what harm could there be in it?

She paused to examine the picture she had drawn. Her skill with words had always far outstripped her abilities with lines and shading, and this effort was no exception. The portrait was, to use Mr. Dawkins's words, all shadow, no light. Lord Ashborough's eyes and hair were, well, *darker* than was strictly just, dark enough that her pulse quickened ever so slightly under the force of his scowl. He looked more menacing than she had intended. The real man was more... She hardly knew what word to apply. Sensual? Seductive?

Realizing she was in danger of lapsing once more into caricature, she turned the paper over and prepared to begin again, only to discover that she had made her sketch on the back of Mr. Dawkins's letter. With a shake of her head, she put aside the drawing and took up a clean sheet of foolscap. Mustering her neatest hand, she wrote:

Mr. Dawkins,
I thank you for your very kind words about The Wild Irish Rose. *I shall begin the revisions you have requested immediately.*
C. Burke

Pulling a tattered copy of her manuscript from her writing desk, she prepared to set to work. But not before tucking the publisher's note into her bodice like the billet-doux it was.

Chapter 3

Given the weather, Cami could only assume that her plan had curried the Almighty's favor. Three fine days in early spring were unheard of—especially three fine days in a row. Yet here she was in Hyde Park beneath a blue sky smudged only by picturesque puffs of cloud, walking four steps behind Felicity and Lord Ashborough.

She walked alone, but she did not mind in the slightest. Although the park was crowded, this was almost as good as a solitary stroll, a pleasure that had been denied her since coming to London. Such moments—among people, yet apart from them—were a writer's bread and butter, the food on which she fed her imagination. She loved to observe the fashions, the mannerisms, the way the afternoon sunlight turned the rippling surface of the Serpentine into a diamond-crusted path. She breathed deeply and drew in the scent of grass and new leaves and delicate flowers—and underneath those brighter notes, the musky smell of decay and manure and coal smoke that gave the spring air its piquancy.

Under ordinary circumstances, she might have whiled away the time dreaming up new stories, a plot to pair the elegant, fair-haired gentleman with the mousy governess who watched him surreptitiously when her eyes should have been on her charges; another to match the lady wearing too much rouge, trying desperately to look young to her circle of admirers, with the balding but sincere older gentleman who hung back just a bit from the brilliant rays of her wit. Whatever else its failings, London did not lack characters.

But today her attention was focused squarely on the most interesting character of all.

The Marquess of Ashborough walked with his hands crossed behind his back. He had not, to Cami's surprise and Felicity's evident relief, offered Felicity his arm. In fact, he kept himself ever so slightly apart from his companion—perhaps to avoid being poked in the eye by the ferrule of her parasol, which Felicity had a habit of twirling nervously. Thanks to that confection of muslin and lace, Cami could not see her cousin's face; she could only imagine her expression, seeing it refracted through Lord Ash's attention.

To overcome the slight distance between their bodies, his head was tilted perpetually toward Felicity's, so much so that Cami began to suspect he would end the day with an uncomfortable crick in his neck. He moved with grace, despite the awkward posture necessitated by walking beside someone so much shorter than he; his stride was easily twice the length of Felicity's, yet Cami observed no hitch in his gait, no restraint in his movements. He listened far more than he spoke, nodded encouragingly now and then, and if his smile could not precisely be called genuine, she saw no trace of the lupine in it either. He seemed determined to put her cousin at ease.

With eager fingers Cami reached for the little notebook she had once worn on a chain around her neck, forgetting for a moment that her brother had put a stop to it the day she had wandered into the roadway while scribbling and was nearly struck by a passing hack. She would just have to save her notes on these encounters for the privacy of her room.

But before she could commit to memory the way Lord Ashborough's gray duster rippled over the breadth of his shoulders, like sheepskin over a wolf's back, she saw Mr. Fox at last hie into view, walking—correction: being dragged along by—four large dogs, and the blood in her veins turned to ice.

"Foxy!" Lord Ashborough called and tipped his hat to his friend.

The gesture of greeting drove the dogs wild. Three pulled harder in his direction, while one shied sharply away. It looked for a moment as if Mr. Fox's arm might be wrenched from its socket. Somehow, he managed to separate the tangled leashes, so that each arm now bore a share of the strain. At the same time, he spoke to the dogs in a calm voice, with none of that fierce authority one expected from a handler of unruly animals and all of the good-natured affability one might expect of Mr. Fox.

Miraculously, blessedly, his quiet words had some effect.

Just a few feet away now, one dog sat abruptly, still leaning against his restraint. The other three stopped and stood, leaving Mr. Fox surrounded by a quivering mass of canines, their tongues lolling almost to the ground.

"Good afternoon, Lady Felicity. Miss Burke. Ash," he said, nodding to each in turn.

Apparently having been reminded of her existence by his friend's greeting, Lord Ashborough turned slightly to invite her into their circle. Mr. Fox smiled in welcome, clearly considering her a part of the group. *Oh, God...*what if he expected her to walk with him?

She knew her fear of dogs was irrational. Why, if others had not repeated the story, she would not even remember the details of the childhood trauma that had led to it.

But she could not make herself move closer.

Closing her parasol, Felicity extended one hand to the sitting dog. "Oh, you darling thing," she cooed. The dog's tail thumped the ground, but he did not rise. "What's your name?"

"That's Tiresias," Lord Ash supplied on behalf of the dog.

Lady Felicity did not look up. "Are you a sportsman, then, Mr. Fox?"

Mr. Fox, already pink from the exertion of keeping the dogs in check, colored further. "Oh, er, I—that is, well... No," he managed finally.

"No? Then how did you happen to come into possession of four such fine animals?"

"Oh, well, they're not, you see. Not fine dogs, I mean." A frown sketched across Felicity's brow, and she drew back her hand. "That is, not to my brother's way of thinking." He gestured with his chin to the trio on his left. "Achilles was the runt. Lelantos won't point. And Medea here has lost two litters already."

Despite herself, Cami smiled at the fanciful names, the warrior's for the weakest of the litter, the legendary hunter's to the dog who could not spot his prey. Felicity only shook her head. "And this one?" she asked, ruffling the sitting dog's ears. But if the name of a blind prophet proved an insufficient clue, Tiresias's cloudy eyes revealed quite clearly the liability that kept him from the field.

"They were all to be put down," Fox explained, "so I—"

"You rescued them?" she interjected.

Fox demurred. "Foolish, I know."

It might have been foolish—in the extreme, to Cami's way of thinking— but it was difficult not to like Mr. Fox in the face of further evidence of his kind heart. She wished there were any hope at all that her cousin could marry such a man, rather than Lord Ashborough.

Felicity was looking up at Fox with an expression of admiration. "Generous, I should say. Your brother is Lord Branthwaite, is he not? I have not the pleasure of his acquaintance."

Fox nodded. "I will introduce you, if you would like."

"Very much," she replied with an enthusiastic nod. "Then I will be at liberty to give him a proper dressing down for his negligence." Her gloved fingers traveled along Tiresias's leash, clearly intending to snake it from Mr. Fox's grasp.

He hesitated. "I don't know, ma'am. They're not very well mannered."

"Then they must learn how to behave around ladies," she insisted, tucking her parasol under her arm and grasping the lead more firmly. As Cami knew very well, and Mr. Fox was about to discover, Felicity was unaccustomed to being gainsaid.

His grip on the other three dogs slackened slightly, but before they could take advantage of their shocked master's moment of leniency, he had reined them in again. A puff of breath escaped Cami's lips, and she allowed herself to relax ever so slightly.

As she watched Felicity and Mr. Fox walk back in the direction from which he had come, she realized she was being left behind with Lord Ashborough. He seemed to have reached the same conclusion at the same moment, for he stepped closer to her. Too close. One could not *observe* at such proximity. It distorted the vision and muddled the senses. She could not seem to raise her eyes past the green-striped silk of his waistcoat, or clear her nose of the warm, spicy scent that lingered about him.

Then he spoke, and she would have been willing to swear that she felt his voice as much as heard it. "We'll have to hurry to catch them, Miss Burke. Unless, of course, you'd rather we be left alone?"

* * * *

Miss Burke stood frozen, face pale, shoulders raised and tense, hands balled into fists at her side. Her posture put him in mind of a small woodland creature hoping to escape the notice of a predator. *Vulnerable*, just as he had said.

But he found himself suddenly disgusted by the thought. He much preferred yesterday's show of strength. Despite the obvious alarm Fox's revelation had produced, he did not think it was he—or at least, not he alone—that she feared.

"Do Foxy's dogs bother you?" he ventured, keeping his voice light.

She stiffened further, this time in righteous indignation. "I haven't the faintest notion what you mean, my lord. Whatever would make you say such a thing?"

Her denial was too sharp, too swift, to be entirely honest. "The, er, enthusiasm shown by the pups seemed to startle you," he explained. "You are no doubt accustomed to the more sedate behavior of your aunt's pug."

Her throat worked up and down. "I have reached a—an accommodation with Chien, yes."

Chien? He could not prevent his eyes from rolling. Who named a dog Dog? Good God, Lady Merrick was lazier than he had thought. Lazy, and also so callous that she ignored her niece's terror in favor of her own ease. A flicker of anger kindled in his belly.

Against his better judgment, he held out his arm to her. It was not an intimate gesture, per se, but nevertheless one he generally avoided. He was a gentleman in nothing but name, and women ought not to be encouraged to entertain romantic notions to the contrary. Whatever he had to offer them, it was not safety.

He noted the tremble of her hand as it grazed his forearm, fancied he could feel the chill of her gloved fingertips through the layers of his coats. Although she had followed them through the park as diligently, as unobtrusively, as a shadow, her mud-brown pelisse was as ineffective as yesterday's dress at disguising what lay beneath. He easily identified the swell of her breast, the gentle curve of her waist. A straw bonnet at least as unbecoming as the pelisse hid her hair almost entirely, but a few wayward black wisps refused to be contained. Had she adopted this costume to ward off unwanted attention? Were there men who did not see past it?

"We needn't follow them too closely, Miss Burke," he assured her. "You can have no concern for your cousin's reputation in Fox's company."

She shook her head. "You seem perfectly at your ease around dogs," she said after they had walked a few steps, drawing no nearer to the others. "I suppose you *are* a sportsman."

Gabriel shrugged. "That sort of hunt has never captured my interest. The hounds, the horses…a ridiculous extravagance. Only rarely do I take on the responsibility for another's care and feeding, Miss Burke," he explained. "And when I do, I expect more than a few partridges as recompense."

If she suspected the conversation had lapsed into metaphor, she did not blush at it, though her dark brows rose.

"Yes," he continued, testing, "any pet of mine must do something to earn her keep."

"I suppose that is only fair. Perhaps it is the lack of useful occupation that renders lap dogs so vicious," Miss Burke countered, the fear in her voice now replaced by the more familiar bite.

"They are tame enough when well handled."

"You are never treated to bared teeth or a snarl, then?"

"A nip now and then can be a sign of affection," he said, his lips twisting wryly. "Or so I'm told."

Such banter was foolhardy, for more reasons than one. He was meant to be charming her, gaining a measure of her trust. Not scandalizing her further. Certainly not flirting with her. But he could not seem to help himself. He stole a glance in her direction, but she had turned her face away. The brim of her bonnet hid all from his view but the silvery rim of her spectacles.

"You needn't walk with me, you know," she said after a moment. "It was not my intention to deprive you of more interesting company."

He narrowly suppressed a laugh. Miss Burke was even more innocent than he supposed if she imagined his conversation with her cousin had been anywhere near as interesting as this one. "If I resumed my stroll with Lady Felicity, would you then walk with Fox and his dogs?"

He felt, rather than heard, her sharp intake of breath. "That would not be necessary," she insisted in a small, rough voice. "I am quite used to being alone."

"No matter," he said, covering her hand with his where it lay along his arm. He had not schemed for this outcome. But he meant to take advantage of it. "I for one am perfectly satisfied with the present arrangement." They walked a few cautious steps in silence. "How do you pass your time in your uncle's house?"

Her head tilted quizzically as she turned toward him. "Pass my time? I read and answer Lady Merrick's letters, respond to her invitations, and so forth."

"Do she and Lady Felicity receive a great number of invitations?"

"I have no standard against which to measure such things. It certainly seems so to me."

He tried to decide whether she sounded petulant. "As Lady Merrick's niece, you are included in them, I hope."

"As Lady Merrick's *companion*, it would be perfectly inappropriate for me to attend social functions with the family." A soft breeze fluttered the ribbons of her bonnet, and she jerked them firmly back into place. "I did not mean to make it seem as if I fault my aunt and cousin for making merry while they can. My uncle has indicated that this will be the family's last London Season for some time. Because of Lord Trenton's…indiscretions."

"Ah. I see." He ought to have been surprised by her forthrightness. He was not. In fact, he found it rather attractive.

A few steps farther, then she stopped once more. When he followed her gaze he saw that their absence had been noted by the others, who were returning to join them. His brief tête-à-tête with Miss Burke was coming to a close.

Before he could decide the best use to make of their waning moments of privacy, she spoke. "I—I wish to know, Lord Ashborough," she stammered, twisting around as if to face him but refusing to meet his eyes. "Is it true?"

It was on the tip of his tongue to feign ignorance, although he knew full well what she meant. No one had ever dared ask him before—at least, not for a very long time. Her insistence on confronting him seemed in keeping with what he had seen of her character, however. He suspected very few challenges went unmet by this woman.

In any case, it would serve no purpose to deny his guilt, for there was very little of which he was not guilty.

When he made no reply, she at last lifted her chin. Her eyes darted over his face, as if she were making a mental sketch of the hard lines into which he had schooled his expression.

"I do not know all you have heard of me, Miss Burke," he said softly, holding her curious green gaze until she blushed. "But I believe I can safely say yes."

Relieving her from the burden of a response, he released her hand and strode quickly toward the others. "I'll take the mutts, Foxy," he said, extending a hand. "You walk with the ladies."

Fox was clearly surprised by Gabriel's request—and clearly reluctant to accede to it. Despite the conventional wisdom that sporting dogs were never to be thought of as pets, that their sole value lay in their ability to be led or bred, Fox lived with these dogs—in his house, not a kennel. Ate with them. Likely slept with them. In short, since their rescue, he had taken all their care and handling to himself, trusting no one else with the task. Until today, upon Lady Felicity's request.

"What? Why?" Fox demanded. Then he spotted the fourth member of their party, hanging well back. "Oh, did the pups give you a turn, Miss Burke?"

Lady Felicity laughed. "Cousin Camellia, afraid of dogs? Nonsense! She takes admirable care of Mama's pug, you know," she added by way of explanation. "Feeding him, walking him, even bathing him."

Gabriel felt his brows knit together but quickly wiped the frown away. Lady Merrick's treatment of her companion was *not* his concern. "Indeed, ma'am. Utter nonsense," he acknowledged, allowing himself one backward glance as he added, "Miss Burke is afraid of nothing."

What accounted for her expression of bewilderment, Gabriel would not venture a guess. He certainly did not allow himself to dwell on the delicately carved angles of her upturned face, the inviting softness of her parted lips as they searched for the right words to form.

Ridiculous, really, for him to be making such a show over the comfort of a woman who was little more than a servant. After all, he had arranged this outing on behalf of the woman he intended to marry, to begin to accustom her to his presence. Nevertheless, he grabbed the tangle of leashes from his friend's hand and gestured for Fox to lead the way out of the park. Ever the true gentleman, Fox quickly recovered and offered one arm to Lady Felicity, the other to Miss Burke.

To *Camellia*.

The name was unusual…befitting the uncommon woman to whom it belonged.

Separated from the others by a distance conducive to her ease, rather than his own, he made his way back to Trenton House. Half an hour after that, he was home. Alone. Settled in his customary chair, listening to Remy tut-tut over the dog hair that clung stubbornly to everything it touched.

The guide to the peerage was still perched somewhat precariously on the chair's broad, rolled arm. Absently, he tapped one finger against the book's worn cover. Then, flipping easily to the page bearing the Trenton family tree, he found Felicity's name.

Her ancient family lineage bid fair to match his own. A noble English bride perfectly suited to a man in his position. Innocent. Lovely, yet not so delicate that one might fear for her ability to bear him a son.

And when he thought of her, he felt…nothing.

No fire in his blood. No spark of interest in his mind.

Nothing.

In other words, she was the ideal woman for a man with a history of killing those he loved. He might at least be able to spare the girl that fate.

Tracing his way upward along the delicate web of lines, his fingertip moved from Felicity to her father, from Merrick to his only sibling, a sister who must be Miss Burke's mother, although the book contained no information about her marriage or children. But if she had wed without her family's approval, wed an Irishman, and been disowned… Well, that would explain much.

Miss Burke's dependent position in her uncle's family.

Her fiercely independent streak in spite of it.

This afternoon, as he had watched her study him from behind those spectacles, he had begun to suspect that he was not alone in his reluctant fascination. Hidden behind those drab clothes, she was like a plainly wrapped package, inside which he felt certain lay something bright and sensuous and unexpected. Under the right circumstances, he would quite enjoy unwrapping such an unanticipated gift.

Gabriel snapped the book shut and tossed it aside. He could ill afford to dally with Merrick's niece while planning to marry the man's daughter. A successful gamester could calculate instantly the probabilities for every fall of the cards. And he was a *very* successful gamester. The smart money was on a decorous if expeditious courtship of Lady Felicity, followed by an equally expeditious, if dull, marriage. An entanglement with Camellia Burke was a losing hand.

Why, then, was he so damned tempted to bet against the odds?

Chapter 4

"This dreadful turn in the weather certainly seems to have cooled Lord Ash's ardor. He hasn't called for two days." Aunt Merrick's voice, rendered rough by the sudden onset of a head cold, gouged its way through Cami's consciousness like dull shears through delicate muslin.

Embarrassed at having been caught not attending, Cami blushed. Truth be told, she was not entirely certain she had ever stopped blushing after the walk in the park. In spite of herself and at the most inopportune moments, Lord Ash's words returned to her—along with the memory of the suggestive manner in which he had spoken them, in a voice that had sent a shiver down her spine.

He was a perfect villain, all right. And she had to keep her cousin out of his grasp.

But at that particular moment, she had been turning over in her mind how best to use her conversation with Lord Ash to make the fictional Lord Granville into a more convincing antagonist. The difficulty, she had begun to suspect, was that Lord Ash was too wicked to be believed.

"I—er, I wonder, Aunt, whether we oughtn't to search for some *permanent* way to discourage that gentleman's attentions to my cousin?"

"Discourage him?" A weary sigh deteriorated into a cough. "We have not that luxury. Merrick gave young Trenton too free a rein, I'm afraid."

"But Mr. Fox happened to mention something about Lord Ashborough's past—"

Her aunt's forceful sneeze cut her short. "Oh, not that dreadful story about his father's death again? I am surprised to hear you repeating gossip, Camellia," she reprimanded with a sniffle, her lips thinning. "And in any case, it's old news."

"But you yourself seem to have some reservation about the reputation he has acquired since—"

"He needs a wife." Aunt Merrick spoke across her, as if settling the matter once and for all. "And an heir. The responsibilities of life will settle him down."

But if they do not? Cami longed to ask. How terrible to imagine her young cousin trapped forever in a marriage to a faithless, cruel—perhaps murderous—man. Why, he might prove a veritable Bluebeard!

Well, perhaps that was a bit extreme. She could not truly believe he kept a locked room filled with the bloody corpses of his conquests. But he surely would not scruple to keep a mistress, perhaps several. Oh, he had not anticipated that she—a woman, and a spinster at that—would understand his bold reference to keeping "pets." She knew very well how men's minds worked, however. Her brother Paris fancied himself quite the young buck about town—even if the town *was* Dublin.

"You have something suitable to wear to the Montlake ball tonight, I trust, Camellia?"

Cami started. "Why?"

"Someone must chaperone Felicity," her aunt explained with an impatient frown at her lack of comprehension. "Lord Ash expects to see her there."

"Surely, you will attend Lady Montlake's ball with Felicity. There can be no question of my needing a dress." Cami tried to modulate the note of panic in her voice. "With a few more hours' rest, you will feel yourself again."

"No, Camellia." Her aunt shook her head. "By the time I'm fit to go out again, Lord Ash is likely to have proposed." A grimly triumphant smile curved her lips. After all, however undesirable Lord Ash's attention might otherwise be, it promised to help her fulfill her primary duty as Felicity's mother: to see her daughter not just wed, but wed to a man of rank and wealth.

But a glance toward the window turned the corners of her mouth downward, into a scowl. "That damp wind still has the teeth of winter in it, despite what the calendar claims." She drew her shawl more tightly around her shoulders and touched her handkerchief to her reddened nose. "I appreciate your reluctance to leave me, in my condition, but you needn't feel guilty. King will attend to me in your place tonight. The matter is settled," she said, her tone brooking no argument. "You will go with your cousin."

As if to underscore the command, rain spattered the window of the parlor where Cami sat with her aunt each morning, reading the bad novels and writing the inane letters against which her father had warned her. Cami shivered.

"Surely you must have *something* to wear," her aunt insisted hoarsely. "Ring the bell. King will assist you." Cami could not help but imagine how the lady's maid would sneer at her meager wardrobe. "It needn't be a ball gown. It's unlikely anyone will ask you to dance, after all."

Though they should not, the words stung. It was not as if Cami had never attracted the notice of a gentleman.

She shook her head in agreement with her aunt's words, but her hesitation had not gone unnoticed. Lady Merrick tipped her chin to the side, studying Cami's face, her ringed fingers hovering in midair above her dog. "Do you *wish* to dance, Camellia?"

With a growl of impatience, Chien stretched to nudge his mistress' hand. Cami jumped. "No, ma'am."

At seventeen, she had been foolish enough to long for a man's attention, his approval. Now, however, ten years later, she knew better. Gentlemen's notice led to courtship, courtship to marriage, and marriage to children and the loss of privacy and…well, a host of other things detrimental to the production of art.

Aunt Merrick looked unconvinced. "You may dance, certainly—when Felicity is suitably partnered. Perhaps Mr. Fox will attend with Lord Ash. He would be an excellent match for you, my dear. Although," she added with something like sincerity as her hand resumed stroking the dog, "I should of course be devastated to lose your companionship."

Cami bowed her head to acknowledge the reluctant compliment. Mr. Fox was a kind and decent gentleman whose friendship she would be glad to cultivate. But further than that, she would not go. And she would not serve as her aunt's companion forever, regardless.

"I envy you the chance to watch Felicity partner with Lord Ash," her aunt observed as Cami walked to the bell. "One rarely sees such good looks and grace combined."

Cami's fingertips twitched involuntarily at the memory of the strength that had flowed through Lord Ashborough's arm. The elegant economy of his every movement. His smooth, confident stride, fitted perfectly to her own.

Her aunt was correct. In the ballroom, at least, he would be a partner to envy.

But in all other respects? Well, marriage was hardly a country dance. If it were, a lady might at least be granted the power of refusal.

* * * *

"I must admit I was surprised you received an invitation for tonight's ball," Fox said, shaking the rain from his hat as he stepped into Gabriel's marble-tiled foyer.

"I haven't."

"No invitation! Then just how do you expect to get in?"

"Like as not he means to wait until the receiving line has ended and the majordomo has left his post, then brazen his way past some poor, unsuspecting footman," Remy muttered as he held out Gabriel's opera cloak.

"Your concern for your fellow soldiers in domestic service is admirable, Remy," he said as he lifted the dark garment from his manservant's outstretched hands. "But do not worry. No footman's career will be cut short by my doings tonight."

Remy cast a chary glance over Gabriel before accepting the words as dismissal. "I'll just hail a cab, shall I, my lord?"

Gabriel suspected the man's uncharacteristically sullen demeanor was the result of being required to partner his employer through the intricate steps of the cotillion for half the afternoon. But practice had been an absolute necessity. Gabriel hadn't set foot in a Mayfair ballroom in…well, in forever.

"But how *do* you mean to manage it?" Fox asked. "When it comes to defending the citadel of polite society, Lady Montlake is a veritable dragon."

"And you find me ill suited to play St. George?"

Fox's expression was something between a laugh and a frown as he settled his hat on his head again. "Oh, your tongue is sharp enough for battle, I'll wager, but what of your sword?"

"I assure you my blade is kept in constant readiness," Gabriel replied with a twitch of his lips.

"For God's sake, Ash!" Fox snapped as Remy snorted with laughter and suggestively thrust the battered black umbrella through the door ahead of him. "If rumors are to be believed, half this town is well acquainted with your…blade."

"The female half, I hope?" Gabriel winked and stepped past his friend, out the door.

Remington awaited them on the top step beneath the umbrella, while the cab stood in the street below. "It's down to you to keep his nose clean, lad," the man said, handing the umbrella to Fox. "My old bones don't fancy having to fetch him home on a night like this."

Fox smiled and accepted the worn handle. "I'll do my best," he promised.

"Why is it no one ever asks me to watch over Fox?" Gabriel grumbled, peering through the curtain of rain that sluiced from the narrow portico's roof.

"He's got brothers aplenty for that, my lord."

Gabriel could not properly be said to envy his friend. After all, to most people's way of thinking, he already had everything a man could want: good looks, intelligence, wealth. And without meddling parents or siblings, he had been doing largely as he pleased for most of his life.

Still, he sometimes felt the absence of those deeper human bonds, a connection he seemed destined to be denied.

Fox was the closest Gabriel would ever come to having a brother, and God knew the man had done his best to fill the role, fighting for him and with him as the situation demanded. Over the years, Gabriel had destroyed everyone who had ever cared for him, everyone he had ever loved—or who had loved him. Everyone except Christopher Fox.

But tonight, as he looked out into the utter blackness of the rain-soaked night, Gabriel feared, not for the first time, that even their friendship might not be proof against fate.

"What's the use of siblings if one must spend all one's time keeping others out of trouble?" Gabriel groused as they ducked out into the storm. "The eldest would never know the joy of being the troublemaker."

The umbrella was broad, but not so broad as the width of their combined shoulders, with the result that each had one wet arm by the time they reached the cab. Once inside, Gabriel swore and threw back his cloak to keep the damp from soaking through to his coat, then looked up to see his friend smiling at him.

"There's nothing humorous about rain, Foxy. If there were, every Englishman would die laughing."

"It's not the rain, Ash," he said, brushing droplets off his own shoulders and then wringing water from his glove. "I was just thinking about what you said, about the eldest always having to keep the others in line. It put me in mind of Miss Burke."

"Oh?" *Damn and blast, can the woman's name worm its way into every conversation?* At least he need have no fear—could have no hope—that she would be in attendance tonight. Her duties as chaperone would not extend to the ballroom.

"She's five younger brothers and sisters to shepherd through life, you know."

Gabriel cast a bored glance through the rain-streaked window. "How very virtuous she must be, then." *And how very ripe for a little rebellion...*

In a little while, the hack slowed to a stop before Viscount Montlake's townhouse. Light spilled from every door and window, turning raindrops into hazy prisms. Footmen stood at the ready with umbrellas, waiting to escort the arrivals inside.

"How do you mean to spend your evening once Lady Montlake turns you from her door?" Fox teased.

"She won't." Of this, Gabriel was quite certain.

His friend eyed him suspiciously. "It's hardly gentlemanlike to use your past, er, acquaintance with Lady Montlake to—"

"Lady Montlake has no past acquaintance with my 'blade,' if that's what you're insinuating. Gad, the woman must be fifty! Even I have limits."

"Do you?" One skeptical brow rose. "I confess I am glad to hear it."

"Stow it, Foxy. If your brothers did not teach you the dangers of poking the bear, I shall," he warned.

One footman opened the door and lowered the steps, while another held up a second umbrella.

"So what *is* your hold over the old dame?" Fox asked when the servants had left them under an awning and gone to assist the party in the next carriage.

"Oh, young Montlake got into a spot of trouble."

"In over his head at the tables, was he? I rather thought you preferred to teach those foolish puppies a lesson."

Gabriel had ruined more men over a hand of cards than he cared to count, and if he had wished it, he could have been entering Montlake's house tonight as its owner, rather than a guest. But something about the beads of sweat on the young man's brow, the way his eyes had shied in terror from the cards as they fell, had persuaded Gabriel that the viscount had learned his lesson, beggaring not required.

Unlike, say, Lord Trenton.

Gabriel shrugged. "Makes a nice change from grinding them under my boot heel."

"And you expect Lady Montlake's appreciation to take the form of a warm welcome tonight, do you?"

"Warm? Perhaps not." Gabriel stepped over the threshold and handed his cloak to a footman. "But welcome, nonetheless."

Chapter 5

Cami did not need to feel the sharp dig of Felicity's elbow against her ribs to realize that something had upset the equilibrium of Lady Montlake's ballroom.

The sudden hush would have been enough to catch her attention, but when followed by the snap of fans, the shuffle of feet, and the rustle of whispering voices, she could guess what must have happened. She looked up in time to see Lord Ashborough bringing Lady Montlake's hand to his lips. At this distance, Cami could not be certain that their hostess' sudden pallor was not a trick of the light. But if she did not look precisely pleased at this late arrival, she did not refuse his greeting or deny him entry.

When he raised his head, his lazy gaze swept the ballroom, sending scores of blushing cheeks and curious eyes into cover behind a screen of fans, greenery, and other people's shoulders. But when his dark eyes lit on Cami and Felicity, and that slow, certain smile lifted one corner of his mouth, the collective attention of the ballroom shifted to them, and Felicity gave a squeak of alarm.

"I certainly hope that scoundrel doesn't imagine he'll find such a welcome in this corner of the room," sniffed Mrs. Kendal, a school friend of Lady Merrick's whose hovering presence suggested that she felt—perhaps rightly—that Cami's chaperonage was insufficient for the occasion.

In defiance of Mrs. Kendal's earnest wish and despite the crush, Lord Ash was beside them in a moment. Behind him, the crowd shifted and swirled, like the waters of the Red Sea coming together again after parting. "Lady Montlake's guests were only too happy to allow me to pass," he explained in quiet answer to Cami's unspoken question as he bowed his greeting. He was dressed entirely in black, the brilliant whiteness of his linen the only contrast. Against the more vibrant silks surrounding him, he ought simply to have disappeared. Instead, the sharpness of the contrast drew the eye. The severity of the costume suited him.

Mr. Fox, the next to be greeted by their hostess, was longer in crossing to them. As they recovered from the shock of the Marquess of Ashborough's unexpected appearance, several people stopped Mr. Fox to speak with him. He paused the longest beside another gentleman with sandy-brown hair, who clapped him on the shoulder and, after a brief exchange of words, left his party and joined Mr. Fox in his journey across the room.

"Lovely to see you again, Lady Felicity," Mr. Fox said when he reached them. "And you, Miss Burke." After an uncertain pause, the second gentleman stepped forward. "Oh, er, yes. Lady Felicity, Miss Burke, may I introduce my brother, Lord Branthwaite? "

"Pleased to make your acquaintance." Branthwaite's bow lacked both his brother's endearing awkwardness and his enthusiasm.

Cami curtsied deeply and tipped her chin in acknowledgment of the greeting. "My lord."

But Felicity's shallower dip was succeeded by a flurry of words. "Branthwaite? I believe, my lord, I have a bone to pick with you."

A frown of bewilderment. "With me?"

"Over Foxy's pups," said Lord Ashborough from his place near Cami's elbow. She wished he would stand farther off.

"Pups?" Branthwaite's brows rose. "I don't—"

"Tiresias, Lelantos, Achilles, and Medea." Felicity ticked off each dog's name on the tip of one silk-gloved finger.

Branthwaite's bemused expression was tinged with something like disapproval. "Your doing, I suppose, Ash?" he asked, his voice low.

To Cami's surprise, Lord Ashborough's head dipped slightly in acknowledgment.

"The dogs' *names* are not at issue, my lord," Felicity insisted, turning the gentlemen's attention back to her. "Did you really mean to—to be rid of them?"

Branthwaite's eyes darted toward his brother and, after a moment's consideration, his lips twitched in amusement. In the gallery, the musicians picked up their instruments. "I believe the set is starting, Lady Felicity. Perhaps that will give me time to explain myself," he said, extending his hand.

Fox looked pleased. "And you, Miss Burke—will you partner me? I wish to make amends for the other day."

"Then for God's sake, spare her your dancing," Lord Ashborough said as he held out one hand, offering to lead her onto the floor. A flicker of surprise crossed Mr. Fox's face; then he bowed, deferring to his friend.

Over his shoulder, Mrs. Kendal scowled and shook her head at Cami. Strangers surreptitiously awaited her reply. But Felicity's blue eyes flooded with relief. This was the supper dance. If Cami accepted him, it would spare her cousin the marquess' attentions for an hour or more.

To say nothing of providing a golden opportunity to mine his conversation for greater insights into his character.

In order to help her readers understand the motives of the fictional Lord Granville, she had been making rather free with Lord Ash in her mind, on paper. And in the process, she had found herself growing curious about the real man. Dangerously curious. About why, or even *whether*, he did the shocking things he was said to do.

About how it might feel to do some of those shocking things with him.

She smoothed her hand over her borrowed skirts, then laid it on Lord Ashborough's outstretched palm. In recent years, her dancing had been limited to impromptu evenings in a neighbor's drawing room, partnered by one of her brothers or perhaps a sister, if at all. Now, under the glow of a hundred candles and amid the whirl of fashionable gowns and sparkling gems, the familiar comfort of those home entertainments felt very far away. Anticipation fluttered in her belly, tingled through her fingertips.

Swallowing against the sensation, she allowed herself to be led onto the floor. She was not doing this to please herself, after all.

Dancing with him was simply the best way to keep Felicity safe.

* * * *

As he led her to her place in the ladies' line and then bowed to her from the gentlemen's, he could sense the eyes of the other dancers on them. He had fully expected his presence to invite attention, even speculation. He was accustomed to stares and whispers wherever he went.

But if he had imagined that it would be freeing to share the weight of scrutiny for once, he had certainly not anticipated the unfamiliar rush of protectiveness that replaced it, the desire to retrieve that heavy burden from the more delicate frame onto which it had unfairly fallen.

Not that he imagined Camellia too weak to bear it. But it could not have been clearer that she was unaccustomed to the load.

"I had not expected to dance this evening," she confessed with a nervous twitch of her lips that might have been meant for a smile. "At least, not with you, Lord Ashborough."

"You prefer to avoid the public eye." His offer had been a selfish one, then. No, not even that, for dancing with her was against his own interests too.

He would much prefer to study her in private.

Her brow wrinkled. "The public eye? Why, I'm sure not a soul in this room has marked my existence. Their attention is all for you."

Had he merely projected his own weakness onto every other man in the ballroom? He might have glanced around him to see if she was right—if he had been capable of looking away from her.

In contrast to the other women present, her dark hair was dressed simply, to the point of severity. Her spectacles caught the glare of the candlelight, effectively masking her best feature. And her dress was ill fitting, unbecoming, and at least a decade out of fashion, hastily made over from one of the countess' castoffs, if he had to guess, and by someone with little skill with a needle, or else under orders not to reveal Miss Burke's charms.

Further proof that Lady Merrick recognized the dangers of displaying her niece beside her daughter, of inviting comparison between interesting and insipid, sharp and dull.

Despite the dress, and despite her assurances, he could not quite convince himself that the collective eye of the assembly could overlook what was growing obvious to him: Camellia Burke's extraordinary beauty. The blue-black sheen of her raven hair. The sparkle of her grass-green eyes. The promise of her slender body.

But would it be so surprising if the two hundred or so guests in Lady Montlake's ballroom failed to see it? After all, she was teetering dangerously on the brink of spinsterhood; other men clearly had passed over this treasure of the Emerald Isle. By contrast, he had spent too much time since their stroll through Hyde Park imagining what it would be like to toss those wire-rimmed spectacles aside, tangle his fingers in the black silk of her hair, and put her curious tongue to better use than asking impertinent questions.

"You attend such entertainments frequently, I suppose?" she asked when the music began and the steps brought them together.

After their last encounter, he had not known whether to expect conversation—or rather, since she seemed never to be at a loss for words, he had not known what sort of conversation to expect. "No. My own small circle rarely intersects the broader realm of polite society," he replied. "Foxy is my nearest brush with respectability."

Pursed lips warred between amusement and disapproval. "One wonders which of you is more tarred by that brush."

Fox. Unquestionably. If only she knew the number of times Gabriel had pleaded with him to forgo their friendship and save his own reputation. He surely would have had a preferment by now, perhaps something even more lucrative than the place that had been promised him, if not for his association with the infamous Lord Ash.

"Can you doubt how I suffer, Miss Burke?" he replied with forced glibness. "Ever under the watchful eye of our future clergyman? It's a wonder I can dance at all."

"Then I find myself doubly glad you asked me before my cousin," she replied. "Once to save Lady Felicity from the uncomfortable scrutiny any partner of yours must endure."

"Yes?" he encouraged, deliberately turning her toward him, rather than away as the dance demanded.

"And once to save her the embarrassment of dancing with a man who has forgotten the steps," she chided, slipping back into her proper place.

When the dance at last ended, he ushered her through the curious but disapproving crowd, which again parted to make way for his passage, as if he were pitch and they wary of being defiled. In the crowded supper room, competing aromas of perfume and sturgeon and bodies combined to form a haze of scent that hung over the assembled company. He saw no sign of either Fox or Lady Felicity, so he steered Miss Burke to the last empty seats he could find, on the far side of the room. A nearby couple scraped their chairs across the floor, drawing away to avoid any appearance of association.

"May I fetch you some refreshment, Miss Burke?"

"No, thank you, my lord. I am not hungry."

A pity. He so enjoyed satisfying a woman's appetite. "Some wine, then?"

She conceded to that offer with a dip of her dark head. When he returned, she had drawn off her gloves and laid them aside. As her slender fingers curled around the goblet and lifted it to her lips, he spied a dark smudge of ink along the side of her right hand and speckling her first and second fingers—the mark of someone who had spent hours with her pen. Lady Merrick's correspondence must be voluminous.

He had had similar stains himself, once, too stubborn for pumice. At school, translations of Latin and Greek had absorbed him, coming as they had at a time when he was desperate to find some meaning in those old adages about beauty in tragedy, desperate to find a way to allay his own suffering.

All his efforts had only proved that those grand truths were nothing more than lies.

"I assumed every English schoolboy was taught the classics," she remarked as he seated himself beside her. An almost uncanny observation, given the direction of his own thoughts. But her conversation, like everything about her, seemed to be something out of the ordinary.

"Tortured into learning them, more like," he corrected.

"Then I wonder why Lord Branthwaite should suspect you in particular of naming Mr. Fox's dogs."

Gabriel did not fool himself into thinking Branthwaite had meant the remark as a compliment to his wit. "Merely a jest between..." Fox's eldest brother tolerated Gabriel better than most, knew his love for an ironic turn, though they could by no stretch of the imagination be called "...old friends."

She was studying him from behind the rim of her cup, watching memories sketch across his brow as if they were written there and she could easily read them. Brushing away that utterly nonsensical notion, he leaned back in his chair and returned her regard. "Speaking of names," he ventured, "your own is certainly unusual."

"My brothers and sisters and I are all named after plants. The Linnaean classifications." As she spoke, she returned her goblet to the table, though her fingertips continued to trace its curves. "Camellia, Paris, Erica, Galen, Daphne, and Bellis. My father is something of an amateur botanist, you see. He calls us his little garden." That revelation was accompanied by a little spasm of embarrassment and a becoming flush. "Although not a terribly exotic one: just herbs and heather, laurel and daisy."

"*Camellia* is the exception, it would seem," he murmured, caressing her name with his voice. "A rare bloom indeed in this part of the world."

Once more, she took refuge behind her goblet.

For a long moment, neither spoke. "Forgive me," he said at last, rousing himself from thoughts that persisted in wandering in directions they ought not. "I have been imagining you tasked with keeping five tender shoots in a neat row. A difficult undertaking, I suppose. I have no siblings, you see. I am perfectly—"

"—independent," she supplied, her voice tinged with something very like envy.

But certainly he had imagined it, for how could anyone envy his isolation?

At that moment, a mother and her three daughters approached their table, stopped short, and turned back in the direction from which they had come—no easy feat in the crowded supper room. Above the din of chatter and the clatter of silver against china, nothing more of their conversation could be heard than two shocked words, part recognition, part warning.

Gabriel gave a wry smile. In his experience, there were only two types of women: those who sought him out, and those who shunned him. The society matron clearly belonged to the latter camp—or wanted everyone around her to believe that she did.

"Why do they do it?" Camellia asked when the foursome was well out of earshot. "Why do they all call you 'Lord Ash'?"

She was studying him again, her head tilted ever so slightly to one side. She seemed to be one of those women who was drawn to his darkness. But what drew her? Some misguided hope to save him from his sins?

Or a far worldlier—and more interesting—desire to share in them?

"I believe the general consensus is that I earned the name by blackening reputations and charring hopes." Would the answer warn her off, or intrigue her? Which effect was he hoping to produce?

In fact, Fox had fallen into the habit of addressing him as "Ash" when they were boys at school and "Ashborough" had seemed a pretentious mouthful. At the time, Gabriel had been glad of the respite from the weight of a title he had never expected, and certainly had not wanted, to bear so soon.

Others had taken up the nickname afterward, for far less genial reasons. He might have challenged them, called out their blatant disrespect, but why trouble himself to deny such a fitting soubriquet? Everything he touched turned to cinder.

He *was* Ash.

Her skirts rustled as she uncrossed her ankles and sat more upright. Her right forearm flattened against the table. She was preparing to take flight. *As she should.*

Unwilling to let her go, however, he lifted his chin and said, "My father had me christened Gabriel. Perhaps you think that better suits?"

He could feel her eyes on him, accepting his invitation to study his profile. "I—I cannot say, my lord."

"'My lord'? Come now, Camellia. We are to be cousins, after all, are we not?" Ridiculous, really, how he longed to hear his name on her lips. It was courting an intimacy on which he dared not act.

"I—" The catch in her voice tugged his chin back into its proper place, and he lowered his gaze to hers. She did not blush at having been caught in her inspection of his face. He could almost fancy she liked what she saw. "I believe an angel's name is entirely fitting, my lord."

"Oh?" More breath than speech. He cursed the hopefulness in the sound.

"Of course. After all, even the devil was an angel once."

Damn her. Even hardened gamblers did not trick him into letting down his guard. A familiar wave of cynicism swept over him like a domino at a masquerade, hiding what he never meant to reveal, curling the corners of his lips. "I see. By all means, call me Ash, then. All the best people do."

A rather schoolmarmish grimace quirked her lips. "What nonsense, my lord. I most certainly will not resort to spiteful nicknames." There was an odd sort of reassurance in her refusal. "I simply meant that even the worst of men were innocent children once, and deserving of compassion, not mockery." Her restive fingertips plucked up a wrinkle in the tablecloth, then smoothed it away. "Which reminds me. The other day, in the park, you stepped away before I could—that is, I wished to say…"

His heart knocked against his breastbone, urging him to stop her from speaking her piece. But how foolish. Words had long ago lost the power to wound him. Why should her words, spoken with that soft Irish lilt, somehow be different?

At least she seemed to be choosing them with care. "On the matter of your late father, may I—?" A pause. "May I offer my condolences?"

Condolences? Had anyone ever thought to offer him any such thing? He dipped his head to hide his confusion and spied her hand still lying along the edge of the table. Covering it with his own, he squeezed and murmured, "Thank you."

Then, an impulse—he could not call it gallantry—prompted him to lift those ink-stained fingers to his mouth, to brush his lips across the rough ridge that ran along the side of her middle finger, a callus worn by a firm and regular grip on a pen.

"Ash!"

Fox's voice cut through the swelling hum. Against the stream of guests beginning to file from the supper room, he was bearing down on them, Lady Felicity on his arm. Quickly, Gabriel rose to his feet, drawing Camellia up with him.

"Why are you hiding in this corner, Ash? We'd begun to think you'd got quite away."

Camellia's fingers twitched again. Suddenly aware he was still gripping her hand, he released his hold and stepped toward his friend. "Nonsense, Foxy. You can't have looked very hard. And Lady Felicity has promised me the next dance," he added, holding out his arm to her. "What could possibly drag me away?"

Felicity promptly let go Fox's arm and took Gabriel's instead. He did not fool himself into thinking she took pleasure in bestowing her attention on him. But neither did she resist.

Her complaisance was to be expected, given his hold over her family. Having recently been reminded of the delights of the unexpected, however, he found himself wondering whether they might not get on better if she'd slapped his face and told him to take a swim in the Thames instead. Then again, he knew better than to wish for some sort of grand passion to flare between him and his soon-to-be bride.

"Shall we join them in a turn about the ballroom, Miss Burke?" Fox asked, offering his arm to Camellia.

A bright spark of jealousy crackled through Gabriel once more, like the glow at the end of a cheroot being smoked in the dark. This time, however, he could not step between them without cutting the woman who was meant to be his intended.

Out of the corner of his eye, he caught the sharp movement of Camellia's dark head. "I'm afraid you must excuse me, Mr. Fox. Another time, perhaps?"

Relief coursed through him, followed quickly by remorse. Good God, did he lack the decency to set aside his own decidedly illicit interests in favor of even the momentary happiness of the most honorable man he knew?

But Camellia was already gone, murmuring something about the ladies' retiring room to her cousin as she passed, not sparing any of them a backward glance.

* * * *

Thwarted by the crush, Cami ducked through one of the disguised doors at the back of the room, those through which servants discreetly came and went. The narrow passageway behind was unlit and, for the moment, empty. She had no notion of where it might lead. But she kept walking, hurrying away from what she had just done. It had been one thing to divert the marquess from Felicity for an hour, another thing entirely to discover herself the sole focus of his attentions.

To discover those attentions were not entirely unwelcome.

When she could bear the heat of his gaze, the intimate murmur of his deep voice, no longer, she had tried to turn the tables. She had not set out to be cruel. It was only a silly game she sometimes played with herself, saying the most outrageous, unexpected things, merely to observe the response they produced—a sort of study in human nature. A way to understand how characters ought to act and react. She had prompted him to recall his boyhood, then offered unexpected words of consolation, thinking to see…guilt? Or anger?

Something, anything other than the raw grief that had streaked across his face, making her feel as if, with the crack of one whiplike sentence, she had flayed the tough hide from his heart. A heart everyone—even the man himself—seemed persuaded he did not have.

At the end of the dark corridor, a dim rectangle of light suggested a doorway, promised an escape. When she reached it, however, she paused to choose: go through it into the unknown, or turn around? Her hand trembled as she reached for the handle. The soft glow of unseen candles in the room beyond limned her hand, the ink-stained fingertips he had kissed in…in gratitude? As if he believed she understood, as if he imagined she cared.

Oh, God. That was the worst of it—the suspicion he might be right.

He…he intrigued her.

There. She had admitted it. She had set out to study him with the same detached, practiced observation a painter might apply to the subject of a still life. But Lord Ash—no, *Gabriel*—was not a plate of fruit, a loaf of bread, or a glassy-eyed fish waiting to be gutted. He moved. He spoke. He *charmed*.

A dark angel, indeed.

Nothing she had seen of him had increased her alarm on Felicity's behalf. In fact, she was no longer certain he was the villain he had been painted. Cami balled her hand into a fist and scrubbed the pad of her thumb over the callus on her middle finger, where his lips had been.

No, this sudden rush of fear was all for herself.

"Your fears are entirely justified."

She jerked her hand from the door and stuffed her knuckles into her mouth to stifle a scream. The voice was rough, low, breathless. And the speaker to whom it belonged was standing just inches away, on the other side of the service door.

"I am not afraid of him." A second, younger man's voice. Frightened, for all his bravado.

"You should be."

Almost unwillingly, Cami leaned forward, drawn by the drama unfolding beyond the wall. Closer to the door now, she pressed one lens of her spectacles to the peep, a tiny square through which the parlor maid might look to make certain the room was empty before entering to clean it. Although her vision was partly obscured by the man leaning against the door, she could just glimpse the younger speaker, Lord Montlake, their host.

"I understand you had quite a near brush with him not long ago," the rough-voiced man continued. The words seemed to be whispered in her own ear. "And emerged unscathed only through his…*mercy*, shall we call it?"

"I am determined he shall never have another chance to harm me or mine."

A bark of sound that might have been meant for a laugh. "Given up the game, have you? Rather too late. The damage has already been done. You saw him tonight. With her. As did every guest in that ballroom." Every few words, the man paused to draw a shallow, ragged breath. "They were all already imagining the worst."

Lord Montlake swore.

"I may count on your support, then?" the other man asked.

Hesitation pushed the young viscount back onto his heels.

"Think of it as a vote for the safety of all you hold dear," he prodded. "Desperate times call for desperate measures."

"He's a right villain, but I cannot believe—"

"Let me make it simple." The other man stepped away from the wall, blocking her view entirely. "If you do not vote to ruin him, I will ruin you." His erratic breathing made the chilling words more threatening still. "God save the king."

"God save the king," Lord Montlake mumbled after a moment.

When the two men had left the room, closing the door behind them, Cami's breath left her lungs in a rush. She had never caught a glimpse of the second man's face. She did not know that she ever wanted to.

For as long as she could remember, she had been interested in what went on in Westminster and how it shaped the lives of those who lived so far from it. The Lord Lieutenant and the policies he issued from Dublin Castle. And from outside its walls, the responses, calls first for an independent Irish parliament, then more recently, and more shockingly, for an independent nation. Her father read the papers aloud and encouraged her questions. Paris hoped someday to stand for election. Politics had always seemed to her to be imbued with honor and pride and…yes, a bit of glamor, as she had put it to Mr. Fox. Oh, even ladies heard whispers of backroom deals and shady doings, of course. But she had never observed such things firsthand.

Until now.

Lord Montlake and the unknown man were conspiring to destroy someone. Was the man truly guilty of whatever crime they intended to charge against his character? Or were they determined to ruin him merely because they had the power to do so?

With a shiver, she fumbled in the dark for the latch and pushed open the door, emerging into the study, a masculine room smelling of brandy and leather and books. A sudden longing for home, for Papa and the cozy safety of the family sitting room, struck her like a blow to the belly.

But Merrion Square was a long way off. And she was not charged with protecting some stranger, a man who had frightened Lord Montlake and angered another man to the point of provocation. When she tried to imagine what he had done, her mind conjured Gabriel's dangerous, cynical smile. *I earned the name by blackening reputations and charring hopes.* Perhaps the stranger did not deserve protecting. Almost certainly, such a man did not require *her* protection.

Felicity, however, did.

Briskly, Cami shook off the strange apprehension that had settled over her with the unknown man's bitter words. No...earlier. With the touch of Gabriel's hand, the brush of his lips.

In a half dozen strides, she was to the study door, and once a quick check had reassured her that her departure would go unobserved, she slipped through it and into a broad, well-lighted corridor. If she hurried, she could be back to the ballroom before the dance had ended.

Chapter 6

The flower shop hummed with the sounds of buying and selling, the snip of shears and shouted directions. Despite the alarmingly early hour, Gabriel welcomed the noise, first because it meant that he might at last have found a place of business capable of filling his order, and second because, amid the commotion, he could hope to remain relatively anonymous.

"I don't know what was wrong with the last three shops, Ash," Fox said, warily eyeing a cactus. "What can you want with all these hothouse blooms? I told you, simple and sweet will be the way to Lady Felicity's heart. Wildflowers and the like."

Gabriel nodded, only half attending. When at last it was his turn to place an order, he laid a carefully written note on the counter. The clerk glanced first at it, then at him. "This'll cost a pretty penny," he said, looking Gabriel up and down as if deciding whether he could afford the extravagance.

"But you can deliver these items as requested?" Gabriel demanded.

Something about him—his voice, his air, the cut of his coat—must have satisfied the young man, for the clerk nodded crisply. "We'll have them there yet this morning, sir."

While he was tallying the order, a rack of bright ribbons caught Gabriel's eye. "For the nosegay," he said to the young man, pointing to one.

"Red? Rather a bold choice for the lady in question, Ash." Fox abandoned his inspection of an odd-looking orchid to peer over Gabriel's shoulder.

"Coquelicot," Gabriel corrected. At Fox's amused expression, he explained, "Named after the poppy. The latest fashion from France."

"I won't ask how you come to know such a thing. I'm quite sure I wouldn't like the answer."

Gabriel drew a length of the orange-red silk between his fingers; the spool wobbled on the rack as the ribbon unfurled. "It behooves the intrepid explorer to study the habits of the natives, my dear Foxy—to learn their language."

"The language of ribbons and flowers?" Fox gave a bewildered shake of his head.

"It's a language I feel certain the lady in question will understand."

"Well, you know best, Ash."

No. No, he most certainly did not. He was not, by nature, a risk taker, whatever his opponents at the table persuaded themselves to believe. And he never tipped his hand until he was certain of the outcome of the game. Excitement, apprehension rushed through his veins, unfamiliar and more than a little unwelcome.

Once the order had been placed, Gabriel left the shop with Fox in tow. Oxford Street rippled before them, a river of humanity into which the two of them managed to merge on their second attempt. Though the air still felt raw after two days of cold rain, a few feeble rays of something that passed for sunshine seemed to have convinced fully half of the residents of London that spring had returned.

They had not taken many steps when a hoarse voice spoke in his ear. "So, the rumors are true, Gabriel."

He would have recognized the voice anywhere, even without the troublingly familiar use of his given name. "And what rumors are those, Uncle Finch?" he asked without turning to look at his interlocutor.

"For one, the rumor that you have crawled out from under the rock where you have been lurking these many years."

Gabriel squinted into a gray sky pierced here and there with the promise of blue. "I suppose you hoped I would shrivel and die in the sunlight." He dropped his gaze and met his uncle's sneer with one of his own. "So sorry to disappoint."

More than a year had passed since Gabriel had seen his uncle last. Automatically, he steeled himself against the discomfort that always slithered down his spine when he was forced to confront that face—his father's face, but attached to another man entirely. He recalled having once felt the briefest glimmer of hope that the two men would resemble one another in more than the physical, a spark that had flared and been stamped out long ago.

"Make no mistake, Gabriel. I *am* disappointed—"

"Lord Sebastian Finch." Fox's calm tones cut across their more heated voices as he gave a slight bow.

"This doesn't concern you, Mr. Fox," Uncle Finch declared. "I can't think why you continue to associate with my nephew, under the circumstances. 'He that toucheth pitch shall be defiled therewith,'" he quoted piously. "A man of God should surround himself with more fitting acquaintances."

Gabriel very nearly nodded his agreement.

"Sage advice," Fox replied, unperturbed. He folded his arms across his chest and rocked back on his heels. "Fortunately for us sinners, our Lord and Savior did not see fit to take it, either."

"Was there something you wanted of me?" Gabriel asked, forcing himself to study his uncle's pallid face; the man's health had always been poor, but appeared now to be failing at a rapid pace.

"Certainly not." The mere suggestion that he had sought Gabriel out seemed to horrify him. "I was on my way to my club to discuss the news of the day. You have heard, of course, about the attempt on His Highness's life? Terrible, terrible. But one can hardly claim to be surprised, when we welcome these Frenchmen—and women—into our country and believe their sad tales of persecution, their claims of opposition to that republican monstrosity they're concocting across the Channel." As he spoke, he watched Gabriel closely.

A certain sly uplift in his uncle's brows, as if he anticipated some reaction to his words, prompted Fox to ask, "What has any of that to do with Ash?"

The old man gulped an anticipatory breath so sharp it sent his lungs into a paroxysm of shock. When the coughing fit had passed, he rasped out, "*Ash?* How—how dare—you—?"

Gabriel watched him struggle to breathe, impassive. "I cannot see that my title is any particular concern of yours, Uncle Finch," he said, lifting one hand to stay the tide of vitriol. "As to the other, Foxy, I would not be surprised if my dear uncle intends to suggest I am in league with a den of French spies. Killing a king is of a piece with my past crimes against the nobility, I dare say."

Uncle Finch favored him with a bitter stare that he managed, after a moment, to twist into a condescending smile. "If the shoe fits, Gabriel. Alas," he said, crossing his hands over the knob of his walking stick, "the charges I have heard laid at your door are not quite so damning. Rumor has it you were vulgar enough to seek admittance to Lady Montlake's ballroom without an invitation. And there are those who claim you intend to offer for some poor innocent girl, merely in hopes of depriving Julian of his rightful inheritance." Between each accusation, his uncle paused to wheeze out one useless breath and replace it with another.

"Rightful—?" Fox sputtered. Gabriel gave an almost imperceptible shake of the head to silence him.

"It would seem the girl's family has forgotten your...*history.*"

"Forgotten?" Gabriel brushed an imaginary speck of lint from his sleeve. Given the frequency with which his uncle had denounced him as a murderer over the last twenty years, the charge ought to have lost its sting. But it had not. "I very much doubt it can have escaped anyone's recollection, given how you persist in bringing it up."

His uncle shrugged. "Society has a regrettably short memory. Someone must refresh it from time to time. Although really," he added, "all my efforts seem to have been perfectly unnecessary. You have always been determined to prove me right about you."

Gabriel could feel his anger rising, and Fox must have sensed it. "Let's go, Ash. I cannot think you will wish to be seen engaging in a family squabble in full view of every shop on Oxford Street."

With a cold bow to his uncle, Gabriel agreed. "Yes. Unless you've something more original and interesting, Uncle Finch, I'll be on my way."

Before his uncle could gather the strength to rasp out a reply, Gabriel began to walk in the direction of St. James's. Footsteps scuffed behind him—one set, and by the lightness of their tread, they belonged to Fox. Still, he did not slow his stride. In another moment, he would have done the thing he had been longing to do since he was ten years old: smash his fist into his uncle's face.

When he reached his rooms, Gabriel opened the door himself, swinging it inward with such force that it struck the wall behind and shuddered almost closed again. Remington stopped its motion with one hand and studied the mark its handle had made on the wallpaper. "All right, then?"

"No." His hat sliced through the air and landed on a nearby table. "I just had the dubious pleasure of an encounter with my Uncle Finch on Oxford Street. He's up to something. See what you can find out. Anything... *useful,* you understand?"

Remy nodded once, not a hint of surprise in his face. In all his years with Gabriel, he had been asked to perform tasks far outside a manservant's normal sphere of duty, many of them unsavory. And he had never blinked at any of them. On occasion, Gabriel wondered what it would take to shock him.

Without pausing to remove his greatcoat, he marched down the corridor to his study. Fox found him there a moment later. "Killing the king? You cannot seriously believe your uncle would make such an accusation," he demanded, breathless from the pace Gabriel had set.

"God knows what he has up his sleeve."

Gabriel had not realized he was pacing until Fox stepped into his path and brought him up short. "But you also cannot deny you have helped him blacken your reputation over the years. For the sake of your future, then, isn't it time to move ahead with your plans to turn over a new leaf?"

Fox was right, of course. Whatever Gabriel's desires where a certain lady's companion was concerned, he must put them aside in favor of the only proper match he was ever likely to make—and with it, the hope of saving Stoke and its people from future devastation. Better his bollocks than his neck in a noose.

Without replying, Gabriel turned and strode back toward the window.

"I am fully prepared to stand before you at the altar, if you will have me, and celebrate the union of my oldest and dearest friend to a woman worthy of his regard," Fox vowed, his solemnity entirely in keeping with his future as a clergyman. Gabriel did not doubt his sincerity.

But the earnest note in his voice—Gabriel might have been tempted to call it longing—forced Gabriel to meet his friend's eyes. What he saw there sliced open his veins as neatly as the bloodletter's lance. He thought of Fox walking with Felicity, talking with Felicity, dancing with Felicity. Oh, from a practical standpoint it was a perfectly ineligible match: a younger son could not afford to fall in love with a dowerless girl. But love was not a practical matter. Or so Gabriel had heard.

Fox was willing to give up a woman for whom he obviously was coming to care deeply. Give her up for Gabriel. For a man who did not deserve such a woman—or such a friend.

"From here on out, though, I expect you to be on your best behavior," Fox concluded. "Felicity Trenton is a lady, Ash. So you must be a gentleman."

"For once," added Gabriel wryly. Compared to Fox's sacrifice, it was a trivial request, really. It was only giving up a flirtation in which it was ridiculous to indulge.

It would go badly for him and rather worse for Miss Burke if he should offer anything more.

His feet once more began to wear a path across the rug. For the first time since he had rented these rooms, the moment he had been of age and legally entitled to do so, the flat felt like a prison to him.

Remington backed into the room carrying the breakfast tray. "When you have finished with the other matter," Gabriel said to him, "see that the Grosvenor Square house is opened and prepare to move us there at the earliest opportunity."

The tray clattered onto the desktop. "You—you mean to—to relocate to Finch House?" Remy stammered.

"Rented rooms are an appalling waste of money when a man owns several perfectly good homes," he said, echoing the words his trustee had spoken to him on the morning of his twenty-first birthday, as he had handed over the last of Gabriel's dreadful inheritance. Finch House was an elegant, luxurious townhouse nestled in the heart of the beau monde—entirely out of keeping with the life he lived. Gabriel had resolutely refused to occupy it.

But orchestrating a campaign to thumb his nose at his uncle and take his rightful place in society would benefit from a proper base of operations. The home of a gentleman. "And besides, I cannot very well bring my bride here."

At that announcement, Remy positively goggled.

"That's the spirit." Fox clapped Gabriel on the back. "I shall rejoice to see you settled at last. And on the way to restoring the thing fate stole from you all those years ago."

Gabriel hesitated. "And what would that be?"

"A family." With a sharp squeeze of his shoulder, as if for encouragement, Fox urged him toward his customary chair and came to sit beside him.

Remy approached with a cup in one hand and the teapot in the other. Neither hand seemed as steady as was wont. Gabriel had at last contrived to shock his manservant. "Tea, sir?" Remy asked Fox.

Absently, Fox nodded at Remy, his attention still focused on Gabriel. "I firmly believe Lady Felicity will make you…"

"Happy?" he suggested, a little wryly. What business had he dwelling on coquelicot ribbon and Camellia Burke?

"Of course," Fox agreed. "But I was going to say, 'a better man.'"

Laughable, really, to imagine that bland, blonde slip of a girl taming him. Nevertheless, in a matter of weeks, Gabriel intended to be a married man. With a proper wife, living in a proper household, forming proper habits.

Giving up his larks, just as Fox had said.

Swallowing against a sudden drought in his throat, he watched as the dark, steaming liquid poured from the spout into the cup Fox held. Gabriel never drank the stuff. But his recent discovery that those brownish bits of chaff were actually the dark, glossy leaves of the camellia plant made the beverage suddenly, surprisingly…tempting.

"Just a moment, my lord, and I'll bring your coffee," Remy said, returning to the tray.

But he knew coffee would not do the trick this time. Only one thing would slake this powerful thirst. And though he well knew its tendency to scald, surely he could dare just a sip.

"On second thought, Remy," he murmured, "I believe I'll have tea."

Chapter 7

Cami reached under her spectacles to press her fingertips to her eyelids, hoping for relief. Instead the grit of exhaustion pricked her eyes and made them water. The third cup of coffee had done little more than make her irritable. The mere thought of a fourth made her stomach churn.

"Lady Montlake's ball would seem to have done you in," Felicity said, looking up from her perusal of her papa's newspaper.

It was not the ball that had exhausted her, though they had arrived home only shortly before the hour at which Cami generally rose. No, her muse had been demanding. Or restless, at least. Pages and pages of corrections, additions, investing Lord Granville with a tragic past—father killed in a suspicious accident, a cruel uncle for a guardian—that made his present villainy believable, if not excusable. After breakfast, she would reread those scribbled words and pray that the energy with which they had spilled from her pen was matched by their quality.

"A headache, merely," Cami lied, covering her ink-stained fingers—the ones *he* had kissed—with her napkin. No matter how she scrubbed, they never came clean. Fortunately, Aunt Merrick's cold had made her so fretful that only King's presence could be tolerated this morning, else she would already have been chided for her slovenliness.

Felicity's eyes flicked anxiously across the page. "Oh, my. How dreadful."

"What is it?" Cami demanded as she twitched the paper away. Her pulse leaped along with her imagination. A riot? Another assassination attempt? Some news from Dublin?

No. Merely a gossip column. Clearly, it would have been wiser to have stopped at two cups of coffee.

Your eyes did not deceive you last night, dear readers. It seems a certain sooty peer roams among us once more. Rumor has it, the Beast has even chosen a bride! One wonders if the lady in question has any notion of the Frogs he is said to have kissed....

"Oh, Felicity. Why do you read this nonsense? You can only expect to hear the worst."

An inelegant shrug. "There seems to be nothing but the worst to be heard. I ought to know what I'm getting myself into, oughtn't I? Why, last night I was reduced to begging Mr. Fox to tell me some good of him. As Lord Ash's oldest friend, he must know *something*, even if it's hidden from everyone else."

Impatience itched at Cami. "And what did he say?"

"After a bit of hemming and hawing, he managed to recollect that Lord Ash had been something of a scholar when they were at university." Felicity was clearly nonplussed by the revelation. "Apparently, he took top honors in mathematics at Cambridge."

Of course. A successful gambler would have to have some facility for numbers. "At least you may take some comfort in the knowledge that he is not entirely—or at least, not only—a scoundrel," Cami said, smoothing her napkin across her lap, then picking up her fork. "Though I confess I am somewhat surprised to hear that he bothered with university at all." His description of learning the classics as *torture* suggested the sort of man who wasted little time on such activities. But then, from what she had heard and what Cousin Stephen's experience had confirmed, a gentleman's university experience had very little to do with books.

"Mrs. Kendal said his guardian—his uncle, that is—insisted upon it."

His uncle? Cami's fork slipped from her suddenly nerveless fingers and clattered onto her plate.

Some of the details of Lord Granville's story had been drawn unabashedly from Lord Ashborough's life. But the idea that she had accidentally hit on such a striking similarity gave her qualms. What would he do if he ever suspected she had used him as the model for her villain?

A moment's reflection made her see the ridiculousness of her worry. After all, how likely was it that the Marquess of Ashborough would read *The Wild Irish Rose* and see himself in its pages?

"I really do not think you should be listening to Mrs. Kendal's, or anyone else's, ridiculous gossip," Cami said firmly, retrieving her fork, forcing a bite of cold, rubbery egg past her lips, then immediately regretting the decision.

"Well, I would not need to put so much store in her titbits if you would only tell me what you and he discussed. You spent more than an hour in his company last night." As she spoke, Felicity curled the corner of the newspaper around her fingertip, then frowned at the black smudge it left behind. "Surely, in all that time, he must have said something worth repeating."

Had he? Their talk had been commonplace, yet a strange sort of intimacy had surrounded their exchange, a cocoon of calm amid the noise and bustle of the ballroom and the supper room. Talk of childhood and family. The sound of her name on his lips. Those lips pressed impertinently, improperly to her hand...

A wave of heat swept up her chest to her cheeks, chasing some sensation, some emotion for which she had no words.

"Lord Ashborough is courting *you*, Cousin Felicity. He had no particular call to make himself agreeable to me."

"He is not *courting* me, Cousin Camellia," Felicity corrected, an uncharacteristic sharpness in her voice. "I'm a bought bride, and we both know it. Though I doubt he feels much obligation to make himself agreeable to anyone, come to that."

"Was he disagreeable?"

"No." Felicity sounded nonplussed. "Merely...distracted."

At that moment, Tom the second footman entered, bearing an enormous bouquet in one hand and a salver on the other and extending them both to Felicity.

"How lovely! Why, they look just as if they had been gathered from a meadow." Felicity's expression of surprised delight was nearly obscured by a profusion of what looked like wildflowers, although it was really too early in the year for them to be any such thing. The splendid riot of pink and yellow and lavender blooms came together in an artful arrangement that appeared free of artifice, perfectly suited to a young lady of Felicity's romantic tastes and nothing like the nosegays more typically sent by eager young men the morning after a ball.

"Who could have sent them?" she exclaimed, though the answer seemed obvious enough. "Who knows me so well as to choose all of my favorites? Do open the note, Cousin Camellia."

Tom's face was contorted in what might have been intended as a speaking glance, though its message was opaque. Wordlessly, Cami motioned for him to give her the letter.

> *My dear lady,*
>   *Thank you for the favor of your company last evening.*
> *Though these blooms cannot rival the bloom of your cheeks, I*
> *hope this small token, and the memory of my esteem it carries,*
> *will call up the luster of your charming smile.*
>   *Yours &c.*
>   *Ash——*

Only the first three letters of his signature were legible, as if he too thought of himself by the shortened version of his title. The hand was as bold and dark and strong as the words themselves were, well, flowery. "The bloom of your cheeks"? "The luster of your smile"? Did such obvious and hackneyed sentiment produce the desired results? Were women really wooed with such utter nonsense? Although she had little experience with rakes on which to draw, Cami had somehow imagined their techniques a bit more refined.

"Lord Ashborough sent them, of course," she told Felicity, dropping the note onto the table. A flicker of something—disappointment?—crossed her cousin's face, but Cami's attention was claimed once more by Tom, who was standing just out of the line of Felicity's vision, nodding first at Cami, then jerking his head in the direction of the door.

Cami frowned. "Is something the matter with your neck, Tom?"

"No, miss." But while Felicity examined each petal and leaf, he went through the same elaborate routine, this time moving only his eyes. Torn between exasperation and worry that he might do himself an injury if allowed to continue this pantomime, Cami rose from the table. "I promised my sister a letter," she said, excusing herself.

"Goodness, Tom," she scolded as soon as the door to the breakfast room shut behind her. "What are you about, making such dumbshow? Is it another letter from Mr. Dawkins?"

"No, miss." With a more restrained tip of his chin, he indicated the florist's boy standing just inside the front door.

Cami walked slowly down the stairs and across the marble-tiled foyer, stopping in front of him. "Have you a message? If it's money you want, you'll have to wait for the butler."

"You're Miss Burke?" Before she could even nod, he drew a second, smaller bouquet from behind his back. "I was 'structed to give these into your hand, direct."

"For Lady Felicity?"

"No, ma'am. For you."

Wide eyed, she took the flowers from his outstretched hand. With a touch to the brim of his cap, the boy was gone.

"Well, I never," Cami gasped to no one in particular, as Tom had already made himself scarce and the hall was otherwise empty.

She had taken three swishing strides back to the staircase before her curiosity got the better of her and she glanced down at the bouquet she carried. At first, she saw only what she expected to see: a proper, predictable nosegay. A small, neat arrangement of hothouse flowers that might have been meant for any woman who merited some little notice. A kind gesture from the always thoughtful Mr. Fox, perhaps. Certainly nothing that required subterfuge or secrecy. Merely ordinary blooms bound with a length of ribbon.

Silk ribbon, she realized as her fingers curled more tightly around the stems. An almost unthinkable luxury for a woman in her position. Oh, Aunt Merrick saw to it that Cami had everything she truly required. A lady's companion simply did not *require* silk ribbon.

Especially not silk ribbon in the most glorious shade of red she had ever seen.

The flowers were no less extraordinary than the ribbon that bound them. Creamy petals ordered themselves precisely around feathery yellow stamens, a golden treasure at the heart of each sweetly scented blossom.

Camellias.

A rare bloom in this part of the world, he had said, the sound of her name on his lips as real to her now as the touch of those lips against her skin.

She glimpsed a card tucked amid the shining green leaves, and her fingers trembled—drat that coffee!—as she withdrew it carefully from its nest. A calling card. The Marquess of Ashborough's calling card. With a calm she did not feel, she palmed the rectangle of stiffened paper, feeling its sharp corners bite into her hand, and ascended the stairs to her room.

Safely within the privacy of its four walls, she admired the nosegay once more. What had he intended to buy with these flowers? Her silence? Or something else entirely?

She turned her attention to his card as if it could reveal the answer to her question. Embossed lettering rose from it, the print surprisingly plain. Slowly, she turned it over, wondering whether it bore any message even as she despised her curiosity.

Just one word, scrawled by a confident hand.

Gabriel.

Her eyelids fell as she lifted the card almost to her lips. Carried in his breast pocket, against the heat of his chest, it had absorbed his unique fragrance. From the ivory paper wafted the warm scents of tobacco and bergamot and something she could not identify. It smelled like…an invitation to sin.

Her pulse ticked upward and her eyes popped open, but she did not immediately thrust away that invitation.

She had no illusions about why he fascinated her. He was unlike anyone she had ever known, except perhaps in the pages of the sort of novels she generally denied reading. Powerful. Free to do as he pleased. Dismissive of the world's scorn. He represented everything she had ever desired. He could give her a taste of things that she, as a woman, had always been denied.

Oh, but every story ever told taught that the price of such knowledge was dear. Too dear. Her hand dropped to her side. She could not, would not, pay it.

Still, might she not enjoy the flowers while they lasted? Like as not, Gabriel had had no hand in their purchase, but had given the task to some servant. And as the petals faded and fell, they would serve as a reminder of the fleeting nature of men's affections.

At the washstand, she filled a tumbler with water; the flowers' thick green leaves would disguise its chipped edge. Seating herself at the worktable that filled one wall of her narrow room, she began painstakingly to unpick the exquisite poppy-colored ribbon and arrange the stems in the makeshift vase.

* * * *

Gabriel's knock on the door to Trenton House was opened by the butler. "You are expected, my lord."

By whom? Gabriel had not known himself that he would call until the hubbub of sorting and packing had driven him from his rooms, and his restless feet had carried him into Mayfair. And he did not delude himself into thinking that Felicity was any more eager for his visit than he was to make it.

Disapproval radiated from the butler as he bowed Gabriel inside and led him stiffly up the stairs to the doorway of an unfamiliar room. Before Gabriel could decide whether the servant's demeanor simply inhered to his species or was directed toward him specifically, the man bowed once more. "Wait here, my lord. I shall inform her ladyship you have arrived."

He opened the door to reveal a sitting room. Lady Merrick's, he guessed, by the plump chairs and primrose draperies. More knickknacks than books lined the shelves on either side of an empty marble fireplace. And before the window stood a delicately carved lady's writing desk with a matching chair, whose occupant did not raise her head from her work.

"Oh, Miss Burke," the butler said. "I did not know you were here. Lord Ashborough has come to call."

If the butler's voice, or the sound of Gabriel's name, produced any reaction, she did not show it. No start of recognition. No turn of her head, even, until she had put the point to whatever she was writing and laid her pen aside. When she rose, she stayed standing before the escritoire, her back to it, her ink-stained hands folded demurely in front of her. "Then you must tell Lady Merrick he has arrived, Wafford," she prompted.

With another stiff bow in Gabriel's direction, the butler left.

For a moment, Gabriel stood in the doorway and simply soaked in the sight of her, a chiaroscuro of bright and dark, her head tilted slightly to the side, the light from the window behind limning her body and shooting through wisps of her black hair like stars in the night sky. Then he stepped closer, skirting a table with curving legs whose marquetry top was almost entirely obscured by an enormous bouquet of rather ordinary-looking spring flowers arranged incongruously in a crystal vase.

Another three steps and he could see that her spectacles had slid down to perch at the end of her nose. A smudge of ink along her cheekbone, near her ear, suggested that impatient fingers had brushed away an errant lock of hair, perhaps more than once. Scattered across the desktop behind her lay a half dozen sheets of closely printed paper, with lines scored through and words crammed in between to replace them. At this distance, he could not read what she had written, but she caught the direction of his gaze and shifted nonetheless, blocking his view.

"I am sorry to have disturbed you," he said, returning his eyes to her face.

Camellia dipped her head to acknowledge his apology but did not demure as ladies often did. Obviously, she had been hard at work, and she resented his interruption. She made no move to sit down again nor offered him a chair. She did not curtsy. He did not bow.

Hang good manners. He wanted to kiss her, and not just on the hand.

And he was used to getting what he wanted.

While he struggled to bring his basest impulses under control, she spoke. "I must thank you for the flowers." The cadence of her voice curled through him like soft music. "Your servant must have been put to some trouble to find camellias in London, in May."

"I've sent my man to do many things for me, and he rarely disappoints."
He allowed himself one step closer, close enough that he might easily
reach out and take her hand in his, though he did not. "But when the task
concerns pleasing a woman, I do it myself."

Understanding chased through her eyes, followed closely by pleasure.
Yes, it pleased her that he had chosen the flowers—and her own pleasure
seemed to catch her unawares. Oh, she was better than most at hiding her
telltales. He would not want to sit down at the card table across from such
a one. But fortunately—or unfortunately—for them both, he was equally
adept at reading the signs.

"And they did, did they not?" he murmured. "Please you, I mean."

Unlocking her intertwined fingers, she reached up to adjust her
spectacles. "I was *surprised* by them."

She might bear the name of a flower with smooth, glossy leaves and
sweet-smelling petals, but then children were generally christened before
their personalities were either known or developed. Gabriel had the distinct
impression her father might better have chosen to name her after some
plant with thorns.

Something rumbled in his chest. A laugh of amusement or a growl of
frustration? Before he could decide which, and whether to let it escape,
she added a prim concession.

"Though I suppose it would be fair to say I was *pleasantly* surprised."

A small triumph, but still it left him almost giddy. She was not indifferent
to him. He dipped his head, partly in a bow of acknowledgment, and partly
to hide what he feared might be a foolish grin. "Then I shall consider myself
amply rewarded for the trouble of finding camellias in London, in May."

When he raised his eyes to her once more, she was studying his
expression. "Wildflowers cannot have been much easier to come by," she
said after a moment.

Wildflowers?

Gabriel, who had built his reputation on never revealing more than he
meant to reveal, blinked. Twice.

A dreadful tell. Little old ladies who played nothing more daring than
loo would have tittered at him knowingly behind their cards. A sharp
would have called his bluff on the spot.

Camellia did neither. But she knew he had come up empty this hand.
Of that, he had no doubt. The corners of her brows drew together ever so
slightly, and her gaze slid past him, to the extravagant arrangement on
the table.

Oh. *Wildflowers.*

"And was Lady Felicity also...pleased?" he heard himself say.

"You must ask her yourself." Camellia's bright eyes were still focused on some point behind him, but higher now. The object of her gaze was something other than the flowers.

They were no longer alone.

"My lord. How good of you to call." On silent feet, Felicity crossed the room, her voice brittle and dull, like the wintry leaves on a tree from which the sap of life had been sucked. No, she was certainly not eager. But she had come, nonetheless.

When she stopped and stood beside her cousin, comparison between them was inevitable. In the unforgiving morning light, filtered through yellow draperies, Camellia looked drawn and tired, every bit ten years Felicity's senior. Dark and more than a little defiant.

Next to her, the daughter of the Earl of Merrick glowed gold, like a beam of sunlight herself. She was not smiling; in fact, her expression was so blank, he suspected she had spent some time in the looking glass perfecting it, having seen the animation in her face when she spoke with others. An English rose, which he was to prune and train and pluck as he saw fit. She would never shock or scold him. She would never, never tell him no.

No other man of his acquaintance would have thought it a decision worth weighing. Felicity was in every respect the ideal toward which marriage-minded English gentlemen strived, and if not for her brother's foolishness and her father's weakness, he would have lost any chance at her hand long ago. His choice was clear. So clear, he ought not even call it a choice.

But oh, he craved something quite different in a woman. A challenge. A contest of wits, of wills—one he was not certain to win. The companionship of one as sharp and cynical as he. For beneath that diamond-honed edge of defiance that glittered in Camellia's green eyes, he saw passion. Throbbing, aching, scratching, clawing, dangerous, deadly passion. It might destroy him, but he would revel in his destruction.

Worse, though, he would destroy her.

Turning slightly, he bowed to Felicity. He thought of the promise Fox had extorted from him. He must be a gentleman. He must marry this girl and do his duty by Stoke and the memory of his father. "How lovely you look this morning, ma'am," he said to her.

A curtsy, accompanied by a careful smile. "Thank you, my lord. You are too kind." With the wave of one arm, she gestured him to the chairs behind her, then cleared her throat nervously. "Mama wishes to speak with you, Cousin."

So, they were to have a moment's privacy. Time enough for him to speak his piece, if he chose. A glance darted between the two women. He expected to see desperation in Felicity's eyes, a plea not to be left alone with this monster. But she was braver than he had realized. He saw only resignation to her fate.

Camellia gave a sharp nod. "Of course. I'll just..." She turned and hastily gathered her papers, so dense with ink they crinkled and crackled in her hands. In another moment, she was gone, the door left open behind her.

"I fear I disturbed Miss Burke at her work," he said as he sat. Rather than giving under his weight, the overstuffed cushion resisted, as if trying to push him onto the rug. Onto one knee, perhaps. Firmly, he planted the soles of his boots flat against the floor.

"Oh, it is nearly impossible not to disturb her work. She's always writing. Mama says she goes through paper and ink at an alarming rate."

Bristling at the implied criticism of Camellia, he said, rather more loftily than he had intended, "On Lady Merrick's behalf, I suppose."

"On occasion, yes. But my mother is..."

Too lazy for letter writing, Gabriel silently supplied.

After pausing and pressing her lips together, giving the unexpected impression that she had restrained a similar observation, Felicity began again. "The letters, I believe, go to some Irish correspondent of my cousin's. She has several family members in Dublin."

Gabriel nodded. "Yes. I believe Fox mentioned something about it."

But those overwritten outpourings of Camellia's pen surely were not destined for a doting parent or a curious sibling. *A lover*, jealousy whispered petulantly in his ear.

Damn it, why did he care to whom she wrote?

Because he did not like to imagine those eyes scouring some other man's face. Because he wanted to believe that she too had spent a lifetime seeking a match she had never found, a game of chess in which she would not have to resort to swiping at the pieces like a bored house cat merely to liven up the contest. Because when he thought of her a thrill of something like terror chased through his veins, and because he knew he didn't frighten her at all.

Though God knew, she should be frightened.

"My dear Felicity," he began, determined to do the thing he must do. Utter madness to be thinking of anything other than his duty. Utter madness to be thinking of Camellia.

Her breath caught. Anticipation, but not of the pleasurable sort. "Yes, my lord?"

My lord. He might have corrected her. After all, they were to be married, were they not?

Curious that he had no particular desire to hear his given name on *her* lips.

Afterward, he could not have said what his next words to her had been. Some commonplace about the weather, he thought, and after she had recovered from her surprise, Felicity had turned the conversation toward Lady Penhurst's musical evening, which promised to be dread... er, *delightful.*

Once five endless, respectable minutes had ticked and tocked their way into ten, he allowed the chair to propel him to his feet. "I will wish you good morning, ma'am. I will be disrupting your plans for the day, otherwise."

She rose with him, bewildered though not disappointed. "You could do no such thing, my lord," she insisted, curtsying. "My time is at your disposal."

True, of course. Everything of hers was at his disposal. Lord Trenton had played the game and lost. Gabriel had played and...won, as he almost always did. One final card to toss on the table, and he would have everything he needed.

And nothing he wanted.

Better that way, his conscience scolded. Yes, yes...but he was finding it damned difficult to force himself to the point, nonetheless. He bowed and excused himself from the room. Only when the butler had shown him out the door and he was striding freely down Brook Street did he realize Felicity had never mentioned the flowers, conspicuous though they had been in the cozy sitting room.

It was as well. After all, they had as good as been chosen for her by Fox.

Chapter 8

"Miss, the carriage is here."

At Betsy's shout, Cami's hand jerked. "Drat!" She had pressed down so fiercely on the tip of her pen, it had left a little blot and nearly made a hole in the paper.

Most of the manuscript will have to be recopied anyway, she consoled herself as she laid the pen in its tray. Mr. Dawkins could not be expected to make heads nor tails of her scribbles. Once it was legible, however, she felt certain he would agree that she had transformed her villain utterly, from a pasteboard shadow in a pantomime to a complex and compelling man. The changes to Lord Granville would make his attempt to destroy Róisín more forceful, more heart-wrenching. Surely even an English audience would grant that much.

From time to time, though, she found herself wondering if the closing scene as she had first written it was consistent with the character he had become. Would readers feel too much sympathy for Granville? Would it blunt the savage critique of England's treatment of Ireland that lay behind Róisín's tragic story?

"Miss?"

Betsy was still in the stairwell, but closer now, and the note of anxiety in her voice meant Cami would not have long before the door opened. After wiping her hands, she laid the still-damp page atop the rest of the manuscript of *The Wild Irish Rose*, already safely ensconced in her lap desk. Those last pages would have to wait until tomorrow.

Though Aunt Merrick had never been noted for her equanimity, since her head cold the servants had gone out of their way to avoid trying her patience further. Her increased peevishness, as everyone knew, was entirely a consequence of Lord Ashborough's failure to come to the point. Three outings in the last week, three opportunties discreetly provided for him to propose to Felicity, and still nothing.

Cami had not been required to accompany them on those outings. She had, however, received a minute recounting—once from her aunt, and once from her cousin—of both his behavior and his appearance. As a consequence, Gabriel had been constantly in her thoughts; even her dreams had not been safe from him. More than once, she had awakened with her pulse pounding and damp sheets tangled around her limbs. And it had not been fear that had made her heart race.

Never one to waste an experience, however, she had used every detail she gleaned, every moment of the time she had spent in his imagined company, to better her book.

From her aunt, she had learned that Lord Ashborough did not even glance into the card room at the Crawfords' ball. "Proof," she had insisted, "that he means to turn over a new leaf." Privately, Cami suspected that the card room at a ton ball was not up to his usual standards. Or at least, his usual stakes. Felicity had revealed his unexpected but similarly portentous move to Grosvenor Square, into the previously abandoned Finch House. "Not *abandoned*," Lady Merrick had corrected her. Apparently, he had always kept a full complement of servants employed to care for the place, even though he did not live there. Aunt Merrick seemed to regard it as proof of his munificence, and certainly it would be futile to argue about pointless displays of wealth with a woman who seemed determined to live so that no one would suspect the Trenton family was teetering on the brink of ruin.

Unlike her mother, Felicity never rhapsodized about his good looks or his gallant behavior. Instead, her accounts of the time she spent with the marquess were frequently interspersed with some mention of Mr. Fox, who must, it seemed to Cami, be hovering over his friend like a guardian angel determined to keep him on the straight and narrow path. Felicity was always quick to recall some pleasant remark he had made, to recount an amusing story about his dogs, or once, to remark, quite apropos of nothing, that she had always thought gray eyes expressed uncommon intelligence.

Not content to watch her cousin sacrifice either her affections or herself, Cami was determined to make certain that Felicity did not suffer in real life the way Róisín had in the pages of fiction. So she had formulated a plan.

"Miss?" Betsy sounded almost desperate.

"I'm coming." Cami shook the wrinkles from her skirts as she rose to leave the room. The movement stirred the air and brought the scent of camellias to her nose. Lord Ashborough had, through word and deed, revealed his interest in her, an interest she dared not reciprocate anywhere but in her dreams.

But with any luck, Lady Penhurst's musical evening would provide the perfect opportunity to exploit that interest.

Inside the carriage, she took the place beside her cousin. Aunt Merrick looked her up and down before tapping on the ceiling to order the driver to move on. "I would gladly have sent King to dress your hair, Camellia."

"Thank you, Aunt. But there was no need."

"I think it's quite..." Felicity reached up to tuck a wayward lock into the loose arrangement. "Is it an Irish fashion, Cousin?"

Cami smiled. "You may say so. It is entirely my own invention." Aunt Merrick huffed in disapproval and turned to look out the window.

Given her own way, Cami would have walked the short distance to Lady Penhurst's, rather than be confined in the now silent, increasingly stuffy carriage. Though dusk was falling, the sky was still light, the air unseasonably warm—perfect for a meandering stroll through Mayfair. Aunt Merrick would have protested that the weather was changeable and, worse, the behavior was unseemly. But Cami cared little for the consequence conveyed by the crest on the door of the coach or the well-matched team of horses that drew it.

When the carriage slowed just a few moments later, Aunt Merrick remarked on the number of arriving guests. "Lady Penhurst should be pleased. She could not have been sure of a crush after last spring's scandal about her niece, the one they called the Disappearing Duchess."

A scandal? That explained Cami's inclusion in the invitation. Lady Penhurst must have been eager to fill out her guest list. For her own part, Cami could imagine little worse than an evening designed to showcase the dubious musical talents of assorted young ladies. And as for the young men before whom those talents were to be displayed...were there not more important things to discover about a potential wife than her ability to perform on the pianoforte?

A footman opened the carriage door and lowered the step. Cami was the last to descend. The steady trickle of arriving guests suggested that at least some of London society did not share her reservations about the evening's entertainment. Or perhaps they were just hoping for another scandal. "What of Lord Penhurst?" she asked.

"Lady Penhurst's son. He was at school with Stephen," Felicity explained in a whisper. "Rather wild. I doubt we'll see him tonight."

He was standing beside his mother in the receiving line, however, offering up words of greeting tinged with boredom. "Will you be favoring us with a song tonight, Lady Felicity?" he asked, clearly uninterested in the answer. Cami wondered if his future bride had the misfortune to be among the performers.

Before Felicity could speak or shake her head, his mother broke in. She was a thin, sharp-eyed woman with such coarse gray curls Cami hoped they were false. "No need. She's made her match already, as I heard tell," she said, with a suggestive lift to her brows. The last scandal did not seem to have dulled Lady Penhurst's appetite for gossip.

Felicity's cheeks flushed red. Immediately following Lady Montlake's ball, her name had begun to be paired publicly with Lord Ash's, and tongues had begun to wag, much to her chagrin.

"Oh?" Lord Penhurst was already looking past them to the next guests. "And who is the fortunate gentleman?"

"If the rumors are true, she's expecting an offer from Lord Ashborough," declared Lady Penhurst in a sham whisper that carried along the receiving line. "Though it's really not done, I invited him tonight. Strictly on your behalf, you know," she told Felicity. "He arrived not long ago."

The name returned Penhurst's gaze to her face as he paled and offered her a stiff bow. "Indeed he did. I wish you the best of luck, ma'am."

The doors that usually separated the dining room and receiving room had been opened to create one large space, and all the ordinary furniture had been removed in favor of spindly gilt chairs. In neat rows, they faced a slightly raised dais surrounded by plants and upon which sat a pianoforte, two more chairs, and a harp. As yet, no musicians occupied the stage, but the seats for the audience were filling rapidly, making the empty chairs around Lord Ashborough conspicuous.

He rose and stepped toward them, holding out an arm for Lady Merrick and smiling at Felicity. "Good evening. There are seats just here. Please, join me."

"Mr. Fox does not accompany you this evening, my lord?" Felicity asked. Cami ached at the hopeful note in her voice.

"His sister, Lady Dalrymple, holds a weekly salon, to which he is promised in perpetuity, I'm afraid." The words were accompanied by a sweeping glance that settled for the merest moment on Cami before he returned his attention to leading Lady Merrick to a chair.

The flash of heat, of hardness, in his eyes made Cami's knees wobble beneath her skirts. She reached a self-conscious hand to the silk ribbon that wound its way through her hair and circled her throat. What had felt like cleverness half an hour past now felt decidedly dangerous.

Drawing a steadying breath, she looped her arm through Felicity's elbow and pushed onward. She must do whatever was necessary to keep her cousin safe. Even if it meant throwing herself onto the fire.

* * * *

My God. Was she taunting him?

Loosely curled locks of black hair hung softly about her face and shoulders; no difficulty picturing them spread across his pillow after a tumble. A token effort to contain the mass of dark waves came in the form of a band of coquelicot silk. A collar of the same bright ribbon encircled her slender neck. His ribbon.

A possessive growl rumbled through him.

His.

The last thing he needed was a woman who inspired those sorts of thoughts. His desires were a furnace best not stoked. Carefully, he arranged the seating so as to put as much distance between him and Camellia as possible, to ward off any further temptation. Felicity to his right, her mother beyond that, Camellia at the end. Entirely out of his range of vision—unless he sat up straighter than was comfortable and leaned slightly backward in his chair to catch a glimpse of her profile. Felicity's darting frown caught him at it more than once.

To distract himself, he called up the memory of Uncle Finch's gray-tinged face, wheezing out his taunts. Empty threats, surely. But a timely reminder of the man's determination to see his useless son inherit the marquessate. Gabriel could put a stop to all of it with a bride of good birth and good breeding. Better still if she was too meek to complain about the unfortunate necessity of marrying a rogue.

Forcing his attention to the program, he assessed the tortures that lay ahead. Four pieces before the interval, four afterward. Would the vocalist or the violinist screech worse? He clapped politely for the young woman who faced the pianoforte as if she had a plank stuffed down the back of her dress. He studied the reflection of the chandelier in the high polish of his boot during an overly ambitious aria, while silently praying its composer might deign to make an appearance—from the beyond if necessary—to prevent Miss Blaise from further tarnishing his good name.

The first rippling notes of the harp were soothing, a welcome change. Beside him, Felicity smiled and shifted, leaning to murmur something to her mother, who nodded approvingly. Without any contortion on his part, their movements opened up his line of sight to Camellia, who sat almost as stiffly as the piano player, the corners of her mouth turned down.

"Do you dislike the harp, Miss Burke?" he asked when they came together between the performances. It would be churlish to ignore her entirely, he excused himself. And likely to draw the notice of others.

"Camellia dislikes anything that smacks of frivolity, Lord Ash," Lady Merrick asserted before she could answer for herself.

He expected to see disapproval in Camellia's expression—disapproval either of the performance or her aunt's charge. But the countess' words seemed to have caught her off guard, so that her full lips were parted in half shock, half pout. The pose gave the very briefest of glimpses at the woman she hid behind that mask of severity.

Then those mobile lips curved ever so slightly upward at the ends and she said, "I have no objection at all to the harp, my lord. When it is well played."

It was Lady Felicity's turn to gasp in surprise. "You do not mean to fault Miss Cunningham's talent, surely."

"She plays well enough, I'm sure. Not so well as many I have had the pleasure of hearing. Those who have a sort of *native* feeling for the instrument, if you will," she added. "As an Irishwoman, I cannot bear to see harpistry classed among the merely fashionable accomplishments, like painting screens or netting purses."

"Surely you would not deny us access to your country's finest exports?" Gabriel prodded devilishly.

"Such as linen?" she suggested, glancing from him to her aunt as she replied. "Or salmon? Or a ridiculous stage brogue at which you may laugh when you choose to while away an hour at the theatre?" Lady Merrick's complacent nod of agreement became a frown. "Indeed not," Camellia finished, her defiance cast as reassurance. "I would deny no one anything to which they have earned the right."

"A patriot, eh?" Gabriel began, but her aunt's scold cut him short.

"Really, Camellia. A fling at politics? I would expect a niece of the Earl of Merrick to know enough to keep her opinions on such matters to herself."

"Which is to say, to have no opinions at all," Camellia countered.

Lady Merrick made no effort to deny the claim, but instead looked toward Gabriel for confirmation. He could see out of the corner of his eye that Lady Felicity, that specimen of ideal English womanhood, had turned away, clearly and properly bored by the direction the conversation had taken.

"I have always considered it remarkably shortsighted to believe that a woman exists to cater to a man's pleasure," Gabriel said, forcing himself to look only at the countess, "but then to expect she ought to know nothing about what pleases him—what interests him, what occupies him in his daily life."

"Indeed, my lord, his interests, his desires, should be her daily study," Lady Merrick said. "But to form an opinion counter to his own on any matter of importance? Surely you would not tolerate—"

"A gentleman who cannot bear to have his opinions countered is not worthy of having them," he declared. "Surely you would not require a lady to respect beliefs that cannot be defended?"

Before her aunt could reply, Camellia spoke, and he could no longer avoid her eyes. Something in them suggested disappointment—no, not that, but rather confusion, as if she were having to revise some long-held opinion and found the process trying. "What of the lady?" she asked. "Are her beliefs entitled to the same respect?"

"If they are sincerely held and can be rationally defended, then yes. But the passion of a moment, or an unthinking prejudice—"

"National pride, perhaps?" Her chin jutted forward.

"Precisely. One's emotions must be kept under good regulation," he insisted, wondering when he had become such an idealist. Or perhaps a fool. After all, it was emotion that had brought him to this pass to begin with. "Certainly, they have no place in the world of politics."

"Which is why," Lady Merrick interjected with a note of finality, clearly intending to bring the distasteful subject to a close, "God has ordained politics to be the province of rational men, and not such poor, weak creatures as we women who are too easily swayed by our hearts."

Camellia's lips parted again. This time, however, he suspected that the words struggling to force their way past them might cause her to lose her place entirely—or at least cause her to lose the privilege of leaving the house.

So he spoke over her. "Lady Felicity, may I escort you to the refreshment room?"

Although he would have been willing to swear that she had not heard a word that had passed among her cousin, her mother, and him, she responded with alacrity to his offer. "Yes, of course, my lord."

Lady Merrick sent a triumphant glance in her niece's direction, as if his attention to Lady Felicity confirmed the countess' opinion that men preferred empty-headed females.

She could be forgiven for thinking it, he supposed. She was not even entirely wrong. There were such men, certainly.

Unfortunately for Lady Felicity, he was not one of them.

With a polite nod toward the others, he offered Felicity his arm. As her gloved hand slid along his sleeve, he could not help but wonder whether Camellia's touch would feel similarly cool. He rather suspected it would scorch. Her indignation radiated from her in waves, like heat rising from the baked earth on a late summer day.

Never, never had he wanted so badly to be burned.

"Camellia," he heard Lady Merrick command after they had walked a few steps away, "fetch me a lemonade."

Ordinarily, he might have turned back and offered to bring it himself. But as he glanced toward the refreshment room, at the milling crowds awaiting the next performance, another plan began to form in his mind. A dangerous, delectable sort of plan. And he held his tongue.

"Which of the performances did you most enjoy, Lord Ash?" Felicity asked, after a moment's silence.

"Sadly, I have no judgment in matters of music," he said, mustering his most charming demeanor. "You must teach me which I ought to have liked best."

Lady Felicity looked up at him, her blue gaze awash in consternation. It was not that she did not have an opinion, he realized. Any fool could see that she did. But she had been scolded once too often for offering it. He could not help but think that if someone like Christopher Fox, someone safe, had asked the question, she would have been only too eager to speak her mind.

It had been difficult enough to follow through with this marriage scheme when he had thought her dull and dumb. God help him if he were to discover she was more like her cousin than first met the eye.

"I quite liked the harp, actually," she said at last, "until Cousin Camellia said—"

"Shall I let you in on a little secret?" He tilted his head toward her as if to impart a confidence. "Miss Burke quite liked it as well."

"Oh, do you think so?" Her face brightened. "I found it wonderful. I would like to have learned, but Papa said the pianoforte was sufficient. And even then, I—I am not very good." That admission was accompanied by a demure lowering of her gaze.

"Your modesty becomes you," he said, although he suspected she was not merely being modest. "But I will not permit you to find fault with these perfect fingers," he murmured, taking them in his and lifting them almost to his mouth as he spoke.

He did not kiss her hand. And, as was proper, she gently withdrew from his grasp and blushed as if he had. "What nonsense you speak, Lord Ash," she protested.

Ah, God, she was sweet innocence itself, and he was the basest cad in existence for using her for it. But such a revelation would surprise no one.

Out of the corner of his eye, he caught a glimpse of Camellia waiting at the nearby table. "Yes. I fear I have quite taken leave of my senses," he said as whatever good intentions he possessed rapidly abandoned him and set to work paving the road to hell—or at least, opening a path to the punch bowl. "In fact, I'm afraid I've just remembered a prior engagement. I will have to leave soon, if I am not to be late."

"Of course, my lord. I would not wish to be the cause of your breaking a promise."

Those gentle words were almost enough to stay him from his course. Almost.

But they were accompanied by a slight easing of her posture. Relief. She wanted to escape as much as he did. "You are too generous, my dear." The endearment fell from his lips with only the slightest hesitation. "May I bring you a glass of champagne before I go?"

She was tempted, he could see. "Mama never permits it." She paused, considering, and then dutifully shook her head. "Just lemonade, if you please."

And in another moment, he was looking down at the blue-black twists of Camellia's hair, imagining what it would be like to untie the ribbon that held it and watch it tumble free to tease her breasts.

He leaned forward under the guise of reaching for a cup—the same cup for which she had reached. His fingers brushed hers—both gloved, this time—and then retreated. "I do beg your pardon, Miss Burke." Her hand dropped to her side, so he picked up the cup and offered it to her with a bow. "Will you be so kind as to deliver a message to Lady Merrick on my behalf?"

She took the drink from his hand and nodded, but she did not meet his eye.

"I have just remembered another commitment and must take my leave. Please give her ladyship my regards and extend my apologies for this abrupt departure."

"You ought to speak for yourself, my lord," she said, straightening her spectacles with her free hand. "Are you quite certain my feeble, female brain is capable of remembering such an important commission?"

He felt a smile tug at his lips. "Quite." Leaning forward on the pretense of taking a second cup, he spoke again, but this time, his whispered words were for her ears only. "When the music resumes, meet me in the gallery at the rear of the house." A request he had no business making. In a tone that ought to cause her to take flight, if she truly possessed even an ounce of the good sense he thought she did. As he straightened up, he raised his voice again. "Let me take you to your cousin. You and she can return to Lady Merrick's side together."

A high flush of color had spread across Camellia's cheekbones, and her eyes were focused unseeingly on the cup in her hands. For a moment, he feared he had played the wrong card and lost everything.

But those hands did not tremble. No golden drop threatened to overspill the rim of the crystal cup. No, he did not think he had not misjudged her desires entirely.

Long before anyone could notice anything unusual about her behavior, she was herself again, walking toward her cousin with firmness of purpose that would cause a lesser man—or perhaps a better man—to quail.

"Lord Ashborough wishes me to return you to your mama," she said to Felicity, her voice prim and only slightly higher pitched than usual. "We should go, before the music resumes."

"Oh, yes, of course," Felicity agreed, separating herself from a cluster of young women, including the unfortunate harpist. "I will wish you a good evening, Lord Ash," she said as she curtsied. "I hope the rest of it proves enjoyable."

"You are too kind, ma'am. It would be unforgiveable in me to hope for more pleasure than I have already received," he said, bowing first to her and then to Camellia. Unforgiveable—nevertheless, more pleasure was precisely what he sought. "Lady Felicity. Miss Burke. Till we meet again."

Camellia's curtsy seemed slightly unsteady, and her lips were parted, as they had been earlier, weighing her words. Her tongue peeked out and swiped at their fullness, as though her mouth had suddenly gone dry. Apparently forgetting that the beverage she carried was intended for her aunt, she took a careful sip before finally and simply saying, "My lord." Then she linked her arm with her cousin's and walked back to Lady Merrick.

He watched them go from a spot near the entryway. Two young women he did not recognize, obviously sisters, rose and walked to the front of the room. The elder one seated herself at the pianoforte while the other readied her voice. Her preparatory scale ascended in a haphazard fashion that did not bode well for the performance. Still, Gabriel turned to leave with reluctance as other guests began to return to their seats. As he scanned the faces around him for some sign of Lady Penhurst—who, he suspected, would protest his departure; the woman did so love a scandal—his eye caught a movement farther off. A dark-haired woman slipping through one of the doors at the back, probably looking for the ladies' retiring room. Nothing remarkable in that.

Nevertheless, his pulse ticked upward at the sight.

Before the footman could open the door and show him out, Gabriel bid a hasty retreat, following Camellia.

Chapter 9

Cami listened, unmoving, to the slow tap of his footsteps as he crossed the empty gallery and came to stand behind her. It was hardly a sneak attack. This was what she had planned, what she had hoped for, was it not? But at the sound of his voice, she jumped nonetheless.

"You came."

Was it her imagination, or did disappointment edge his words?

Cami wished now that she had turned around before he had reached her, stepped away from the deep window alcove where she had taken shelter. She needed to see his face, to read the expression in his eyes. Raising her gaze to the glass, she sought their reflection instead. But the window was just a window, no mirrored portal into his mind. The gallery behind them was too dark, clearly not intended to be among the public spaces for this evening's entertainment. And the last violet light of day still illumined the garden before them. Topiaries cast eerie, jagged shadows along the gravel paths.

"Why?" he whispered when she did not speak.

Because you asked me to.

Caught off guard by her own unspoken confession, she flinched again. *Could* that be the reason? Was everything she had ever said about independence, self-determination, autonomy, a lie? Had she been waiting all her life for a man merely to *ask?*

No. She most certainly had not.

Forcing herself to stand a bit taller, she spun on one foot to face him and found him standing so close it was an effort not to touch him.

"Because I wanted to."

His eyes flickered over her face, searching. "I felt certain you would prove too wise to do such a foolish thing."

"*Was* it foolish, then?" The words were a whisper on her lips.

Another sweeping glance along the ribbon at her throat; she could have sworn she felt the heat of that look like a touch. "Very."

She fought to keep from cutting her gaze away. "Yes, well..." Speaking was an effort. "My brother Paris delights in telling me I am too smart for my own good." The smile that rose to her lips at the memory was genuine, if weak. "But no one has ever accused me of being too wise." His answering expression, a sort of half smile that mirrored her own, did nothing to settle her jangling nerves. "I came because I wish to speak with you about Lady Felicity," she said finally. "She does not wish to marry you."

The revelation did not seem to surprise him. "She will be a marchioness," he reminded her. "Fine clothes, beautiful homes, jewels to make the queen herself envious. Society would say that a dowerless girl should account herself fortunate."

"Ah, yes." Cami nodded again, growing braver. "But Society is not being asked to make a devil's bargain."

At that, a soft laugh tinged with bitterness parted his lips. "So you met me here to plead on her behalf."

Her head began to bob of its own volition. But she would not lie....

Not even to herself.

Oh, she had set out this evening with a plan in mind, a plan to help Felicity. But somewhere along the way, on the long journey from her writing table to where she stood now, she had been forced to admit she was doing this for herself. Because he wanted her, and his desire gave her a new, heady power that flushed through her veins and left her trembling. Because he was sardonic and rakish and forbidden...and she wanted him, just the same.

His head tilted to the side as he studied her expression. Cami feared her face revealed more than it should.

"If I did not know better, I would suspect you of trying to compromise me, Camellia," he said, softly teasing. "Wearing that ribbon. Luring me here. Were you hoping to save your cousin by exposing me for a rogue? I can assure you, everyone already knows." One hand rose to sweep a lock of her hair out of her eyes. The same wayward curl that Felicity had tried to restrain, perhaps. But the brush of his fingers behind her ear, the warmth of his palm beside her cheek were not at all the same. "You should be considerably more worried that I will compromise you."

Her mouth was dry, too parched for speech. She longed for a glass of the ice-cold champagne that had been flowing so freely in the other room, though she feared if one were in her grasp now, she would have tossed it back like a trollop.

"Y-you couldn't," she managed to say at last, all the while a prisoner to his heated gaze.

"Is that a challenge?" His hand slid forward and he traced the curves and dips of her upper lip with the pad of his thumb, then dragged it across the fullness of the lower. Inexplicably, her tongue longed to dart out and chase the sensation of his touch. Not the first time, certainly, that her Irish tongue had got her in trouble. She did not part her lips until she could be certain it was under her control.

"You cannot compromise me," she declared. And she meant it. "No one gives a fig about my reputation. I am a woman of mature years— almost eight and twenty of them, if you must know—no green girl whose innocence must be carefully guarded. And most important of all, I am a lady's companion, not a lady."

He took in her words without blinking, without releasing her, without reacting in any way. As if he expected them, or accepted them in any case. Until she reached the end of her litany.

"You are a niece of the Earl of Merrick." His voice was firm, correcting her error. "A granddaughter of the late earl, if my understanding of your family tree is not faulty. Therefore, by birth, a lady."

If he had not been touching her, she would have shaken her head in denial. But the gesture would only have nestled her cheek into his palm. "I am the daughter of a noblewoman, it is true, but one severed from her family with the neatness and completeness that ordinarily requires a surgeon's scalpel. I am also the daughter of a Dublin solicitor," she reminded him. "Not a gentleman, in the common usage of the term. I cherish no hope of rising to a rank to which I have never belonged."

"Why then did you come to London?"

"Partly for my mother. My uncle expressed a desire to heal the rift in their family."

"But you are skeptical of his success?"

"At present, he is in no position even to help himself. As you well know."

Those words did produce some reaction. For the briefest of moments, his eyes slid away from hers. But almost before she had noticed their movement, they were once more focused sharply on her face. "If not only for your family, then why?"

It was her turn to shift her gaze, to let it drift over his lips to settle in the vicinity of his cravat. "I have reasons of my own."

"Which are not to be divulged..."

"Not at present."

"And never to me." Once more, she heard disappointment in his voice. Along with a note of certainty that he deserved to be disappointed.

She longed to smooth a cool hand over his brow, to wipe away the cynicism etched there. But how foolish, really, to imagine that she of all people—sharp tongued, skeptical—had such a gift. If he *could* be soothed, improved, sweet Felicity would be far better suited to the task, would she not? "I came here to speak with you about the fate of my cousin," she insisted. "Her brother and her parents have behaved shockingly. And I do not wish to see her hurt." That, at least, was the truth. Certainly Cami did not want to be the one causing her pain.

"Lady Felicity will be perfectly safe," he vowed. His thumb now traced the edge of her jaw, then slipped lower to brush back and forth across the silk ribbon encircling her throat. Reflexively, she swallowed, though she knew he would feel that proof of her nervousness, could not miss the flutter of her pulse. A wicked smile curved his lips, and the pressure of his hand increased. He was drawing her closer, lowering his mouth to hers. "You, on the other hand..."

Awareness of what was to come hovered like a freshly dipped quill suspended above a blank page. Her fingertips, the ones he had once kissed, tingled. When she laid that hand against his chest and slid her palm upward to his shoulder, anticipation gathered and grew, trembled at the edge for a moment, then tumbled headlong, chasing through every vein, every fiber of her being, the way a droplet of ink fell from a pen, seeped into the very fibers of the paper, and could never be erased.

The slightest movement—she would not even have to stretch onto her tiptoes—and she would be kissing him.

Instinct told her to close her eyes but the writer in her resisted, determined to absorb every detail of this moment: the unexpected softening of his expression, the sparkle in his heavy-lidded eyes, the grain of beard peppering his skin.

"You should go." His breath whispered across her lips. "Now."

But she was not even wise enough to heed the warning in his voice.

Did he move, or did she? In that moment, all that mattered was the meeting of their lips, gentler than she had expected. Gentler than she needed. Sliding her hand higher, around his neck, she pressed closer to him and was rewarded with the hard length of his body, fitted perfectly against her softness. His other arm came around her waist, his palm settling on the flare of her hip, his fingertips tracing lightly along her curves. Oh, yes. He was a rake. He was not in the habit of denying himself pleasure, and a woman's body was no mystery to him. And she would revel in that knowledge. Just this once. Just this once.

The kiss deepened, grew firm. When his tongue touched the seam of her lips, she parted them eagerly to his invasion. But he pressed no further. Instead he teased her, little flicks of slick sensation that had her chasing and darting after them, until her tongue was right inside his mouth, and he was sucking on it, drawing her in, drawing her down. Proving she could be tempted. A moan of longing rumbled in her throat, and she was not ashamed.

Still, she did not close her eyes. He held her gaze as she held his, and it was more intense, more intimate than the dance of their tongues, the kneading hand at her bottom, the hot weight of his erection against her belly. She was lost, utterly lost in his dark eyes. This was the descent, the fall. The end. She had been wrong about not being ruined. This was not her first kiss, but it would surely be her last. It would ruin her for any other.

Her left hand rose and met her right at his nape, fingertips tangling together in his hair where it fell over his collar. Did the tug of her searching fingers give him pain? If so, his only answer was to hitch her higher against him, to plunder her mouth with a kiss so greedy, breath was an afterthought. Then his eyelids drifted closed at last, breaking the spell.

Before she knew it was over, she was standing apart, her feet flat on the floor, her hands sinking to her sides. As free of his embrace as if it had never happened. Cooler air slipped between them.

He tugged one coat sleeve into place, an entirely unnecessary gesture. Did she look as unmussed, unrumpled, unaffected by their kiss as he? Well, she might lack his expertise in such matters, but she would not be bested by his practiced composure. She forced her ragged breathing to slow, though her nostrils flared at the effort. Perhaps, in the dimly lit room, such a small detail would go unnoticed.

No such luck. A smile quirked at the corner of his mouth as he reached up to straighten her skewed spectacles. The movement made her aware of smudges across each lens. Mastering her annoyance, the way her fingers itched to tug them off and wipe them clean, she met his gaze. Squarely. Sternly.

In answer, the curve of his lips shifted into something that threatened to melt her insides. "Am I always to be the subject of such careful study, Camellia? Well, the next time I kiss you, you'll close those eyes."

It wasn't a threat, or even a command. It was a promise. A promise that one day, he would offer safety enough to conquer her fears, knowledge to quench the thirst of her curiosity. A promise that part of her longed for him to keep right that moment. Her breath came faster, despite her best efforts. "Next time? But we can't—"

"Don't be tiresome, my dear. Obviously we can. We did." He crossed his arms over his chest and arced one brow. "The only question now is whether we will do it again."

What about Felicity? her conscience prompted. She tried to shake off the question. Felicity did not want his kisses. But one day soon, she'd have them, whether she wanted them or not. Something very like jealousy flickered through Cami at the thought. Oh, how could she be attracted to the man who was supposed to be her perfect villain? What had she done?

She squared her shoulders and tipped her chin upward. "We *must* not."

The familiar sardonic mask slipped over his face as he bowed and stepped aside, freeing her to walk away. "You see, I was right. You *are* a wise woman."

Not truly wise, no—but wise enough to take the avenue of escape he offered this time, her steps measured at first, then quicker as she drew closer to the door. What had she been thinking when she had left the safety of the salon to meet him?

On the one hand, she had extracted an unexpected promise that Felicity would come to no harm. Truth be told, Felicity might be better off as Lady Ashborough than she was now, the pawn of a family driven to desperation. And strange though it might seem, Cami trusted him to keep his word. He had always been honest with her, even about his villainy. And she had never been certain that all of the things that looked like villainy really were.

On the other hand, he had behaved as badly as she had hoped he might, touching her, kissing her.... But what did it change? As he himself had pointed out, no one had ever denied his reputation for petticoat chasing, or anything else. Her aunt and uncle had known of it from the first and were still resigned to his suit; Felicity grew more so every day.

On the...well, she was out of hands, but there was still a third point to be raised in this internal, infernal debate: She had wanted his kiss. Still did. Fought with each footstep not to whirl around and race back to his arms and betray her weaknesses, rather than expose his.

In the end, she had mustered proof not of his wicked nature, but of her own.

As she exchanged the dimness of the gallery for the brightness of the salon, she paused to polish her spectacles, stopping near two gentlemen in earnest conversation at the back of the room. Who could be blamed for seeking some distraction from the shrill yet flat notes of a duet that was hopefully winding to a close? She would have gone by without a thought if she had not caught a few whispered words—whispered not just because the speaker feared to be overheard or to interrupt the performance, but because he could not seem to fill his lungs to put sufficient breath behind them.

"I trust I can count on your vote, Penhurst."

The words themselves were almost as familiar as the rough voice. Another deal, no doubt accompanied by another threat. Another young nobleman at someone's mercy. The man seemed confident he would get his way.

She kept walking, did not turn to look at the speaker until she was back at her aunt's side. Under cover of tepid applause, she leaned toward Lady Merrick and asked, "Who is that gentleman conversing with Lord Penhurst?"

Making no effort to disguise her intentions, Lady Merrick twisted in her chair. "Where? I don't—oh, at the back. Hmm...one doesn't often seem *him* out and about, especially at functions like this. Come, come," she said, nudging Felicity to her feet. "We ought to make our curtsies."

With her thoughts still on Gabriel, Cami followed in their wake, not having been instructed to stay put.

"Ah, Lord Sebastian. I hope your attendance here this evening is a sign you are in good health."

"Lady Merrick," he gasped out, the words followed by the slightest dip of his head. He did not seem inclined to waste his precious breath on a response to her remark, and indeed, it was perfectly unnecessary. He obviously was not a healthy man. He was thin, too thin, and his skin had both the color and texture of chalk.

"May I introduce my daughter, Lady Felicity Trenton? And Merrick's niece, Miss Burke?"

One shallow bow sufficed for both of them, and his surprisingly sharp-eyed gaze was reserved entirely for Felicity. "Sebastian Finch."

"Uncle to Lord Ash," Aunt Merrick explained, low, to her daughter.

Whatever his other ailments, Lord Sebastian's hearing seemed to be perfectly acute, and the shortened form of his family title did not sit well with the man. Though he did not scold with words, the scowl he shot in her aunt's direction was sufficient to send a chill through Cami too.

Gabriel's uncle was the man she had twice overheard plotting to ruin some unknown gentleman. And he did not strike her as the kind of man who would scruple to make even his own nephew miserable.

Or worse.

"Then you and I may soon be—" Felicity began, speaking more to herself than to him. Now that cold, ruthless look turned to her, and her words squeaked to a halt. Rather than acknowledge the rumors of his nephew's pending engagement to the young woman standing before him, Lord Sebastian cut her instead. With a sharp jerk of his chin he gave silent orders to a goggling Lord Penhurst to show him to a chair.

Felicity paled, then flushed red. Tears glittered along her eyelashes. Instead of returning to their seats, Aunt Merrick huffed and marched them toward the door. The footman was just returning to his post.

"The Trenton carriage. Immediately."

"Yes, ma'am."

Though the footman moved with alacrity, the carriage's arrival was not immediate. They had to wait several long, awkward minutes for their coach to be sorted from the others and brought around to the front of the house. Ample time for Felicity's embarrassment to advance from crimson-cheeked embarrassment to pale, trembling mortification. Meanwhile, Lady Merrick's indignity seethed and boiled and began to spill from her lips like a foaming pot the cook had forgotten to remove from the fire.

"I don't—how dare—who would think—wait until Merrick hears of this!"

When they arrived at Trenton House, Wafford bowed them in, and Lady Merrick marched past, still muttering a half-voiced tirade against the bad behavior of both Lord Sebastian Finch and his nephew. "Tell King to make up one of her special tisanes for my headache," she barked, then pressed the fingertips of her free hand to her temple with a moan.

Both Tom and Wafford were only too willing to believe that the order had been directed at them, if it provided an excuse to escape her ladyship's black mood. With quick steps, they tried to hurry past one another to deliver the message. Linking elbows with her daughter, she began slowly to ascend the stairs, leaning heavily on Felicity's arm, though Felicity's wan face and stumbling steps suggested she might really be the one in need of assistance.

Cami waited until the creak on the stairs rose high enough that she did not think she would be called upon to follow, then strode to the back of the house to take the servants' stairs to her attic room. When she opened the door, warm air, heavy with the scent of camellias, greeted her. Without even pausing to light a candle, she crossed the room, thrust open the small, high window, and tossed the bouquet out, chipped tumbler and all. The satisfying crash of glass against cobblestones never reached her ears, however. The street was too far below.

And the flowers' distinctive aroma lingered in her small, stuffy chamber.

Pacing back to her desk, she caught a shadowy glimpse of herself in the looking glass above the washstand. The ribbon. That damned ribbon. Scratching at her throat, spearing her fingers into her hair, she struggled to free herself from it. But it only wound itself tighter, tangling, snarling. Oh, what had she done? To Felicity? To herself?

After dragging a deep breath into her lungs, she lit a candle, then began again, methodically unwinding and unthreading until the silk coiled on her palm like a living thing. Her eyes darted to the open window, but this time her fingers gripped convulsively and would not obey her rash command to be rid of it. With a sigh, she let the ribbon spill into a drawer. It would be a reminder of his touch, of his tempting kiss. A reminder of her foolishness.

Desperate for something to distract her, she opened her writing desk and looked at her book. She had heeded Mr. Dawkins's directive to make the villain more realistic, more believable. He was real all right. Real enough that she swore she could still feel the heat of his palm where it circled her hip, smell the sinful lure of his cologne, taste his lips on hers. But readers were supposed to despise Granville, not desire him. Had she saved her book, or ruined it? With unaccustomed hesitation, she withdrew the final pages of the manuscript, the scene in which Róisín saved herself and secured her freedom through Lord Granville's death.

Did Cami have the strength to face the story's inevitably tragic end?

She picked up her pen, but before she could dip it into the ink, there was a soft rap at the door. Hurriedly, she stuffed the few loose sheets of paper into the drawer atop the ribbon and closed the lid to her writing desk. Who could be knocking at this hour?

"Yes?"

"May I come in, Cousin?" Though muffled by the thick oak panel, Felicity's voice betrayed her exhaustion.

Cami rose and opened the door. Even by the light of the single candle, Cami could see that Felicity's eyes were still rimmed with red. "Are you all right?"

"I shall be, if a certain gentleman will find the courage to defy his uncle and come to the point."

Cami did not think it was courage Lord Ashborough lacked. "The, uh, the uncle who served as his guardian?"

"No. That was his mother's brother. The gentleman we met this evening is his father's. Mama says he disapproves most strenuously of the reputation his nephew has acquired and has been quite public with his protestations."

"That is unfortunate," Cami said. *Though perhaps understandable.* "Still, has he any particular claim to authority over…?"

Felicity bristled. "Lord Ash may do as he pleases, of course, with or without Lord Sebastian Finch's consent. So it cannot be for that reason he refuses to propose."

"Refuses?" Cami cursed the spark of something very like hope that flickered to life inside her. No. *No.* He was not free. And she ought not to want him, even if he were. "I thought all had been arranged?"

"There has been no offer, no announcement of our betrothal. But our names are already linked. You heard them tonight. The gossip is on everyone's tongue." Lowering her gaze, she began to twist her fingers in her skirt. "I begin to fear he has set out to punish our family further by humiliating me."

Cami recalled Lady Penhurst's smirk. If Lord Ashborough did not propose marriage soon, Felicity would be an object of derision among the ton, perhaps even unmarriageable, depending on the quantity of venom in those wagging tongues.

"But I thought you did not *wish* to marry Lord Ashborough?"

"Well, I—I don't," Felicity admitted, flustered. "It would be misery."

"Misery? Surely not." Cami spoke, as she so often did, before she thought how it would sound. Rather, she had been thinking of his kiss. Felicity's eyes flared with surprise at her denial. "Unless there is another to whom your heart belongs," Cami added hastily. Although they were alone, she dropped her voice to a whisper. "I have thought, perhaps, that you and Mr. Fox..."

Now, Felicity fixed her with eyes that burned. "Do not speak of it. Only Lord Ash can save my family. I would be an utter fool to think of anyone else."

Cami reached out and took her cousin's icy hands in hers. "Oh, Felicity, I am sorry. But I do believe he is an honorable man...." A soft scoffing noise scraped the back of Felicity's throat. It *was* a rather ridiculous claim to make; Lord Ash was a rogue, a rake, a murderer. And if her guess was right, his uncle intended to accuse of him of yet another terrible crime. A man of honor? What a laughable notion. Except that she felt the truth of those words in her very core.

Unless the hard, hot ache behind her breastbone was merely her deep desire that those words were true?

"He will keep his promise to your father, and to you," she said. *His promise to me.*

Although marrying Felicity was not *quite* what she had asked of him.

Through sheer dint of will, Cami had kept her voice even, her expression calm, her posture relaxed as she spoke. If the riot inside her stomach, her brain, her heart was revealed anywhere, it could only be in her eyes. Thank God, her spectacles had always provided some shield when others sought to pry.

Not enough, though. Not this time. Felicity was studying her, precisely in the way Cami often took the liberty of studying everyone else. And she saw...something. Something that made her brows, her lips, her fingertips twitch. But whatever it was she had imagined she glimpsed, she did not speak of it.

Instead, she freed herself from Cami's hands and stepped back across the threshold. "I should leave you to your rest, Cousin. Mama is likely to be a bear in the morning." Cami nodded her understanding of the warning and closed the door behind Felicity as she left.

Ought she to have confessed what she had done? Confession was good for the soul, it was said. But not as good, perhaps, for Felicity, who would rightfully feel betrayed. Cami had set out with the intention of protecting her. Oh, where had it all gone wrong?

Her eyes darted about the room as if seeking an answer and settled at last on her worktable.

With the book.

She had let herself be drawn to a flesh and blood man merely through the power of her own pen. She pulled the closing pages of the manuscript from the drawer with trembling fingers.

She could fix this. She must.

Chapter 10

As he walked back to St. James's, Gabriel found himself wishing for more seasonable weather. Cold, damp. The sort of air that would cool a man's ardor in half a moment, or at least half a mile. Instead, the balmy warmth encouraged his thoughts to persist in untoward directions.

After a while, he gave up and let himself think of her. Of Camellia. Dark hair spilling from a band of poppy-red ribbon. Another flash of color, another glimpse of the woman inside. On her lips, he had tasted the lemonade she had drunk—or perhaps that delicious combination of tart and sweet had simply been the taste of *her*. God, but he wanted to kiss her senseless. Every inch of her. But worse than that, he wanted to talk with her. Tease out her thoughts on import tariffs, the value of native culture, and Irish independence—issues about which he had never troubled himself before. Before making love to her. After. Perhaps even *while* making love to her, if that's what it took to put a spark in those green eyes…though there were a few other things he'd want to try first.

Instead, he forced himself to imagine sitting opposite Felicity in the breakfast parlor at Finch House, a twelvemonth hence, discussing…nothing of importance. They would have risen from their separate beds and met there quite by accident. She would be poring over her invitations. He would only too gladly offer to breakfast at his club instead.

Better yet, she would be at Stoke by next spring. A baby in the nursery, or on the way. He would stay in town, of course, and—and what? Visit Tattersalls and pretend to care about horseflesh? God, he could hardly imagine anything more boring.

But boredom was his goal in a way, was it not? No more gambles. Just a life of quiet respectability until he passed Stoke Abbey, his title, and all the rest, whole and—well, not unblemished, but hopefully polished up a bit—to his own son.

And to do that, he need only spend the rest of his life with Lady Felicity Trenton, for whom he did not, and thank God would never, feel anything like passion. If that seemed like too great a price to pay, then he had forgotten the most important lesson of his childhood: the sort of wretched bills that came due when a man wagered with his heart instead of his head.

When he let himself into his rooms with his key, all was quiet. His footsteps echoed along the corridor; the rugs had been rolled up in preparation for his move to Finch House. Here and there sat a half-full packing crate. Skirting them with care, he made his way to his study, expecting to find more crates, hoping at least that his chair still sat by the window.

It did. But it was not empty.

Clad in the sort of clothes that would allow him to slip in unnoticed almost anywhere, Remington sat hunched forward, elbows on his knees, an unlit pipe clutched in one hand. Fox sat in the chair opposite, in a similar posture of defeat. When Remy offered to rise, Gabriel waved him off. They had never really stood on the normal ceremony of master and servant; he saw no need to start tonight.

"What is it, then?"

Fox raised hollow eyes to his face. "I've come straight from Victoria's. Lord Havisham was there, bending Dalrymple's ear about the assassination attempt on the king. Seems the culprits have been caught. A French girl and two men claiming to be her brothers."

French. Just as Uncle Finch had suggested. "Oh?" It was a struggle to keep his voice flat, uninterested. Had the man made a lucky guess, or was he in a position to know something? "That's good news, I presume?"

"For some." Remy fiddled with his pipe.

Crossing his arms over his chest, Gabriel looked from one to the other expectantly. "Out with it."

"The girl's name is Adele Vallon."

Gabriel dropped like a stone onto the footstool. "Damn."

"So it's true?" Fox demanded. "You do know her?"

"In a manner of speaking."

"Now is not the time for mincing words, Ash. Was she your mistress?" His friend did not meet his eye, clearly wary of the answer.

"No. No!" But even the second, more forceful denial was met with skepticism, a slight raising of the shoulders, like a man warding off a blow. Or a lie. "I met her at a gaming establishment—"

"One of those wretched hells, I suppose you mean?"

"Yes." One of the seediest. The sort he frequented only when his prey could not be run to ground elsewhere. "She was working the floor. When Viscount Steyne made her a, ah, *proposal*, I…intervened." He had spoken to her in French as she passed on Steyne's arm, and relief had flooded her expression. Her dark eyes, overlarge in a narrow, sallow face, had been enough to confirm his suspicion: she was too young and knew too little English to be making the devilish sort of bargain he had just overheard her making with that libertine. Spurning the viscount, she had latched onto Gabriel instead, clinging to his arm, treating him as a sort of protector.

Foolish, foolish girl.

"Did you think how it would look?"

"What did I care? I had nothing to lose, while she had everything." At that, Fox, who had been studying the scuffed toe of one boot with a frown, lifted his gaze, and Gabriel thought he glimpsed a slight softening in his steely eyes. "It's nonsense, of course," he declared. "Adele an assassin?" She was incapable of such a crime.

Still, he had to force a note of conviction into his voice. He *could* believe she might be guilty of poor judgment. Despite his efforts, had she fallen in with those of her countrymen who were less than fond of the English monarch, those less deserving of compassion? He could not help but ask, "Where is she now?"

"The Tower."

The image of hulking stone walls rose in his mind, and he had to suppress a shiver, as if their chill pressed against his own flesh. "But she's no more than a girl."

"Sadly, children are not always innocent, my lord."

Remy's words were an unfortunate echo of Uncle Finch's familiar charge, and they pushed his mind back once again to that odd encounter on the street. *Chance*, some would have called it. But he was too experienced a gambler to believe in any such thing. Understanding dawned with all the cruel clarity of sunrise after a night of too much brandy and too few scruples. When he spoke, his voice sounded curiously distant in his own ears. "My uncle has trumped up some relationship between me and the girl, has he?"

Remy shook his head, but not in denial. "Beggin' your pardon, sir. But you made it dead easy to do."

Gabriel nodded grimly. The owner of the hell, embittered over the loss of the girl, would have reported with a skeptical leer that Gabriel claimed to have found her a place in a milliner's shop and rented her a respectable room— truth, but the sort of truth that was easily twisted. And Lord Steyne would have been only too happy to tell anyone who would listen that Gabriel had made Adele Vallon his mistress—a lie, but that mattered precious little now.

Any supposed evidence against Adele was likely fabricated too. She was merely convenient to his uncle's purpose. Another victim of Lord Ash's reputation.

"When we met him the other day..." Fox's eyes narrowed. "You suspected something of this nature."

Gabriel said nothing. Over the years, he had grown accustomed to his uncle embroidering on his misdeeds. Now, however, the man had begun to fashion them out of whole cloth, it seemed. And Gabriel rather feared he had planted the suggestion in his uncle's mind with his mocking words: *Killing a king is of a piece with my past crimes against the nobility.*

"I think he must've done, Mr. Fox," Remy answered on his behalf. "You sent me right out to see which way the wind blew, my lord. Remember? Didn't take long to discover that Lord Sebastian had been making the rounds among your enemies and stirring up discontent."

"And as you say, I made it dead easy." Gabriel's enemies were legion. He had bested too many men at the tables for it to be otherwise.

"You did, at that," Remy agreed grimly. "But it took a bit more digging to find out about the girl. And then Mr. Fox said—"

His friend readily took up the story. "Dalrymple told me that if Havisham's tale has even a grain of truth to it, you'll likely be charged with treason." Another man would have shied away from revealing it; Fox had been his friend too long to be anything but blunt. Still, the words brought him to his feet, and he paced as he spoke. "There's talk of a writ of attainder."

"Attainder?" Remy repeated uncertainly, his eyes following Fox.

Gabriel was not surprised at his servant's lack of familiarity with the term; the charge was rare. "Corruption of blood," he explained. "It's a fairly obscure provision of the law used to eliminate perceived threats to the monarch. All rather neat and tidy, actually. I need not even be convicted of treason—merely condemned for it. If attainted, I would be stripped of the marquessate, left a commoner, subject to all the punishments from which the nobility are usually protected."

Fox stopped and folded his arms across his chest. "Including execution."

Remington paled. "What sort of monster would destroy his nephew, his own flesh and blood?"

But the answer to that question was too obvious to require an answer.

For twenty years, Sebastian Finch had been railing against a patricide that had gone unpunished. Now, he meant to give Gabriel's peers another chance to convict. His father's death had eventually been dismissed as an accident. But he could not count on being forgiven for his crime the second time around. Especially in these dark days. People would take a rather dim view of an English nobleman who was said to have consorted with French assassins.

"What can he hope to gain by it?" Fox demanded.

"Everything," said Gabriel simply. "He must hope that once he has disposed of me, the king can be persuaded to allow the title to pass to another branch of the family, rather than die out entirely."

"To him, you mean. A sort of reward for his…loyalty."

Gabriel nodded. It had been disconcerting enough to think of Stoke falling into his cousin's hands. But if it somehow fell into his uncle's first…? The thought did not bear completing.

"Remy, it'll be down to you to help the girl. There must be some way to prove she's innocent. But my hand must not be seen to be behind any of it, or it will only go worse for everyone involved."

One crisp nod. No hesitation. And Remy was gone.

"Surely you can muster an ally in the Lords?" Fox suggested when they were alone. He did not add, though he might fairly have done so, that the task would have been easier if Gabriel had ever taken his own seat there. "My father, perhaps?"

How like Foxy to overlook the problem posed by the Earl of Wickersham's infrequent assumption of his own seat as his years increased and his health declined. How like Foxy to ignore his father's patent distaste for his son's choice of friend.

Gabriel's gaze fell on his desk. A towering stack of books awaiting crating. Topmost was the battered guide to the peerage. "I have another candidate in mind," he said.

"Merrick." Fox's gaze must have followed his own. "You cannot mean to go ahead with your scheme to wed Lady Felicity?"

If the attainder were successful, it would touch his wife and any child of his she bore. He had no business marrying now, when he might condemn an innocent woman to life as an outcast, a sort of social death.

On the other hand, Merrick's desire to save his daughter's pretty neck would ensure he'd do his damnedest to see that the charges against Gabriel came to naught. And perhaps, when presented with the possibility of destroying a blameless young bride rather than Gabriel alone, his peers would turn a deaf ear on Lord Sebastian Finch's complaints.

In a long career of dastardly deeds, he had done worse than marry Felicity Trenton.

But not by much.

He had not realized he had risen to his feet until Fox faced him, toe to toe. "God forbid your uncle's plot succeeds, and you are…" This time, he could not seem to bring himself to finish the sentence. But he did not need to. "What would happen to her?"

"I will see that she is well taken care of," Gabriel insisted. "I have a substantial private fortune. I will find a way to arrange a settlement the attainder cannot touch. If the worst comes to pass, she would be left a very wealthy, and I daresay, a very eligible widow—perhaps more eligible even than she is now. After all, pity moves people in ways that prudence does not."

Fox still looked understandably dissatisfied. It was in his nature to protect, as much as it was in Gabriel's nature to harm whatever he touched. "But if her heart should be broken," he concluded, forcing a smile, "you have my blessing to swoop in and pick up the pieces, old thing."

"I do not wish her heart to be broken, Ash," Fox said, his eyes suddenly cold. "Not even bruised. Lady Felicity deserves better. Her family will demand it."

He would never deny that she deserved better. But neither her father nor her brother was in a position to demand anything.

Gabriel had for some time suspected that Fox had another champion in mind, however.

"What about you, my friend?" he asked softly, testing. "Do you demand it?"

At his side, Fox's hand curled into a surprisingly formidable-looking fist. He did not look like a clergyman now. "I do," he said, with unaccustomed resoluteness.

"Careful, Foxy. A better man might take that as a challenge." Gabriel had met more than one opponent at dawn, and he suspected Fox well knew the outcome of those encounters, although he had never asked. "Unless, of course, you've grown such a patriot you mean to spare His Highness the cost of a bullet."

Fox's answering glare forced Gabriel to look away. Gabriel had thought himself fully prepared to make sacrifices to save Stoke from his uncle. Was his friendship with Fox to be one of them?

"You've made quite a reputation for yourself, my friend. And I've never been one for violence," Fox said. Slowly, his hand relaxed, though the set of jaw remained hard as granite. "But I think it's time to remind you that, while I may not be a sportsman, I'm still reckoned a fair shot."

Gabriel shuddered in sympathy with the heavy oak doors as Fox slammed his way first out of the room, then out of the house.

Out of his life.

Chapter 11

With a sigh of annoyance, Cami rose to shut her window against the lark's song and discovered it was morning. Midmorning, in fact. The cool air that had crept into her room overnight had left her stiff. The wick of her candle guttered in a pool of wax; she had not realized she was no longer using its light to write by, but rather that of the sun.

As she stretched to ease the tension in her shoulders, she moved toward the washbasin, removed her spectacles, and splashed her face. Her hair still fell in last night's tangled waves, but after the diligent application of a hairbrush, she soon made quick work of smoothing it into the usual neat, braided coil at the back of her neck. After changing into a fresh dress, she gave a vigorous toss of her head—a desperate attempt to restore her good sense to its rightful place at the forepart of her brain, from wherever it had scattered at the touch of Gabriel's lips. All night her jumbled thoughts had jostled one another, refusing to arrange themselves into anything like sentences on the page. The sheets of paper littering her worktable—the closing scene of *The Wild Irish Rose*—were covered in scratches and spatterings of ink, just as if she had repeatedly thrown down her pen in frustration. Which she had. Gabriel—er, Granville was a problem that resisted a solution.

Gathering up the papers she had rendered almost unreadable, she touched them to the still-glowing wick of her candle, which expired with the effort of setting them alight. A breath of air through pursed lips coaxed forth a genuine flame, and when the pages were burning merrily, she tossed them into the empty hearth. She would start fresh after breakfast.

To her surprise, both Lady Merrick and Felicity were in the breakfast parlor. With one hand shading her eyes from the sunlight pouring through an east-facing window, her aunt moaned softly over tea and toast. Felicity leafed idly through her papa's newspaper.

"Good morning, Cousin." Felicity did not look up as she spoke.

Cami began to fill a plate from the sideboard. Her night's labor, though fruitless, had given her an appetite.

"What makes you such a lie-abed this morning, Camellia?" Aunt Merrick rasped out.

She was spared from having to invent a reply when her aunt held out a stack of correspondence, carelessly smearing the corners through the butter. "Do sort this and see what can be avoided. Merrick will return any day and I do not intend to go out of this house until he's spoken to Lord Ash and made him come to the point. I will not have the Trenton name humiliated."

Cami laid aside her plate, took the letters, and picked up a knife instead of a fork. A pile of invitations soon rose under her hand. Hostesses eager enough for success to court scandal, sending out cards to Lady Merrick and her daughter in hopes they might also secure the notorious Lord Ash. And failing that, to twitter behind their fans over the unfortunate young woman whose reputation had been sacrificed on the altar of her brother's debts.

Three-quarters of the way through her task, she came upon a letter, its direction written so poorly that it had been twice misdelivered. It was addressed to her. And the trembling hand that had penned the direction belonged to her sister Erica. With deliberate motions, so as not to draw attention to the letter, Cami broke the seal and unfolded the paper.

The single sheet was not crowded nor crossed, not even full. Just a few lines that listed forlornly across the page. Despite their mama's best efforts, Erica's hand had never been neat and even and ladylike. Erica herself was of "an energetic disposition," in their mother's gentle phrase. At times it was a great trial to her to sit still long enough to compose a letter; on another day, however, she might cover two sheets with her rambles. But, while this letter's brevity was not entirely out of character, Cami still read signs of distress, or at least hurry, in the omission of Erica's customary embellishments: no stroke of the pen had been turned to leaf or flower or vine. And the words themselves confirmed her fears:

> *Paris and his friends may succeed at last. But, they have lured Galen into their set. I fear for his safety. Of course, he will listen to no one—no one but you. I wish you would come, before it is too late.*
>
> *E.*

Though it might not be readily apparent to the casual reader—deliberately so, Cami suspected—the note conveyed a great deal of information. Paris's "friends," a group of patriots known as the Society of United Irishmen, had been working for years, first publicly, then in secret, to render Ireland a truly independent nation. Two years past, an uprising had failed when promised French support had not materialized. Erica's intimation that they might at last have found a way to succeed sent a thrill of pride through Cami, chased by fear. Paris and the others, including Erica's betrothed, Henry Edgeworth, would be risking their lives on behalf of their country. Was such a sacrifice necessary to reach their goal?

History would answer yes, she supposed. Knowing how often men's lives had been demanded in the cause of freedom, she had written *The Wild Irish Rose* in hopes of making people see Ireland's struggles and forge a solution without bloodshed. Perhaps such a notion had been naïve. She loved Paris dearly, and of course she did not want to lose him, the closest to her of all her siblings, and not only in age. He was smart and determined and—oh, *brave*, so she must be brave in turn. She would try to see the honor in his sacrifice, if it must be made.

But Galen was just a boy, though he would protest to hear himself described as such, no doubt. Young enough to listen to stories of war and hear only tales of thrilling adventure and glory, nothing of pain or loss or even death. Oh, Paris had better hope all was still well when she sailed into the Bay of Dublin, or he would know something of pain firsthand. At *her* hand.

"Cousin Camellia?" Felicity regarded her with a mixture of curiosity and alarm. "What news?"

For the briefest moment, she forgot Felicity's dilemma. Forgot her own contribution to it. "My younger brother is in trouble," she said, dropping the letter onto the table. "My sister has written begging me to come home. I must go immediately."

"Of course you must," Felicity agreed without hesitation. Before his disastrous debts, and the equally disastrous plan to resolve them, she and her brother had been quite close. "But how will you get there?"

"The public stage to Wales," Cami replied matter-of-factly, for she had no money for anything else. Perhaps not even enough for that. "The packet from Holyhead to Dublin."

"But you can't travel all that way alone."

Her uncle had sent a servant to accompany her to London, a fatiguing journey that had taken the better part of a week by private coach. It was a daunting prospect to imagine what the trip might involve if she were by herself. Nevertheless, family must come first. She lifted her chin. "I assure you, I can."

"But you would be...ruined." The last word required a moment's fortification before it could be spoken.

Cami did not know whether to be charmed or annoyed by everyone's sudden concern for her reputation. "You judge from your own experience, dear. No one will pay *me* the least mind, I assure you. I am not 'lady' anything. I am a servant. And a spinster."

A catalog of characteristics remarkably similar to the one she had given to Gabriel, though to prove a drastically different point.

"Go to Ireland?" The hand that had been shading her aunt's eyes fell to the table, making china and silver rattle. "Nonsense."

Felicity frowned with surprise. "But Mama, it must be important or her sister would not ask it of her."

"What good could you possibly do there, Camellia?" Aunt Merrick nodded toward the towering pile of invitations to be answered. "I have need of you here. I forbid it."

Cami had dreamed of the day she would earn enough with her writing to be independent—or, at least as independent as any woman could be. Able to go where and do what she would. She glanced toward Erica's letter where it lay beside her untouched plate. She could not wait around for freedom to be granted. She must seize it. Rising, she laid her hands on the table in front of her for support. "I am sorry to defy you, Aunt. But you leave me little choice. I must go. I can only promise to return as soon as I am able."

Lady Merrick's face grew red. "How dare you behave in this insolent fashion?"

Cami bit her lip to keep from retorting, but to her surprise, her cousin threw off her usual restraint and stood. "Enough, Mama." That lady's face grew darker, beet red, nearly purple, but Felicity turned coolly away. "Come, Cousin. I will help you pack your things."

In the corridor, she squeezed Cami's hand and pulled her toward the staircase. "You needn't fear her."

Cami shook her head. She was not so much afraid *of* her aunt as *for* her. She had looked to be on the verge of an apoplexy.

"Papa will make her understand," Felicity continued. "Oh, Camellia—I do wish I had your bravery. I have so often wanted to prove to her that another person's heart could be stronger than her will."

A reminder, though doubtless not a deliberate one, that by the time Cami returned from Dublin, Felicity would likely be married. Against her inclination. To Gabriel.

Cami swallowed and mustered a smile. "There are many kinds of courage, Felicity."

Felicity went first to her own room in search of a small valise, something a woman could manage on her own. Alone in the quiet attic, Cami withdrew the length of red ribbon from the drawer of her worktable and secreted it in her writing desk, spooling it alongside the sheaf of ink-stained paper.

So, this was the end of their story. Without even a proper good-bye, just a kiss that should never have been.

There were worse fates for a would-be heroine, of course. She had always known that.

Firmly, she closed the lid of her writing desk and snapped shut the latch.

* * * *

Though it was midmorning, Gabriel approached Trenton House with the same sense of nervous dread as a man keeping a dawn appointment. But marriage to Felicity was his last chance to better his odds. He knew the cards his opponent held.

When he reached the steps, he trotted up them. His choices were too few to allow him the luxury of hesitation. Still, as he waited to be admitted, questions lingered in his mind. Would his uncle's charge of treason find purchase among the men whose good opinion Gabriel had never cared to court? Could Adele somehow be saved, or must she join the lengthy tally of lives he had ruined?

And why, *why* had he tortured himself with the taste of Camellia's lips?

Gall, wormwood—those were his portion. Everything bitter. Nothing sweet.

He had to knock twice before the door was opened, and even then the butler ushered him in with an air of distraction. "I'm sorry, my lord. I do not think the family is at home today."

Not at home? Patently an untruth, of the sort butlers all over town were no doubt being asked to utter this fine day. Gabriel's reputation had largely spared him from having to communicate, or rather *not* communicate, with those in good society. Now, however, he would have to learn how to tell such pointless, polite little lies. He cleared his throat and removed his hat. "Mr....Wafford, is it not? Please do me the very great favor of telling Lady

Felicity that I have something to say which I believe she—or at least, her family—will be eager to hear."

"I—" Denial swelled the man's chest, but it could not quite push out his doubt. Even—no, *especially*—the servants must know of the expected proposal of marriage. The butler teetered visibly on the brink of indecision: follow orders to deny all visitors, or follow orders to encourage Lord Ash? With a crisp bow, he decided on the latter course. "Very good, my lord. Will you come up?"

They passed the drawing room, where Gabriel had first met Lord Trenton's unfortunate sister. He had not anticipated an introduction to her cousin as well. But then, who could? The door was open, and he paused to allow his eyes to wander about the empty room. There Camellia had stumbled. There, for the first time, he had touched her. And there she had sat and scorched him with those brilliant eyes and that wicked, wicked tongue.

Wafford cleared his throat, rousing Gabriel from his reverie. "Lady Merrick and Lady Felicity are in the breakfast room, my lord."

Gabriel turned sharply on one heel and followed.

Felicity and her mother could be heard talking—perhaps *arguing* would be the better word—through the closed door. With a resigned expression, Wafford tapped a warning, opened the door for Gabriel, and announced him. The breakfast table was littered with the morning post, newspaper, and dirty dishes. The smell of eggs and kippers still hung on the air. When he entered, Felicity rose and curtsied. "Lord Ash. I was not expecting you this morning."

Lady Merrick shot him a scathing look. "Well, I was. After last night, I trust you're here to propose to Felicity at last." At those words, embarrassment flared in her daughter's eyes, but the countess either did not see it or did not care. Gabriel made no attempt to reply. Did they know what had happened between him and Camellia?

"Your attentions have given the impression that you intend to marry my daughter," the countess continued. "But after your uncle gave her the cut direct last night, I'm sure every tongue in Mayfair is wagging." Fury stiffened Gabriel's spine, though he kept his face impassive. Trust Uncle Finch to find a way to make things worse. "If you do not come up to snuff soon, her reputation will be ruined. *We* will be ruined."

"If we are, Mama," Felicity said, her words considerably more measured than her mother's, "it will have been my brother's doing, not Lord Ash's."

"All Stephen did can be undone with *his* offer," Lady Merrick countered, with a jerk of her chin in Gabriel's direction. "I'll leave you to it," she said with a hard look for him as she marched from the room.

"Please forgive her, my lord," Felicity said when she had gone. "My mother is not feeling well. Coffee?" The offer caught him off guard, but surely he could afford to observe the pleasantries, to delay the inevitable for a moment more. The servants had also disappeared, so at his nod, she poured him a cup from the urn on the sideboard, then gestured him to a chair. "We've had a bit of…excitement this morning," she explained as she resumed her seat. Though the coffee was just this side of tepid, he drank without complaint. "My cousin received an urgent missive asking her to come home." Felicity gestured to a letter half buried by the sheets of newsprint littering the table. "She left this morning."

"Oh?" He aimed for indifference to the news but knew he shot wide of the mark. Camellia was returning to Ireland? He had no right to feel disappointment—to feel anything. Her situation in her uncle's household was far from ideal. And last night, she had spoken true, truer than even she knew. They must not indulge again in the spark of passion that seemed determined to flare between them. Easier to guarantee, certainly, if they never saw one another again.

He found Felicity was studying him when he raised his eyes, and not for the first time did he glimpse some similarity to her cousin's penetrative stare. "I do hope she will have a safe journey." The note of worry in her voice was unmistakable. "I do not like to think of her traveling alone."

"Alone?" The exclamation was sharper than he had intended. "Surely the household could have spared a servant?"

"Mama would not allow it, and though Papa is expected any day now, Camellia would not wait for his return. When I think of the dangers a woman might encounter on such a trip…" Gently, she shook her head. "And even if she makes it to Dublin without harm, her sister's letter hinted at some trouble. I hope it's nothing to do with those rogues who call themselves the United Irishmen."

In spite of himself, Gabriel's brows rose.

"You are surprised I know of such a thing? But I read my father's newspapers every day." Her chin jutted sharply forward. "I am not quite so empty-headed as some would like to believe."

Was the remark directed at her mother? At Camellia? Or at him?

"Miss Burke seems most capable," he said, shifting the subject, though onto equally treacherous ground.

"Yes," Felicity agreed. "Still, I would feel better if I knew she had a gentleman's protection."

Gabriel drew in a slow breath. "What are you suggesting, ma'am?"

"That you go after her, of course," she said simply.

If Felicity wanted to ensure her cousin's safety, he was the last man she ought to consider sending. He could not offer a gently bred woman security or respectability or anything else she needed.

But when he recalled Camellia's kiss, he could not help but wonder whether maybe…just maybe…he had something she wanted.

"For your sake? Or for hers?" he asked gruffly. Noble, unselfish acts were quite out of character for him. She ought not to begin to expect them.

"For your own."

Shock coursed through him. Surely, he had misheard. "I have not the pleasure of understanding you, Lady Felicity."

Her wry laugh revealed perfect, even teeth. "People say you are a legend at the tables, Lord Ashborough, but I cannot credit it. Surely such success as you are reputed to enjoy would require some little skill at bluffing."

All this time, he had been thinking of Felicity as very like her mother. And she was, in looks. But she had not inherited her mother's foolishness and laziness. Those qualities had all gone to her brother, it seemed.

"Your interest in her has not escaped my notice," she continued with a rather sly smile. "Nor has her fascination with you."

He could not very well deny the truth of her words. But this was an attraction that must be discouraged, not encouraged. He shook his head to signify the impossibility of it all. "It matters not," he said. This was not why he had come. He did not need to be tempted to hunt down Camellia and finish what they'd started. And this was the worst possible moment for him to think of leaving London. Such a journey could come to no good end, for any of them, not even Felicity. "You ought to think of your own reputation. Do you not share your mother's concern?" he asked.

"My mother exaggerates. No one would dare to suggest you had reneged on an offer."

Might she be right? People often marveled at his ability to predict the fall of the cards. But only one or two had been foolish enough to accuse him of being a cheat.

"It will simply look as if I would not have you," she continued.

He almost smiled. "Doubtless Society will account you wise."

Especially once the talk of attainder was more generally known.

Felicity looked at him for a long moment without speaking. She gave every impression of waiting patiently for his decision. But her blue eyes were fathomless pools, and he was an unsuspecting sailor being lured to his death by a siren. He began to understand how Fox had wound up so hopelessly besotted with the girl.

"Ring for a footman," he ordered. A plan had begun to form in his mind, a chance for a few more stolen moments with Camellia, and it was just mad enough to work. Felicity moved with alacrity to the bellpull, and a young man in livery appeared in the doorway. "Go to Finch House, in Grosvenor Square," Gabriel said to him, "and tell them Lord Ashborough requires a traveling coach, horses, and a driver as soon as possible." Would the fine carriages that had once filled the mews there all have succumbed to mice and damp? The footman bowed sharply and was gone. "And you." He turned to Felicity as he spoke. "Fetch me pen and paper." At the very least, he knew how she might be spared.

When she had returned with the requested items and left again, he cleared a space at the table and sat down to write, less a letter than legal document. He took care to observe the forms, to leave no loose ends, to press his seal firmly and clearly into the wax so that there could be no doubt of its legitimacy.

Afterward, he dashed off a heartfelt note to Christopher Fox. When it was finished, he sealed it and wrote his friend's name on the outside, along with specific conditions for its delivery, intending to leave it in his rooms in St. James's.

"Your coach is here." Felicity had returned to stand just inside the threshold.

Quickly, before he could think better of it, he extended the first document to her. "This, I hope, will allay your concerns, and those of your family, about the matter of your brother's...situation." It erased Lord Trenton's debts under conditions Gabriel hoped all parties would find favorable—a gamble, he knew. The last he might ever make, since it could easily lead to his ruin. Merrick would no longer be under any obligation to him. Who would be left to plead on his behalf?

She read through its contents and looked up at him with those wide eyes. "I know it is more typically the fashion for a lady to express gratitude upon receipt of a proposal, rather than upon its withdrawal. Nevertheless, I thank you, my lord," she whispered. "I do not think we would have suited."

Which had, of course, very nearly been the point. He mustered a laugh. "There's quite enough misery in the world to be going on with. No need to add yours to the mix."

"Cousin Camellia did try to tell me it would not be miserable to be your wife."

"Did she?" The lurch of his heart against his rib cage was almost painful.

"I shall put this letter into Papa's hand myself." Felicity had folded the parchment and was tracing one edge with her fingertip.

He had a sudden vision of what she might endure from her mother when he left. "He is expected soon, you said?"

"Perhaps even today," she reassured him in a voice that was steady, strong. "Now, come."

The street before Trenton House was nearly filled by an old-fashioned four-in-hand coach, an ancient, heavy thing that looked to be on the verge of collapse. No one who saw it on the road would imagine its occupant a wealthy nobleman.

It was perfectly suited to the reckless journey he was about to undertake.

"She has not been gone an hour," Felicity said. "Surely you will be able to catch her?"

"With a little luck." He eyed the coach dubiously. "In which, let me hasten to add, I do not believe."

"You don't need luck, my lord." To his surprise, she laid one hand on his shoulder and stretched up to brush his cheek with her lips. "You need love."

Sweet words and a sweet gesture that nearly unmanned him, for in a lifetime of scars and sin, he had known very little sweetness. But if she knew what awaited those he loved, or who loved him, she would not wish that fate on anyone.

With a slight bow to the woman who was to have been his bride, Gabriel turned and left.

Chapter 12

With a silent sigh, Cami clutched her portable desk. Along with a dozen other passengers, she sat in the public room of a posting inn, awaiting the northbound stage. The price of a ticket for a place inside the coach had been too dear. Now, however, she was wondering whether she ought not to have paid it, even if it meant bread and water for the rest of the journey. The roof was a notoriously dangerous place aboard a crowded, speeding coach, but she was even more worried about the weather. Through a dirt-streaked window, she eyed the thickening clouds. *Rain.* Could she persuade a fellow passenger to trade places with her? But why should anyone imagine she deserved a place inside, simply because she held a wooden box whose contents she didn't fancy getting wet?

She tried to distract herself with her usual amusement. Who was meeting the stooped old lady with the leathery skin, who clutched an unlit pipe between her teeth and hid what Cami believed must be a live piglet, judging by the grunts and squeals coming from beneath her cloak? And what had possessed that tall, oddly dressed fellow, the one who had proclaimed loudly to his fellow passengers that he was the best wizard now living in Britain, to travel by the public stage rather than taking his broomsti—

Oh, it was no use. Characters they might be, but she was in no humor for making up stories to suit them. Her feet were sore from the long walk through town to reach the inn; she was worried sick about her family; and she was almost certain to get drenched. Was that a rumble of thunder?

No, a coach. A dozen pairs of hope-filled eyes turned toward the sound. A lumbering, old fashioned four-in-hand slowed as it passed the window. Merely some private conveyance stopping to change horses. The jumble of conversation resumed around her, and Cami absently traced the smooth, worn, ink-stained edge of her writing desk. Absorbed in her thoughts, she did not immediately realize that the door to the public room had opened, that the murmur of voices around her had grown louder, that someone was striding in her direction.

"Camellia?"

For a moment, she wondered if the fatigue of the walk had made her weak in the head. It could not possibly be...

Booted feet stopped before her. Between blinks of astonishment, her eyes traveled upward, over an imposing greatcoat and snowy cravat, to Gabriel's face. She saw no trace of his usual sardonic expression. He looked drawn, tired.

"What are you doing here?" he demanded. "Are you mad?"

"No, my—" *My lord*, she had been about to say. But she had a sudden vision of the chaos that might ensue if she revealed to her fellow passengers that the gentleman standing before them was a wealthy nobleman. Already, their curiosity was pressing them closer. "No," she said, rising. "It is not madness to wish to go home."

"Some might beg to differ."

She could not keep her eyes from widening at his words, but his own expression was obscured as he bent to pick up the bag at her feet. Before he could attempt to take the writing desk from her arms, she moved out of his reach. "Pardon me?"

"A woman thinking to travel alone on the public stage is exhibiting a kind of madness. It would serve you bloody well right," he said, each syllable spoken sharply and loudly enough for every one of her fellow passengers to hear, "if you'd been robbed. Or worse. Running off like that. Worrying your family. Worrying me."

Cami knew her mouth had popped open, but she could not seem to muster a retort. And as he had begun to march back in the direction of his carriage, carrying her bag, she had very little choice but to follow him. He tossed her valise to his coachman, then turned back as if prepared to toss her into the carriage with very little more ceremony. "Get in."

"I have no intention of—" she began. Unyielding fingers encircled her upper arm. "Unhand me this instant! How dare you—?"

"That's it, Miss Burke," he said softly, leaning in. Humor glimmered in his dark eyes, though it had not entirely chased away their haunted look. "Now you're getting into the spirit of the thing. Slap me across the face if you'd like. I assure you, it's the only invitation you'll ever get."

"Why, you devil—!" This was all an act. But to what possible end? Though her fingers itched to make good on his offer, she hesitated.

A wicked smile lifted one corner of his mouth. "Unless you'd rather kiss me, instead?"

A bolt of heat passed through her, devastating as a lightning strike. Then rain began pelting from the leaden sky. One thick drop struck her cheek; another dodged the lens of her spectacles to strike her eye, making her blink furiously. Unless she was willing to brave the coming storm aboard the roof of the stage... She clutched her writing desk tighter with one arm, lifted her skirts with her free hand, and stepped into Gabriel's coach unassisted.

As he settled into the opposite seat, the coach jerked into motion. Laughter rumbled in his chest, though she could not help but notice that it did not reach his eyes. "Well, at least we've done them the kindness of leaving them with something to talk about while they wait." He gestured toward a window filled with curious faces. "Shall I figure in their tales as the cruel brother come to drag his sister home, do you suppose? Or as the aggrieved husband whose headstrong bride ran away in the night?"

"I could not say." She understood then that his high-handedness had indeed been a deliberate act, intended to spare her reputation. Bad enough to be a youngish woman, traveling alone; far worse if she seemed to be the sort who leaped into the carriage of the first gentleman who happened along. She squared her writing desk on her lap. "I have very little familiarity with spinning those sorts of stories."

For answer, he laughed again.

"I was not running away," she said when they had traveled some way in silence. "I was on my way back to Ireland. I received an urgent letter from my sister and must get home as soon as possible. You should know I have no intention of going back to London."

"That's as well, since we're headed in the opposite direction."

She glanced out the window to find that the city was indeed receding, the landscape becoming more rural. If he wasn't returning her to Trenton House, then where was he taking her?

Another quarter mile passed with his hazel eyes fixed on her, something almost feverish in their depths. The air of the carriage felt charged, heavy— the weight of the coming storm, perhaps. She fought the impulse to squirm beneath his stare. "I'm bound for Stoke Abbey," he said at last, answering her unspoken question. Then he settled his gaze on the passing scenery, though the carriage windows were blurred with rain. As she studied his profile, she saw that fatigue, or perhaps worry, had etched grooves about his mouth and eyes. "My family estate."

Was it her fancy, or did he name his destination with reluctance? He must have left in a hurry, to be traveling without even a servant. Some pressing matter of business must have called him home. Still, who set out on such a journey all alo—? Well, who *else* would set out on such a journey all alone?

"It lies in Shropshire," he added, "along the border with Wales."

"Why, that cannot be far from Holyhead," she said, naming the Welsh port from which the packet sailed for Dublin.

"Less than a day's journey, I'd say."

Just when she was in need of the means of traveling northward, she had crossed paths with Gabriel, who happened to be headed that way. Surely not a coincidence... But if it were not, then she must confront the fact that Felicity had sent him. And if he had called at Trenton House that morning, had he at last made the offer for which the entire family had been waiting with bated breath? What had been her cousin's reply?

Fear of the answers kept those questions in check.

"What luck!" she managed to exclaim instead.

"Luck?" The force of that one wry word as it left his lips propelled him forward, closer to her. "How very...*Irish* of you."

She pressed her spine against the upholstered cushion of the seat back, putting as much distance between them as possible. "I thought gamblers were great believers in luck."

"A successful gambler deals in probabilities, Miss Burke. Mathematics," he declared, "not luck."

Ah, yes. Gabriel, the mathematician. Certainly, the man's gifts included the ability to divide a woman from her honor and multiply her troubles in the bargain. Well, she could not boast of any particular skill with probabilities, but she knew luck when she saw it. Both good and bad. "I could not think of accompanying you," she murmured, more to herself than to him. The impropriety of traveling by herself paled in comparison to the scandal of traveling unchaperoned with Lord Ash. All alone, trapped in a carriage for days? People would assume they had succumbed to temptation—and when she remembered what she and Gabriel had done just last night, she feared people would be right.

He turned back to face her, and one brow arced. "Perhaps I ought to have left you to the vagaries of the public stage, then." The half smile that turned up his lips did very little to ease the hard lines into which his expression had fallen.

A few miles farther up the road, the driver steered the coach into the yard of a posting inn to change horses. A servant came to the carriage door, carrying a tray laden with meat pies and mugs of ale. Cami pressed her palm against her abdomen to keep her stomach from rumbling. As the young man handed in the food to her, Gabriel dug in the pocket of his coat, retrieved his purse, and spilled coins onto the servant's palm. "And," Gabriel added, "I believe the lady wishes to descend here."

The servant turned to peer up at her inquiringly. "Ma'am? Will I help you down?"

Cami, who had fallen quickly on the simple repast, swallowed noisily, then twisted her head just enough to glance across the carriage at Gabriel. Having had the responsibility of caring for younger siblings, she knew well the old trick of saying one thing, in hopes of prompting the opposite action. By suggesting she leave, did he hope to goad her to stay? He lifted his brows, taunting, mocking…but beneath them, what little she could see of his shadowed expression was haunted. She began to suspect he wanted her company.

And heaven help her, she wanted his too.

Turning back to the waiting servant, she said, "Thank you, but no. You may give the order to drive on as soon as the horses are ready." She could not be expected to give up the comfort and safety of a private carriage, traveling in precisely the direction she wished to go, after all.

Though she would not try to persuade herself that traveling with Gabriel was exactly *safe*.

The young man nodded and folded up the steps again. In a short while he returned for the empty mugs and tray, and moments after the door snapped shut, the carriage spun into motion once more.

Her belly full, she felt her eyelids begin to droop. The various ordeals of the last day had been draining, and the rhythmic sway of the coach was a powerful lullaby. With one fingertip, she traced the erratic path of raindrops down the window to keep herself awake.

"You look tired," he said. A most ungentlemanly observation.

She met his gaze with every intention of denying it. She could not bear for him to discover that she had passed a sleepless night because of him. A yawn caught her off guard. She tried to hide it behind her hand, but he was not fooled.

He leaned forward and placed a hand on either side of her portable desk, clearly intending to relieve her of the burden. When she thought of what he could discover inside, she curled her fingers tighter around its worn corners. Relenting, he reached up to untie the ribbons of her bonnet instead, removed it gently, and laid it next to him. Then, he drew her spectacles carefully from her face and tucked them into the discarded bonnet. Last, he shifted to the seat beside her. "Rest," he said, patting his own shoulder to indicate she might use it as a cushion. Automatically, she shook her head. A sigh of exasperation parted his lips. "You're exhausted, Camellia."

At this distance she did not need to squint to see the smudge of shadow beneath his own eyes. The produce of his usual vices, no doubt. A late night at the tables. Too much drink, too many women. Or...?

How dare she hope he had been kept awake thinking of her?

"It would be most improper," she said, though she really might be too tired to care.

A smile quirked his lips. "Of course it would be improper." Again, she recognized the challenge in his words. "Everything about this is improper, Miss Burke."

She remembered the day they had walked in the park; he had asserted that she feared nothing. Tentatively, she laid her cheek against the point of his shoulder. A hard pillow. Rather damp and cool too. Before she could try to settle into whatever meager comfort the position would allow, she felt his finger brush the underside of her chin. When she lifted her head to look up, he shifted, settled his arm around her shoulders, and nudged open his greatcoat, exposing the plush, dry wool of his coat beneath.

Undeniably more comfortable. Undeniably more dangerous. Had she really tried to claim he could not ruin her? At the time, she had meant it.

But experience was teaching her there were many kinds of ruination.

She allowed herself to lean against him, this time resting her cheek against the curve of his chest, in a little hollow that seemed perfectly fitted to her head. She could feel his breath stir her hair. With the steady *thump-thump* of his heart beneath her ear, she snuggled into his warmth and fell fast asleep.

Chapter 13

Cami awoke with a start. The carriage had stopped; the sky beyond its windows was growing dark. Beneath her cheek, her pillow rose and fell with even, rumbling breaths. Confused, she pushed herself upright to find she had been curled against Gabriel's side like a child. For what must have been hours, through even the changing of horses. She had probably snored. Or worse, drooled.

How could she have let herself sleep so soundly? How could she have let herself—? She clutched automatically for her writing desk and found it missing.

By the light of the inn yard's lanterns, she fumbled searchingly, silently through the carriage's dim interior. Vaguely, she remembered him trying to take the desk from her. Her fingers passed lightly over Gabriel's hard thigh and knee—he wasn't holding it either. With her toes, she felt about the floor—no, it hadn't slid off her lap while she slept. Reaching out, more than half-blind, she slid her hands over the opposite seat until they struck the box's wooden edges. When she grabbed it to her, she heard something else, something light—her bonnet, perhaps—fall to the floor. Where were her spectacles?

Heart racing, she opened the carriage door. She needed more light. She needed air. She needed to come to her senses, to throw off the disorientation of sleep. Without really meaning to, she stepped out into the night, discovering as she did so that the carriage steps had not yet been put down.

A simple misjudgment of distance. If she had realized the situation, she could have jumped down with ease. But now her foot, expecting to meet a level surface some inches above the ground, must stretch out farther. The awkward weight of her lap desk pitched her forward. And before she could reach to catch herself, she was falling. Her desk flew from her hands to land with a crash on the cobblestones some feet away. Twisting and flailing, trying to keep herself from meeting a similar fate, Cami threw up her arms and gave a cry as the ground rushed up to meet her.

"You, boy. Over here with some light." Gabriel's voice was husky with sleep. She could hear the carriage creak as he eased himself through the door, felt his boots strike the ground as he stepped down carefully to avoid her prone form. "Camellia." He knelt beside her head and brushed her hair away from her face with fingers that did not seem to be quite steady. "Can you hear me?"

"Yes," Cami managed to whisper. All the breath seemed to have abandoned her lungs. Oddly, her pain gave her some consolation. She knew she could not be badly injured if she could still feel everything. Scraped palms. Bruised knees. And—oh! "My ankle," she gasped. "I think I must have twisted it."

"Lie still," he ordered. She felt his hands rearranging her skirts to cover her bare legs before he turned her and lifted her with surprising ease, cradling her against his chest as he nodded silent commands to the small crowd that surrounded them: the driver, grooms, servants of the inn, and even, to her deep mortification, some of the inn's other patrons.

As they passed into the inn, she closed her eyes against the light and allowed them to stay closed. "I'm sure I could manage on my own," she murmured, but he did not hear her, or pretended not to, at any rate. Without even an exchange of words, they were shown upstairs to a room, and in another moment, he was bending to seat her on the edge of a neatly made bed.

"I'll just fetch some hot water for your missus, shall I?" An older woman's voice, probably the innkeeper's wife.

When Gabriel replied, she expected him to correct the woman's error. But he merely thanked her. "And have someone bring up our things."

"Very good, sir."

Then they were alone. She peered up at him, a handsome blur. "Do you know what became of my spectacles?"

He lowered himself to her eye level; at this distance, she could make out every feature without squinting. "Tucked inside your bonnet. Which I very much hope I didn't squash as I got out. Now, let's see those hands." Obediently, she held up her palms for his inspection. Some scrapes, but mostly dirt. Already the stinging had begun to abate. "And your ankle?"

Slowly, she rose and tested whether it would support her weight. It ached, to be sure, but she gritted her teeth against the pain. "Bearable."

"Thankfully, there is no need at present for you to bear it." He wrapped his fingers around her elbow to urge her back down to the bed.

A tap at the door gave way to a small parade of people: a maid with a ewer of steaming water in one arm and a stack of towels in the other, a boy with their bags, another carrying her writing desk, and finally the innkeeper's wife to oversee the rest. When they had deposited their loads, the woman flapped them through the door with her hands. "Is there ought else?"

Surely Gabriel would request a second room, would put an end to this charade. Instead, he stepped closer to the door, clearly intending to shut it tight after her. "That will do. Thank you."

Though as far as Cami could tell, Gabriel was making no particular effort to be charming—in fact, to her ear, he sounded rather terse—the innkeeper's wife simpered nonetheless and curtsied on the threshold. "Well, ring if you need me."

"But...but she thinks we're married," Cami whispered when the door closed.

Gabriel turned to face her, but at this distance, his expression was unreadable. "It's for the best. This seems a respectable inn. We might have been turned away if she knew we weren't." She watched as he shrugged out of his greatcoat and slung it over a chair in the corner. "I'll say you needed your rest after the fall and sit up tonight in the pub. It won't be the first time," he added with a self-deprecating laugh as he strode to the washstand and poured water from the ewer into the basin.

"Let's see about getting you cleaned up first, though, shall we?" He approached with a damp cloth and she reached up for it automatically. A blurry smile spread across his face as he caught one wrist in a gentle hold and began carefully wiping the grime of the inn yard from her palms. It stung a bit, but less than submerging her hands in the basin would have. "There, see. Much better. Now..." He rinsed the cloth and wiped her face next. Was it streaked with dirt too? Either way, she could not deny how good the warm water felt against her skin.

"Thank you," she murmured when he returned to the washbasin.

"Don't thank me yet. There's still that ankle to tend."

"It's fine." She perched more upright on the edge of the bed, a position that required her to brace herself with her toes.

Gabriel must have seen the grimace that flickered across her face. "Fine, eh? Well, then, it won't hurt to take a look."

A look? It was not his eyes that worried her, but rather his long, clever fingers traveling over her foot, up her leg. But before she could wipe the image from her mind, or the flare of heat from her cheeks, he was kneeling on the floor before her. Without conscious thought, she drew her foot back under the protection of her skirts.

"Modesty, Camellia? I wouldn't have thought a sensible woman like you would be susceptible to such nonsense."

It wasn't nonsense. Not really. More like self-preservation. With a deep breath, she stuck out her injured right foot. He slipped her shoe off and ran his fingers over her stocking-clad ankle. "A little swelling. Not as bad as I'd feared. Can you undo your stocking? I want to see if there's any bruising." To her relief, he rose and stepped back to the washstand while she hurriedly undid her garter, rolled down her stocking, and tugged it free of her toes with a little gasp of discomfort.

The sound did not escape his notice either. "Let me see," he commanded in a brusque, businesslike voice she had never heard him use before. He dropped to one knee, lifted the hem of her skirt, and took her foot in his hands. "Can you bend it this way? Like that?" Slight pressure of his fingers directed which way she was to flex her ankle. She felt the heat of his palm against the sole of her foot as he asked to her press against him. "Good, good. Clearly not broken. Just strained a bit. It should be easy enough to rest it for a couple of days. By the time you reach Dublin, it should be back to normal. I'll just—" He held up one of the linen towels, ripped it in two neat halves, and began to wind one strip around her foot and up her ankle to support the injured joint. She raised the hem of her dress a little higher to watch him work. How had he acquired this skill? Was it wrong to take pleasure in his touch?

"What's this?" His fingertips skated over an old scar, a series of jagged lines that stood out pearly white against the pale skin of her calf. When she did not answer, he lifted his face to hers, questioning; his hands did not release her leg. His position on the floor before her allowed her to see him quite clearly, even without her spectacles. His dark eyes clouded with uncertainty. A frown notched the space between his brows.

"Nothing," she said, dropping her skirt so that the fabric draped over the scars and his wrists too. "It happened when I was a child."

"*What* happened?" Without looking, he tucked in the end of the bandage to secure it, but still he did not let her go. She could feel his gentle touch tracing the rough edges of the scar over one side of her calf, then the other. "It's shaped like a—"

"Like a dog bite. Yes." Though it sent a twinge through her ankle, she tugged her foot free of his grasp. "I was six—no, seven, I suppose. Erica was almost two. I don't have any memory of it, really. Mama says we were playing in the square, inside the walled garden, when our neighbor's dog broke free of its leash and began to chase us. Erica ran, of course, because she was of an age when she ran everywhere. It made the dog…wild." She'd heard the story so many times, she could almost see and hear what her mind refused to recall—the dog's growls, flecks of spittle flying from its jaws. Erica's squeals. Her own screams. "I picked her up and ran with her to the gate." It hadn't been locked, but panic had made her little fingers fumble nonetheless. "When we couldn't get through, I lifted her over and was just scrambling up after, when—"

His kiss was swift, hard. Intended more to silence than seduce. But not without passion, for all that. When she reached for something to steady herself against the surprise, her hands settled on his shoulders and she felt the tension there. "My God, Camellia." He pulled her closer, buried his lips in her hair. She tried to steel herself against his reaction, his embrace. Tried and failed. "That's why you… Foxy's pups…and that damned Chien. He—he *growled* at you. The day we met. And you were expected to—to—"

It was her turn to quiet him. "Shh," she soothed. "Aunt Merrick said it was high time I conquered my fears, and I daresay she was right."

"It was heartless and cruel!"

She pulled away to look him in the eye. She would not be enticed into wanting—to say nothing of needing—a man's protection. "If there are a hundred ladies' companions in London, ninety-eight of them are surely tasked with worse things than looking after a bad-tempered, gassy pug."

His answering expression was skeptical, but reluctantly amused by her description of the dog. He rocked back on his heels, increasing the distance between them. "I did not mean to… I should leave you to your rest." Standing, he wiped his hands on the remaining scrap of toweling and tossed it over the washstand. "Do you—do you wish for me to call for someone to help you—?" With one hand, he gestured toward her clothes, which were streaked with mud, and likely worse.

"Undress?" She fought down a laugh. So he still imagined she was some sort of grand lady accustomed to having a maid at her beck and call? "I'm sure I can manage."

"Right." He moved hesitantly toward the door. "Anything else?"

"My spectacles?"

She saw his head turn in the direction of the window and the yawning blackness beyond. The little sparkles of light against the glass must be a scattering of raindrops. "Can you manage tonight without them, do you think? It'll be impossible to find anything in the dark. I'll go out at first light to look for them myself."

Hesitantly, she nodded her agreement. She did not *need* them. After all, she was just going to undress and slip into bed.

But when she heard the rattle of the door latch, her pulse quickened. Not fear of being alone. Longing for a few more moments with him. She flailed about for something to stay him. "Did you mean it?"

She watched him turn toward her, wondering about the expression on his face, which at this distance, was unreadable to her. Without her spectacles, she felt slightly nervous. Uncertain.

As though she oughtn't to be held responsible for what happened when she couldn't see straight.

"What you said when you found me at the posting inn," she explained. "Were you really worried? About me?"

* * * *

Worried?

His heart had begun hammering the moment Felicity had told him what Camellia had done. As the old coach had crawled toward the posting inn, he feared she would already have left.

At the first glimpse of her in the public room, he had expected to feel relief. Instead, his heartbeat had turned frantic at the sight of her alone, among the riffraff who traveled on the stage. Desperate to gather her in his arms and never let her out of his sight again, he'd settled for creating a distraction and getting her away.

His plan all along had been to surrender the coach to her at the first opportunity. She could then travel in reasonable comfort. Alone, yes, but the burly coachman would see to it that she came to no harm. And he had fully intended to hire a maid from one place or another, to lend an air of respectability.

When she'd clearly expected some explanation for his being on the road, something other than following her, he'd given Stoke as his destination. Perfectly plausible, though he had no intention of actually going there, of course. Even had he wanted to, which he did not, he needed to return to London and answer his uncle's accusations. Still the mere idea of an excuse to spend three more days in her company, along with—*no*, he had refused to tempt himself with the thought of as many nights—had done nothing to return his heartbeat to normal.

He'd settled for an hour or two, just until the next change of horses. Seated across from her in the confines of a carriage, however, so close that their knees bumped whenever the body of the coach was jostled by the rutted road, which was all too frequently, he had found his desire to touch her had not abated. So he had contrived a way to get closer.

Certainly, he had not meant to fall asleep with her in his arms. In fact, he'd pinched himself to stay awake merely for the chance to watch her. Knowing such a pleasure ought never to be his, and delighting in it all the same.

Then he'd awoken to the sight of her sprawled against the cobblestones, apparently lifeless, and for a moment, he'd been certain his heart meant to stop for good. Cradling her against his chest, washing her, skating his fingers along her soft skin...extraordinary intimacies. He thought he'd known what it was to touch a woman. He had been wrong.

Worry? No, that wasn't the half of what he felt. He could deny it, of course. Continue to be glib, to use wit as a shield—to protect her, as much as himself. He'd been doing that most of his life, after all. But sheer exhaustion had worn down his defenses.

She was studying him intently, as she so often did. How much could she see? Despite her missing spectacles, he felt stripped bare by that look—and not in the way he longed to be.

He turned away from the door and walked toward her. When he stopped beside the bed, just inches away from her, she rose to meet him. With anxious eyes, he searched her face for some flicker of discomfort, but he saw none. Instead, her pupils flared wide until her green gaze was nearly black. *Desire.*

"Yes. I meant it," he answered at last. Setting his hands on the curve of her shoulders, he lowered his mouth to hers.

She did not immediately return his kiss. Her palms slid lightly up his chest along the silk of his waistcoat. Neither pulling him closer nor pushing him away. "I cannot..." she whispered against his lips. "We *must* not. Felicity." The name was barely a breath.

Raising his hands to either side of her head, he lifted her face, made her feel the weight of his stare, so there could be no misunderstanding. "I will not be marrying your cousin."

His words were met with a long silence while she absorbed their significance. He could see other questions forming in her eyes. Wondering, perhaps, what had changed. At last she said, "What about Stephen's debt?"

"Forgiven." He hesitated another moment. "But only after she'd cut me loose and told me to come after you."

A certain tightness—guilt, perhaps—eased from her, and she sagged into his grip. But her breath came more rapidly. He watched her breasts rise and fall. Oh, she wanted him, perhaps almost as much as he wanted her. And one barrier had come crashing down.

It was not, however, the only thing standing between them. "Don't misunderstand me, Camellia," he said firmly. "I am not a free man." Uncertainty streaked across her expression. No matter what happened between them tonight, he did not dare promise to do what society would call—wrongly, in this instance—the honorable thing. "I cannot marry... anyone."

"I don't—" Hesitation caught her next words, held them back. He could sense a war waging within her. "I don't want to marry you, Gabriel," she said finally, watching her fingertips flutter against the folds of his cravat. "I just want—"

"This?" Dropping one hand to her lower back, he brought her hips flush against his, leaving no room for doubt. Crude, but then, he had never claimed to be a gentleman.

She snagged her lower lip between her teeth, then eased it free. "Yes."

Had he imagined his heart raced before? A wild, primal beat pounded inside his chest, almost drowning out the soft knocking, deeper still, of something that might have been disappointment, a flicker of longing that there could have been something more, something lasting between them. Resolutely, he ignored that quiet sound. He could not plan for the future. But he could give her what she wanted in the here and now.

Even positioned as they were, with his erection cradled against her belly, he could not quite convince himself she had said yes. But last night—God, had it been just last night?—she had kissed him with greedy lips and told him she was no innocent miss. He had not taken her at her word then. Now, however...

Curiosity prickled along his spine. Had she...? With whom? When? The questions implied no judgment, no scorn. After all, he was hardly innocent, either. And he had never subscribed to the notion that women did not feel lust, any more than he believed they never felt hunger or thirst, though they were sometimes persuaded to ignore even those urges.

She stretched upward to brush her lips along his jaw, and he turned toward her to meet her mouth with his. He had never given kissing much thought before, other than as a prelude for more interesting things to come, but he felt suddenly as if he could spend a lifetime learning her lips, the sharp bow of the upper as he traced it with little nibbling kisses, the plushness of the lower as he sucked it between his own. With his tongue he stroked deep into her, over her teeth, along her tongue, against the roof of her mouth, and she did not spar with him for once, but let him plunder her with a groan. When she tipped her head back to take him deeper into her mouth, her hair tumbled loose of its pins and cascaded over her back, over his hands, black as a raven's wing and more beautiful than he could have imagined.

As he kissed her, his fingers worked at the fastenings of her gown. Buttons, hooks, ties that had never baffled him before seemed strange, and strangely wonderful, as they forced him to slow down and unwrap her, inch by precious inch. The challis of her dress gave way at last to a plain cambric shift, gathered low across her chest with the bow nestled between her breasts. He ran one finger along the edge of the garment, never dipping beneath its ruched hem, the merest brush of skin against skin. Gooseflesh rose and she shivered, but he could feel it was not from cold.

Nor were her hands still. She loosed the buttons of his waistcoat to clutch at him through the fine lawn of his shirt, then began to tug at the knot in his cravat. "Easy," he murmured, backing ever so slightly away, catching her fingertips and kissing them one by one while she watched with wide, dark eyes. Pleasure could be found in haste, yes. But also in leisure. "Sit down. Rest your ankle."

To his surprise, she did not protest but sank onto the mattress. Her gaze traveled down his body, lower, lower, as if she meant to devour him with her eyes. When he bent to capture her lips again, her eyelids drooped but refused to fall. "What did I tell you, my dear?" he asked, catching her chin in one hand while the other tugged loose his cravat.

"About what?" Already she had a dreamy look about her, her plump lips slightly swollen.

"Those eyes." With a snicker of fabric, he slid the strip of linen free of his collar and dangled it from one hand. "Will you close them? Or shall I?"

Defiance sparked in their green depths. "What?"

For answer, he stretched a length of his cravat between two hands and held it before her at eye level.

"A blindfold?" Her eyes flared when he nodded. "That sounds…" One finger came up to stroke tentatively along the edge of the slick linen. "Wicked."

He'd intended only to tease her with the idea, to shock her a bit. But she was intrigued! "There is very little I have not done in the way of wickedness, I assure you." His voice had dropped so low he struggled to recognize it as his own. "Or in pursuit of pleasure."

"Pleasure?" She tipped her head to the side.

"Yes. Pleasure. You see, every time I catch your eye, Camellia, I find you studying me. Nothing seems to escape your gaze. Always watchful, always alert. You look and look. Have you never wondered what it would be like just to let yourself feel instead?"

Her lips parted and she blinked up at him, then squinted slightly to bring him into focus. "But without my spectacles, I can really see very little as it is, and nothing clearly."

"All the more reason to forgo that faulty sense and let the others have their turn, yes?"

She hung for a moment on the precipice of uncertainty, then shook her hair back behind her shoulders, tipped up her chin, and closed her eyes. "All right."

Good God, this was a woman who never went without a shield of some sort, from her tart tongue always ready with a retort, to that damned writing desk she had refused to relinquish until sleep made her grasp relent. Once, in his mind, he'd called her vulnerable, then later dismissed the word as having nothing to do with Camellia Burke. But in this moment, she was willing to be vulnerable. For him. With him.

He would make sure she did not regret it.

His hands trembled as he wound the strip of linen around her head twice and carefully tied the knot so as not to tangle her wild hair within it. With her head tilted back, her throat was bare to the brush of his lips as he bent to kiss the wild pulse point that hammered just beneath her delicate skin.

He let his hands settle lightly on her shoulders and trailed his fingers down her arms, so that his touch would not startle her. Then, kneeling, he brought his hands to her uninjured ankle and removed her shoe. Easing his hands slowly up her calf, over her knee, he untied her garter and rolled her stocking down over her foot. She shivered. "Sensitive?"

"I—I don't… Yes?"

He understood her uncertainty. His feather-light touch had raised gooseflesh. It could produce a ticklish sensation, if done carelessly. But he intended this to be something else entirely. Pure pleasure, sending a spark along every nerve ending, chasing along skin that had perhaps never known another's touch. Greedy, he longed to run his fingers over her everywhere.

Instead, he released her leg and rose.

"No," came her harsh whisper. "Don't stop."

"I won't." Beneath her eminently practical shift, he could see the tight peaks of her nipples but little else. "Can you stand, just for a moment?"

She rose without any visible difficulty or discomfort, although she listed slightly to one side as she shifted her weight onto her left foot. Again, he ran one fingertip along the gathered edge of her last remaining garment, that same light touch he meant to teach her to crave. Her chest rose, pressing toward his hand. Slowly, he plucked at the tie between her breasts, and when it was loose he eased her shift down over her shoulders. It met no resistance as it came to her hips and slid over them to puddle on the floor at her feet, like the marble gown of some Grecian goddess, draped over the pediment.

"Ah, Camellia. How lovely you are." And she was, with her high, round breasts and skin like fresh cream, though there was a bruise on one shoulder from her fall, and she was far too thin. Had her aunt's cruelty extended to starvation?

The sound of his voice seemed to remind her that his sight was unimpeded, and she moved her arms to cover herself. "Don't," he said, tracing one finger along the angle of her jaw. "If it will make you feel better, I'll douse the candles, while you lie down on the bed."

As he moved around the room, extinguishing the lights until all that was left was the soft glow of one flickering flame near the washstand, he shed his coat, his waistcoat, and his shirt, letting each garment fall where it would. When he reached the bed again, he propped himself against it to tug his boots free. She was lying half curled on her side, imagining, he supposed, that she was shielding herself from his gaze, though the sight of her long legs and the curve of her bottom were more than sufficient to send a bolt of heat straight through his belly and into his cock.

He did not generally let that organ do his thinking for him. It would have been death to do so at any gambling hell, where beautiful women were often employed as distractions. He knew he ought not to be thinking with it now, either. Whenever the right cards simply fell into his lap, he had taught himself to play as if the game were rigged, which it usually was. There had been women who wanted nothing more than a tumble with the notorious Lord Ash, of course, and he'd generally been willing to oblige. But he'd certainly not expected it of this one.

He wished he felt more confident of his ability to read her intentions. Perhaps the blindfold had been a tactical error. No matter—he did not have the strength to deny her, whatever her intentions were. Still, as he kneeled onto the end of the bed beside her feet, the shudder that passed through him was more than desire. A premonition of loss, perhaps.

Except what he feared losing in this gamble was not money or land or some other meaningless bauble that could easily be replaced.

His eyes fell on the scattering of silvery scars just above her makeshift bandage. She had risked at least her limb, perhaps even her life, to save her sister. What was it Fox had said about the burdens of being the eldest sibling? Always responsible, never quite free. He'd witnessed the same protective instinct in her treatment of Felicity. She had given a great deal of herself to so many.

Had anyone ever sacrificed anything for Camellia?

Bending low, he set his lips gently against the curve of her calf. The physical hurt from that incident with the dog was no doubt long gone. But there were other sorts of pain, and he would kiss them away, kiss every inch of her, until she let go of everything she'd been carrying and...flew.

Careful to skirt her injured ankle, he suckled her toes, then moved up her leg, nipping the soft flesh behind her knees, laying kiss after kiss along the back of her thigh till he came to her bottom and paused to pass his hand lightly over its plumpness, feeling her skin prickle to awareness, drawing her womanly scent into his lungs. Then he started again with the other foot, tasting salt. When her hips began to lift eagerly to his touch, he knelt above her and began at the top, sweeping aside her hair to kiss her neck, the slope of her shoulders, down the valley of her spine. Lips, teeth, tongue, over and over again, until she was breathless and so was he.

When he'd given her a moment, and only a moment, to recover, he cupped one shoulder. "The best is yet to come," he said with a low laugh as he coaxed her to turn onto her back.

Chapter 14

As Cami turned, the straw in the mattress crackled beneath her and the faint fragrance of the field rose from it, not unpleasant. The sheets felt coarse against her bare skin, abrading her cheek, her nipples. To her surprise, that feeling was not unpleasant either. She had thought she knew what to expect when he stripped her of her sight, but she could not have anticipated this rush of awareness, the way even ordinary sensations threatened to overwhelm but never did. Touch, scent, sound—they left no room for modesty, crowding out her doubts and the niggling vestiges of guilt.

And she could only be grateful.

Though why should she feel guilt? He was not now Felicity's, any more than he would ever be hers. It was only giving in once—or perhaps, if it was very good, twice—to the practiced seductions of a rake, as heroines were wont to do. But this time she was beholden to no pen but her own to craft a satisfactory conclusion to the affair. Once they reached Shropshire, she would leave him, and they need never see one another again.

She felt the bed shift as he rose, heard the soft sound of some item of clothing being shed. His breeches, almost certainly, for she had already heard his coat hit the floor. *Oh, my.* Heat rushed over her; the nighttime chill of the room was little more than a suggestion to be ignored. Once she was fully on her back, though, uncertainty nudged closer to her consciousness. She didn't know quite what to do with her hands. Press them to her sides? Fold them primly in her lap?

A nervous sort of laugh bubbled in her chest at the mental image that arose. She felt the mattress sink again as Gabriel returned to the bed. "Something amusing, my dear?" His warm voice at her ear made her scalp tingle. The lingering hint of his cologne combined with the elemental scent of his maleness to tickle her nostrils.

"I was wondering where to put my hands," she confessed.

"Mmm." He nuzzled her neck and drew in a deep, hungry breath, granting her permission to do the same. "I have a few thoughts. But to start…" His fingers tangled in hers and he lifted her arms over her head, pinning them to the pillow as he came more fully over her. His mouth sought and found hers, his lips soft, his day's growth of beard rough, his tongue sleek and demanding. And she surrendered to all of it with an eagerness that once would have made her blush.

As before, his kisses did not linger in any one spot. She felt his lips along her jaw, down her throat, over the ridge of her collarbone. What happened when he reached her—?

"Ahhh!" She bucked upward as his mouth closed over her breast. The flickering heat of his tongue was almost too much; then he began to suck. The wet sound filled her ears and spikes of lightning shot from the place where his mouth was through every nerve in her body. When she was absolutely certain she could not survive the pleasure, he shifted his ministrations to her other breast, freeing his hands from hers to run them down her arms and along her body, at last settling to cup the breast he had abandoned, to pluck her tender nipple between finger and thumb.

There could be no better feeling. She was sure of it. Another cry escaped her lips, this time a cry of despair as his mouth shifted once more, now exploring the valley between her breasts before grazing along her ribs and over her belly. When he lifted his body away from hers, she gripped the headboard so tightly the delicately turned spindles dug into her tender palms and gave her pain. Anything, anything to keep herself from begging.

He was at her feet again. A string of pretty little kisses, the scrape of his beard, the sweep of his hands, up her shins, over her knees, to her thighs. Then…

"Open your legs."

Shock shuddered through her at his dark tone of command. That inner voice, the one the blindfold had temporarily succeeded in silencing, wrangled itself free of its restraint and urged her to resist, to maintain some semblance of control. But the second, secret heart at the joining of her thighs pulsed eagerly. Not surprised that it would betray her, she searched the heart lodged safely behind her ribs, the heart that had always been under her sole command. It too throbbed and leaped at his startling demand.

After the briefest hesitation, hardly worthy of the name, she slid one leg over the edge of the bed, opening her very core to him.

With a whisper of touch, his fingertips skated over the soft skin between her thighs, learning this part of her as he had learned all the others. The merest brush against those silky curls, up to the swell of her belly and back down again. Her flesh tingled, anticipating his playful tracery.

His kiss followed, as she had feared—nay, prayed—it would. She was on fire, and yet his mouth burned as it traveled up from her knees to the delicate skin where her thighs joined her body. Hot breath ruffled her curls, then scorched her navel as he rested his rough cheek against her hip and let his fingers slip into her wetness. His touch was sure and steady and maddening, seeking and finding the place where her pleasure was centered. The first few strokes were enough to leave her panting, but when he set his mouth to her there, her body grew rigid with passion. If she screamed, would someone come?

But she did not want to be saved from this.

Without conscious thought, her hands dropped to his head, tangling in his hair as he sucked and licked until she shattered and shuddered into release. Tears leaked from the corners of her eyes, but the blindfold wicked them away.

Her breath was still sawing in and out of her lungs when he reached up to push the cravat away so he could look deep into her eyes as he entered her.

She had not known whether to expect pain the second time, as there had been the first, so long ago. But Gabriel had been born to bring her only pleasure, it seemed. He held her gaze as he filled her, arms at either side of her head, his strokes slow at first, then building and deepening as her desire built and deepened again. Now she could see the slight sheen of perspiration on his skin, the straining and bunching of the muscles that stretched across his shoulders, the way the flickering light of the last candle picked out the coppery gleam of his dark hair, both on his head and on his chest. And his eyes, black now in the shadows, drawing her down into their depths. She could drown in them, and she did not care.

Soon, too soon, she was lifting her hips in time with his thrusts and crying out when another climax overtook her, just as he jerked from her body and spent against the rough sheets.

* * * *

When the sun began to creep over the horizon, Gabriel awoke to find himself tangled in the bed linen and Camellia's black hair, one arm thrown possessively over her naked body. He'd done many things with a woman in his bed, but they had never before included sleep.

Last night had been extraordinary. He'd been delighted to discover she was every bit as passionate as he'd imagined. Had he ever been quite so focused on a woman's pleasure, on making her *feel?* Certainly, he had never taken so much pleasure in doing so.

Somehow, though, even those delicious memories paled in comparison to the experience of waking beside this woman. He was tempted to accompany her on the rest of her journey—he had never been to Ireland, after all—just for the possibility of starting another day, all his days, this way. Barring that, he was tempted to snuggle closer to her right now. To drowse until the sun was high in the sky, and when he woke again, to set his lips to the place where her shoulder and neck met, a spot last night's explorations had revealed to be most sensitive...

Instead, he eased away from her and slid out of the bed, careful not to disturb her rest. He'd delayed too long already. Unless he returned to London and challenged his uncle's accusations, he had no future at all. And for the first time in many years, he wanted to be able to dream about tomorrow. No, he wanted to do more than dream.

A wash with the cold water left in the washbasin made quick work of his lingering arousal, then he set about gathering his discarded clothes. His cravat, however, was still wrapped around Camellia's hair. Well, he had packed a change of linen, just in case it took more than a day to catch her. If only...*ah*, there was his bag, beside hers, beneath the window. Once he was dressed, he would go out to the stables to find her spectacles as he had promised.

First, however, he had to move her battered writing desk. The servant had placed it squarely atop both their bags, which formed a sort of nest for the wounded thing. The worn, ink-stained wood was scarred and chipped in several places. He bent to pick the desk up with all possible care, but it was no use. The latch had been broken by the fall and when it was moved, the front panel, which the latch had once held in place, tipped forward. The desk's contents spilled at his feet: folded letters, quills, a penknife, and what had no doubt once been a neat stack of papers closely covered with dark writing.

He froze with the desk in his hands, then glanced toward the bed to see if the sound had woken her. But she did not stir.

He might have stood admiring her sleeping form indefinitely, until something moved, tickling the top of his bare foot. Startled, he looked down to find a length of ribbon, coquelicot silk ribbon, dangling from the gaping hole in the side of the box, like a tongue lolling almost to the ground. Only its frayed end, threads tangled on the broken latch hinge, kept it from falling.

The sight of it hanging limply ought not to have made his heart lurch. It had made a much more spectacular showing at Lady Penhurst's musical evening, bright and sensual against Camellia's black hair and pale skin.

But to discover that his ribbon had been included among the meager possessions quickly packed for her journey home...

He shifted so that it was no longer touching him, but that only sent paper cascading into the place his foot had been. With an abundance of caution, fearful of causing another minor avalanche of parchment, he set the writing desk down on the floor and stepped back. She had not wanted anyone else to handle the desk, that much had been clear. Its contents were precious to her. Precious and private, and though he had seen every part of her last night, in this matter, he did not intend to pry. He would dress. He would go out to the stables. He regretted leaving a mess for Camellia to straighten, but he *would not look*. On the rare occasions Gabriel was required to offer his vowels, he always made certain to honor them. After all, a gambler was only as good as his word.

But there had never been a time, he realized as he bent over his bag to rummage for a clean shirt and a fresh cravat, that he had been forced to quell the curiosity that surged through him at the sight of his picture among a woman's things.

Dark eyes glowered up at him from the floor, revealed by the shifting of papers that had previously hidden them. Easily recognizable. Proof she had been thinking of him when they were apart.

But hardly a flattering portrait.

She had sketched hastily—on the back of a letter, he discovered as he held it up to the pale morning light for a more thorough study. A letter from a man named Benjamin Dawkins, of the firm Dawkins and Howe. Booksellers on Fleet Street.

Camellia had written a book?

The brief letter bore the date Gabriel had first called at Trenton House. *"A London audience will find your English villain wholly unbelievable, a caricature drawn out of Irish prejudice...."* This Dawkins had prompted Camellia to reimagine her book's antagonist, and her mind had gone immediately to him. Which meant...

He glanced down at the swirl of paper surrounding his feet, the manuscript pages of a novel. A novel in which he, apparently, played some part. No, not just *some* part. Despite himself, he laughed softly. The villain's part. *Of course.*

The letter slipped from his fingers and fluttered once more to the floor to join them. With crisp, efficient motions, he tied his cravat, finished dressing, slid his legs into his boots, then shuffled the disordered papers back into a neat stack. He would go the stables and find her spectacles, though he no longer doubted Camellia's clarity of insight. For a moment, he'd let himself imagine she saw something else, someone else, in him. He'd urged her to think of him as Gabriel, but she had really only ever been interested in Ash. She had known just what she was getting last night.

Only he had been blind.

* * * *

Cami clung stubbornly to the last fragments of sleep. Yawning, she stretched. Her muscles felt stiff and sore, as though she had slept the whole night through without stirring once. She also was not wearing a nightgown.

The previous night's activities came back to her in a rush, and she clutched the sheet to her chest. But when she at last opened her eyes, she discovered the room was empty. Passing a hand over her hair, she found Gabriel's cravat still tangled in it. Deftly, she twisted the strip of linen to keep her unkempt locks out of her face. As she moved, a silvery gleam caught her eye. Her spectacles lay on the table beside the bed. He had found them. With fingers that fumbled in their eagerness, she unfolded them and put them on.

Suddenly all was in sharp relief. The faded floral paper on the walls of the shabby but clean room. Steam rising from the pitcher of water on the washbasin. On the chair in the corner someone had laid out her clothes; her dress had been brushed, the linen was fresh. Her eyes traveled to the place where her bag and writing desk had sat, but someone must already have carried them down to the coach. When had Gabriel risen? Just how long had she been asleep?

She stepped out of bed with caution, but her ankle gave her very little pain. After she had splashed water on her face, dressed, and arranged her hair as best she could, she made her way down to the public room of the inn and found him seated at breakfast. The aromas of toast and coffee and other good things wafted from the table. Yesterday afternoon's meat pie was no more than a distant memory, and she approached the repast with an eager, slightly embarrassed smile.

Gabriel rose. He was handsome as ever in his well-tailored clothes, with his crisp linen, his freshly shaved jaw, and…a look in his eyes she had never seen before. She had not realized how warm their hazel-brown depths had always seemed to her, until she saw their cool, wary expression now.

Suddenly nervous, she dropped her gaze to the table and saw what she had not noticed from across the room. At her place lay the thick stack of paper that made up her life's work, neatly tied with red silk ribbon. Her stomach, which had been growling keenly over the other contents of the table, performed a poorly executed somersault and landed somewhere in the vicinity of the floor.

"Please sit down," he said, as if he suspected how her knees wobbled beneath her skirts. "I regret to say that your writing desk was another casualty of yesterday's fall." The explanation was offered in a voice as distant as his eyes as he resumed his seat opposite. "It was resting atop my valise. I did not realize that the hinge holding the front panel in place had broken. When I picked up the desk to set it aside, everything spilled out. Including that." He gestured toward the stack of bound pages.

She fought the impulse to snatch it up and clutch it protectively to her chest.

"Did you—did you read it?" she managed to whisper.

The wait for his answer was torture, and after last night, she suspected he enjoyed keeping her on edge. "No," he admitted at last. "But I gathered from Mr. Dawkins's letter it is a novel, one in which my own likeness features rather prominently."

She nodded, but hidden beneath the table, she twisted her fingers in her lap. "Are you…are you angry with me?"

"Angry?" His expression of wide-eyed surprise was tinged with mockery. "Why, Miss Burke! What would there be to anger me in your tale? I trust you've told only the truth. Say rather, *flattered*," he corrected, pausing to take a sip of coffee. "Not every villain can hope for the lasting infamy of print."

No, he wasn't angry. That much was true. He was… She raked her eyes over his face as her mind flailed for a word. *Resigned.* Yes, that was it. Resigned to being thought a villain. At the discovery of what she'd done, he'd slipped back into his comfortable role, donned once more the familiar mask.

She'd gone to bed with Gabriel, and woken up to Lord Ash.

He pushed away from the table, as if preparing to rise. Did he intend to punish her presumption by abandoning her in—in—? Why, she didn't even know the name of the village. Almost every coin she'd had to her name had been spent on a ticket for the public stage. She hadn't enough now to return to London, to say nothing of getting home. Her heart rattled in her chest.

Time for a gamble of her own.

"Is there anything more calculated to bring on a bout of ennui than driving through the Midlands?" she asked. He hesitated, and a shadow of confusion flickered across his gaze. After a moment, he gave a cautious nod in acknowledgment of the truth of her observation. "Miles and miles of nothing but fields and sheep. Hours and hours with nothing to amuse the traveler. Fortunately,"—she lifted her hands and laid them, palms down, on her manuscript—"I have had the foresight to bring a book." Now, his dark brow arced. "And so, I wish to make a proposal."

Though he said nothing, she knew from his posture she had his full attention. But as she weighed her next words, his expression smoothed into something unreadable, part and parcel of the skills that made him successful at the card table—an ability to lure others into risking what they could not afford to lose.

"Despite the admirable restraint you have shown, you are curious, I suspect, about what I have written," she said. "If you will agree to convey me at least as far as Shropshire, I will read to you from *The Wild Irish Rose*."

He was much too skilled to allow surprise to show on his face, though she felt sure he had not anticipated such an offer. Would he refuse it? She thought of what she had written about Lord Granville. No, she did not expect Lord Ash to sit quietly through a recital of his sins. But there were certain things he needed to hear.

"As Lady Merrick's companion, I often read novels aloud," she reminded him encouragingly. "She seemed to find my voice pleasant enough." *Despite my accent.*

He stood. "I'll leave you to your breakfast," he said, nodding at the table. A pause, while his long fingers drummed against the back of his chair. "And I will tell the driver to have the carriage ready in a quarter of an hour."

It was not precisely an invitation to accompany him, but it was answer enough. A species of relief curled through her, but its unusually sharp claws dug into her belly, robbing her of any remaining appetite.

Gabriel seemed to read her thoughts. "*Eat*, Camellia." That tone of command again, softened when he added, "You're far too thin."

A flush swept over her skin—embarrassment, yes, yet tinted with the memory of his touch. The strange realization that he had seen more of her than her nakedness. The possibility that in some corner of his charred heart he cared—or would care, if anyone had ever shown him how.

With the slightest of bows, he strode to the door. When he had left the room, she picked up a piece of toast and forced herself to take a bite. For what lay ahead, she was going to need her strength.

Chapter 15

The morning sky was bright without being sunny, damp without being rainy. Gabriel stood beside his coach, glanced at the low hanging clouds on the horizon, and wondered what other nonsensical observations about the weather he could make to pass the time until Camellia came to resume her travel northward.

He had greeted the day with every intention of traveling in the other direction, eager to confront his uncle face-to-face. Determination had burned in his belly, hot and bright. Over the course of the last hour, however, that flame had begun to sputter and smoke. Soon enough, it would be snuffed out entirely.

What did it matter, really, whether he went forward or back? Whether he was charged with treason and hanged? Hadn't he always expected to meet some scandalous end? And as for Stoke, what had possessed him to believe that its people were better off with him as its master, that he ought to fight to keep it out of his uncle's hands? Camellia's reminder, though unintentional, had been timely.

He was and never would be anything more than Ash.

In the doorway of the inn, she appeared in her plain woolen dress, covered by her usual brown pelisse. Once, he had read the loose fit of her garments as a kind of disguise; now, he found himself wondering if they had been cut for a fuller figure that had since been worn away by work or worry or homesickness. In one hand, she carried her bonnet by its ribbons; the stack of papers she held against her breast with the other. Her hair hung over one shoulder in a thick, black braid, and her chin tipped upward when he caught her eye.

Altogether a much more appealing picture than it had any right to be.

With slow steps, but no obvious limp, she crossed the cobbled inn yard to the carriage. To his side. "I hope I did not keep you waiting, my lord."

For answer, Gabriel held out one hand to help her up. Instead, she laid the bundle of papers on his palm, followed by her bonnet, and clambered into the coach—favoring her right ankle, yes, but determinedly unassisted.

Inside the carriage, she arranged her skirts and her bonnet with care to take up the entirety of one bench. When he looked into the coach, she was sitting primly with the bound stack of pages in her lap. He could order the coachman to drive on and send her away, alone. Or he could take the seat facing the rear, facing her, and subject himself to her tale.

You are curious, I suspect, about what I have written. But what sort of man felt curiosity when looking into a mirror?

With a muttered oath, he hoisted himself into the carriage.

Hardly had the coach rolled into motion when she slipped the knot from the ribbon and took up the first sheet of paper, holding it just high enough before her that she could fix him with those sharp green eyes from time to time as she read. He had the distinct impression she was enjoying herself.

With a slight clearing of her throat, she began. "Róisín Nic Uidhir had been born with a fiery spirit to match her red hair, and so it came as no surprise to her brothers, Cathal and Fergus, when she told them she had been invited to the Belfast Harpers Assembly and meant to go, with or without them."

Camellia's voice, which always had a lovely, lyrical quality to it, took on a new and unfamiliar note. There was something at once alienating and compelling about it. On her tongue, the foreign names might have been invocations to a deity—some Celtic god that probably meant Englishmen like Gabriel mischief.

"'Father needs us on the farm,' Fergus said. He had learned to stress what was practical when trying to persuade his sister of anything. 'And it would not be safe for you to go alone.'

"Cathal, the eldest of the three, was more decisive in his refusal. 'You play well enough, for a girl, Róisín, but the festival will bring bards from every county. You cannot hope to compete with the likes of them. There's no need for you to go at all, at all.'"

"So Cathal has not learned how to manage women," Gabriel interrupted, though his tongue felt strangely inadequate to forming the name.

Her gaze flickered up from the paper, then back down. "You assume women need to be managed by men, my lord…or can be," she countered.

He parted his lips to retort but in the end said only, "Go on with the story."

"As you please, my lord."

Oh, she would be the death of him with her prim, distant "my lord" this and "my lord" that. But he supposed there were worse ways to die.

"Róisín merely smiled at her brothers and set to work packing her harp. Fergus argued. Cathal scolded. Nevertheless, on a fine day in June, they left County Fermanagh exactly as she had intended they would, Fergus leading the donkey-cart that carried her precious instrument, while Cathal brought up the rear of the party, muttering dire predictions of the dangers they would face."

The story did not attempt to disguise its allegorical qualities, as the three wide-eyed characters set out on a sort of pilgrimage. While Camellia read, Gabriel allowed his gaze to drift to the window and found himself vaguely disappointed at being surrounded by ordinary English hills and fields, rather than the rugged, green landscape of northern Ireland through which Róisín and her brothers walked. By midday, the siblings' journey had managed to incorporate, with remarkable seamlessness, several lessons in Irish history, a description of traditional Irish clothing, and an encounter with a Catholic priest also bound for Belfast who found some excuse to give his presumably like-minded fellow travelers a lengthy discourse on the many misunderstandings to which their faith was subjected by outsiders.

"Rather heavy-handed, is it not?" Gabriel shifted awkwardly in his seat, stiff from holding himself in a position that kept their knees from brushing. "This panegyric on all things Irish? I am surprised Mr. Dawkins made no complaint."

Camellia laid the page from which she had been reading facedown onto the steadily growing stack beside her. "You didn't."

He should have guessed she had noticed. In truth, he was stiff from having sat through the past three changes of the horses, held spellbound by her tale. And when he watched her plump lips curve in a provoking smile, and remembered the feel of them against his own mouth, certain parts of him grew stiffer yet.

"That's enough for now," he said, crossing one booted foot over the other leg and glancing toward the window. "We'll be at the next village soon, and if the inn's decent, we'll stop for a meal."

"As you wish." She began rearranging the papers, which crinkled as she neatened the two stacks, turning one sideways before placing it atop the other so that the unread pages would not be mixed in with those she had finished.

He felt a sigh of something like relief ease from his lungs. She had at last forgone the damned honorific she'd been wielding all day with the subtlety of a beadle waving a rod at unruly schoolboys to keep them in line. As if they were strangers. As if he had not swept his tongue over every inch of her ivory skin.

Then she lifted her gaze to him and added, with quiet dignity, "My lord."

* * * *

Róisín played for their supper or a room for the night, and all who heard her were enchanted.

When she had written those words, Cami had never imagined they would be a sort of premonition of her own fate. As soon as they sat down to a simple luncheon in the public room of the Green Hart Inn, she drained her cup of tea in a single swallow, though it was hot enough to sear her throat in passing. As soon as she returned her cup and saucer to the table, Gabriel picked up the teapot and refilled it without being asked, looking ever so slightly guilty for having kept her at her task for so long. Lady Merrick's considerably more limited span of attention had never required her to sit and read for hours at a time.

"I have been thinking about our conversation at Lady Penhurst's," he said. "So, you decided to come to London in hopes of finding a publisher for a book I assume you wrote in secret?"

She nodded. No point in denying it now.

"But why not stay in Dublin? A work of such obvious Irish pride, as Dawkins himself noted—"

"My intention was not to reach an Irish audience, my lord, but an English one." Picking up her spoon, she prodded at the bowl of lamb stew the servant set before her. "There are those who know nothing more of my country than what may be displayed on the London stage or sketched in a broadside cartoon. How can they be expected to imagine Ireland as a country with its own culture and traditions, a place quite apart from Britain, and worthy of its independence? I hoped to help them see another side of the story."

As she spoke, she could feel his eyes on her, watching her shift the peas to one side of her dish. A childish habit. Reluctantly, she swirled her spoon through the brown gravy, mixing them back in again. Then she forced down a bite, peas and all, swallowing too quickly to taste them.

"And Dawkins believes he will find readers for that story? To be honest, I had not thought a novel the proper medium for politics."

"I suppose you mean to imply it is an *improper* one?" Crumbs scattered across the table as she gestured impatiently with the hunk of bread she had torn from the loaf to chase the dreadful stew. "Because ladies read novels?"

"And write them, it would seem. As do gentlemen," he added hastily when she reached for the butter knife. "I meant what I said, Camellia. I have no patience with those of my sex who would argue that ladies have neither the brains nor the stomach for politics. The men who hold to such a belief cannot have known many women."

"Whereas you have known a great many, I suppose." The words popped from her mouth before she thought how they would sound. All those months in Aunt Merrick's reproving company and she still had not learned to restrain her tongue.

He did not laugh, as she had half expected, though there was amusement in his eyes as his gaze flickered over her. "Perhaps I only thought I knew them." Before she could revel in her satisfaction at this admission, however, he spoke again. "It is tempting, is it not, to presume greater knowledge of another than we can possibly have, even after intimate study?"

It might have been an allusion to his own behavior of last night. But she felt certain it was intended to be a reprimand of the use she'd made of him in her book.

Why on earth should she be expected to feel remorse for what she had done? He himself had said that everyone knew the extent of his villainy.

Still, she wondered what he would say when he heard the rest of Róisín's tale.

While she poked at the contents of her bowl, Gabriel finished his stew, even wiping the bowl with a bit of bread, then drained his mug of ale. "Order something else, if you'd like. I'm going to stretch my legs."

She could think of several perfectly rational reasons to stay put. For one thing, as he'd pointed out, she hadn't finished eating—or even started, really. And her ankle was tender, though admittedly not so badly injured that a little exercise would harm it. Most of all, she sensed that he wanted time alone.

Hesitating only a moment, she swallowed the dregs of her now tepid tea, picked up a thick slab of the crusty bread and a piece of cheese, and went after him.

She caught up with him just outside the door. Wordlessly, he held out his arm to her, and she took it. Walking slowly, almost certainly for her benefit, he set out in the direction of a tumbling-down pile of stones in the distance that passed for a picturesque ruin, the village's sole attraction to travelers. When they drew within a hundred yards of it, he stopped. "Any closer and the effect will be spoiled entirely."

Already they were close enough to see that the dilapidated structure was too small ever to have been a castle or a church. A byre, more likely. A few sheep wandered among the rocks, nibbling at the weeds.

Cami seated herself on the stile and finished her bread and cheese, while Gabriel stood nearby. The peace and quiet here was nothing like the bustle of London. Not even Dublin. It unsettled her, reminded her that she was meant to be racing home to avert a disaster.

Though he was staring into the distance, Gabriel seemed to read her thoughts. "What do you expect to find when you get to Ireland?"

"I cannot say. My brother Paris may be involved in—well, what he does is entirely his own choosing, of course. The real worry is that he may have involved my brother Galen in something—something—"

"Something dangerous," he finished as he came to sit down beside her. "Your cousin feared that it might have to do with the United Irishmen."

Cami felt her eyes flare and knew her surprised expression was as good as a confession, but she could not stop herself. The United Irishmen had been driven underground years before. The very name was forbidden to be spoken by its members. If Felicity could guess as much, though, how secret could their plots be? How long before her brothers were caught up in one of them?

"Yes." The whispered word was soon lost among the wind rustling through the grasses and the plaintive notes of a ewe bleating to her lambs.

"I see." He looked grave. And very, very English. Good God, he was an aristocrat, a member of the House of Lords. As far as the British government was concerned, the United Irishmen—her brothers—were traitors and criminals. Why on earth had she trusted him with that admission?

Probably because last night she had trusted him with everything else.

"Cathal and Fergus are really Paris and Galen, are they not?" he went on. "With their love of country and eloquent pride in its history…" As he spoke, he took her hands in his, and she realized she must have left her gloves lying on the table in the inn. "Along with an utter inability to see how their sister's gift could save it. And you are the wild Irish rose herself… though I do not think you play the harp." When he lifted her fingers as if to inspect them for the telltale calluses the instrument's strings would produce, he found only ink stains, of course. His thumb brushed across them, but this time, he did not lift them to his lips.

Disappointment tickled in the back of her throat like tears.

Abruptly, she freed her hands from his and rose. "There's a bit of myself in all of my characters, I suppose," she said, brushing the crumbs from her skirt.

"Surely only the virtuous ones."

She flinched at the sardonic edge to his voice. For just a moment, she had forgotten.

He had risen when she did, but he let her walk away without offering his assistance, for which she felt grateful. She suddenly understood his desire to be alone.

All the walking seemed to have done her some good; she could move now with very little difficulty. Always before, though, exercise had also helped to clear her head. Perhaps she had expected too much this time. She had never let her thoughts get into such a muddle before.

She felt confused. Lost.

Somewhere along this winding road from Dublin to London and back again—on which journey she was meant to have spared her innocent cousin, written the book that would transform English opinions of Ireland, and saved her brothers' necks—she had slipped and wrenched something a bit more vital than her ankle. Her head might know that Gabriel was wicked and reckless and in every way unsuited to be a hero. But her spirit craved his quick wit and agile mind, just as her body craved his touch. Last night had resolved nothing in that regard; if anything, the ache was worse.

And now her heart ached right along with it.

Had she made a mistake this morning, offering to read *The Wild Irish Rose* to him?

Or had the mistake been made longer ago, the day she had given in to her aunt's demand and her cousin's plea to sit with them during that first visit from Lord Ash?

When she reached the coach, she glanced back once more at the ruin. At Gabriel, still standing near the ramshackle pile of stones, little more than a speck in the distance.

He was right. Sometimes it was unwise to inspect a thing too minutely.

Chapter 16

The innkeeper studied the register in front of him, frowned, and shook his head. "Haven't got but the one room left, sir. Ye mun share. Sure, then, your…sister, did ye say…? would be willin' to—"

"Cousin," Gabriel corrected. "So you understand, of course, that we do not wish to—"

One brow shot upward. "Aye, sir. I do, that. But I cannot make a room where there isn't one." He appeared to give the matter some thought. "I s'pose you might make your bed in the stable loft with the coachmen and such, if you've a mind to."

"Fine," Gabriel readily agreed. Under no circumstances could last night's interlude be repeated. A second night in her bed would be courting disaster, and not just because it would increase the risk, no matter how much care he took, that she might one day soon find herself carrying a dead man's child.

"Not a word of this to her. My coach will be here any moment."

Unable to bear being cooped up in the carriage any longer, he'd hired a horse after dinner and ridden ahead. It had not been a comfortable journey, but his desire to sit with her, to listen to her, convinced him he had made the only sensible decision. He was not supposed to be enjoying her tale.

Thankfully, this crowded, bustling inn would provide little opportunity for further entertainment, for intimate conversation of any sort.

Gabriel laid a hand on the counter, and the innkeeper looked up. "A private dining parlor is out of the question, I assume?" he asked.

"Th' room has a small parlor adjoinin'. I s'pose I could arrange to serve supper to you and your lady—"

"Cousin—"

"—there. If you wish."

"Yes, thank you. In an hour." He turned toward the door to watch for his coachman, then added over his shoulder, "Oh, and nothing with peas."

The unfamiliar request stymied the innkeeper. "How's that, sir?"

"For supper. Please do not serve any dishes with peas. The lady—"

"Your cousin, you mean?"

Gabriel shot him a look that had persuaded many a gambling man to fold. "The lady does not enjoy them."

"Aye, sir. So that's one bed"—the innkeeper opened the register to make a note—"one private parlor, and no peas."

"Precisely."

A quarter of an hour later, Gabriel's coach rolled to a stop and he reached up to help Camellia down. "Your room awaits you, Cousin," he said, gesturing with his free hand for a servant to carry up her things.

She looked the picture of icy respectability, her long braid now wound beneath her bonnet and the ragged sheaf of papers nowhere in evidence, presumably tucked into the valise she was at that moment reluctantly surrendering to the innkeeper's son. Even her missing gloves had been replaced. "How kind of you." Cool green eyes looked him up and down. "Cousin."

"I'll join you for supper in half an hour, if I may?" An exercise in frustration. She had no real need of his company, and he was a damned fool for wanting hers.

She dipped her head and was gone, leaving him to carry his own things to the stable loft. The accommodations there were spare but clean, though he suspected he still smelled of horse when he returned to the inn to dine.

He found her in a room hardly deserving of the name of parlor; a table and four chairs nearly filled it. Small windows on two sides overlooked the stable and inn yard, while the other two walls boasted doors: one through which he had entered, and one through which he could just glimpse a narrow bed. When she rose and gestured him to a chair, he saw that she had changed into a fresh dress. Her braid once more swung freely across her back as she moved.

"Your room is satisfactory?"

"Yes, thank you. But—" Her gaze darted to the window.

So, she had watched him come from the stables. Before he could offer any explanation, a red-faced young woman backed through the door carrying a laden tray. He very nearly had to step into the bedchamber to make room for her to enter.

An indifferent dinner of roast chicken, underdone potatoes, and wilted greens was accompanied by a bottle of surprisingly good white wine, and by the time he had poured his third glass, and Camellia's second, he had managed to persuade himself the silence that had loomed over them throughout the meal was more companionable than stony. When he poked suspiciously at the wobbly custard that had been sent up for dessert, she covered her mouth with her napkin—hiding a smile, he felt certain.

"Do you know," he said, taking up his glass, "I think I'd rather have another chapter of *The Wild Irish Rose* instead."

She hiccupped, her expression still half-hidden by the square of linen. "Now?"

"Why not?" The last of the day's light was fading from the sky, but the room glowed with the light from a brace of candles.

"I should think the better question would be *why*."

"I thought, my dear, you wished to show me the error of my ways," he said with a mocking smile. "Consider me your test case, the skeptical Englishman to be taught to regard Ireland in a more positive light. Though I must confess I've really given the country very little thought, either good or bad. Until recently."

Her eyes narrowed. "Intolerance is a great ill, certainly. But indifference is worse."

"Well, then…" He eased back in his chair, resting the foot of his wineglass against his waistcoat. "Do your best to correct me."

With an expression he would not exactly call obliging, she rose and went into the other room. When she returned, she was carrying just a few pages—the chapter he had requested and nothing more, signaling that tonight, he ought not to expect carte blanche from her. He applauded her resolve, yet the scoundrel in him warmed to the challenge it represented.

She settled into her chair with the papers in her lap, then took a drink to wet her lips before picking up the topmost sheet. He gestured with the wine bottle for her to begin as he tipped the last of its contents into her glass.

"Róisín had never seen the likes of Belfast," she read. "The city hummed and thrummed with the beats of ten thousand Irish hearts and the notes of a thousand Irish harps. In her ears buzzed the varied accents of her countrymen, who hailed, as Cathal had predicted, from all the four kingdoms. To her great surprise, though, not every voice was Irish. Travelers had come from far and wide to take in the spectacle, and as she pushed through the crowd to the Assembly Room, where the harpists were to convene, she heard an Englishman say to his friends, 'There is the one who will triumph.'

"He was not speaking of her, of course. Rather, the ancient blind bard, Donnchadh Ó hAmhsaigh, had just passed, and a hush had fallen over the crowd, else the Englishman's voice would have gone unheard. Hear it she did, though, and she turned toward the speaker, whose eye had likewise been caught by her flaming red hair."

At last, the arrival of the long-awaited villain.

Gabriel sat up a little straighter in his chair, awaiting the catalog of his own features. But it never came. The man whom Róisín glimpsed above the heads of the other festivalgoers had golden hair and blue eyes. All boyish good looks and charm.

A strange sort of unease settled somewhere behind Gabriel's ribs.

"As the man stood between her and the doorway through which she wished to enter," Camellia read, "Róisín could not avoid his scrutiny. Nor did it occur to her that she ought to avoid it, for though her lips had sung many a song about treachery in the guise of love, she had not lived enough to know that she might be its victim."

Now, suspicion began to prickle along his spine. Difficult as it was to imagine the quick-witted and sharp-spoken Camellia being duped by a rogue, it seemed clear someone else had plied the author of this portrait with seductive wiles. Was it possible she had once been as naïve as her heroine? Had she fallen prey to the same sort of man?

Or, more accurately, had she fallen prey to the wrong sort of man *twice?*

For the first time, the memory of Camellia's body beneath his produced a twinge he might have called regret. The knowledge that some other scoundrel had been the one to take Camellia's innocence offered no salve to his conscience. Twisting the stem of his wineglass between his fingers, he forced himself to return his attention to the story.

"'Do you play?' the man asked as she passed, for he could guess the direction of her steps.

"She paused. 'That I do, sir.'

"He gave her a sweeping bow. 'May I make so bold as to ask the favor of a name? I should like to be able to tell my friends I have seen the one who will win.'"

Inwardly, Gabriel winced on Róisín's behalf. He knew precisely where such flattery led. Camellia resolutely kept her eyes on her paper.

"Róisín turned to look for the harpist who had passed. 'Indeed you have, sir. 'Twas Denis Hempsey you saw.'

"Her modesty brought a smile to his lips. 'I meant *your* name, my dear,' he said.

"'I'm called Róisín Nic Uidhir, sir,' she said, when she could find her tongue. 'In English, Rosie Maguire.'

"'Delighted to meet you, Miss Maguire,' he replied with a bow. 'Granville, at your service. And one day soon, I hope you shall play for me.'"

Pausing, Camellia pressed the page from which she had been reading against her knees. Gabriel cleared his throat. "So Granville's the one, eh?" he asked with false heartiness. "Clearly, a thoroughgoing rake."

"But it is not *too* clear?" She looked up at him with something like alarm in her eyes. "It's essential readers understand that Róisín embodies Ireland, of course, its beauty, its culture, its—"

"Its vulnerability to the rapacious appetites of England, in the form of one despicable Lord Granville?" He did not fault her approach. Readers would devour many things in the guise of a tragic love story. Even politics.

"But Mr. Dawkins disliked my portrayal of Granville, in particular. He thought it a caricature. Hence my need to study the habits and history of someone more...complex."

"Complex." He knew better than to think it a compliment.

"Mm, yes. It seems that England's exceptional villainy with respect to Ireland cannot be represented by a run-of-the-mill rogue."

In spite of himself, Gabriel laughed. What would she say if she knew that her paragon of English vice was suspected of treason against that very crown?

"I'm sure your revisions will satisfy Mr. Dawkins's concerns. Most readers will not share my particular interest in the character," he said, then paused. "To tell the truth, I expected to find him more...familiar."

"He—" She reached for her wine and took one swallow, then another. "I confess I did not have you in mind when I first crafted this portrait," she admitted when she lowered the glass. "He was based on another Englishman I once knew. The son of an old school friend of my father's who stayed with us a few weeks one autumn on his way to join a shooting party in the south." She paused, and the silence told him all he had not wanted to know. "I was young," she added in a rough whisper. "Younger than Róisín. That, at least, is my excuse. We—I—I foolishly imagined we would marry when he returned to Dublin." She restored the empty goblet to the table with fingers that did not look quite steady. "He took another route home."

Gabriel reached out and caught her hand on its way to her lap. Even in the candlelight, he could see that the wine had brought a flush of color to her cheeks, but her fingertips were cold. "How young, Camellia?"

"Not quite seventeen."

"He—he did not—?" He could not seem to push the necessary words past the anger that swelled his throat like the stings of a swarm of bees.

She took pity on him. "Force his attentions where they were not wanted? Oh, no. I threw myself quite willingly into his arms." He could hear the anger in her voice too, the frustration. Along with a ripple of shame. Once more, she freed her hand from his.

"Why did your father not insist he make amends? Or your brother?"

"Paris was fifteen. Had he known, I'm sure he would have gone off half-cocked and got himself killed. And as for Papa...well, what was to be done? A duel? Only brash young men imagine those spectacles can make up for the honor that was lost."

So much for his hope that either Cathal or Fergus would run Granville through to avenge the poor Irish Rose once she'd been plucked. Reluctantly, Gabriel nodded his agreement and tried not to think of Fox's parting words to him.

"Papa found out only later that his friend had sent his son away from London in hopes of separating him from undesirable acquaintances and bad habits. A plan that seemed to have failed quite spectacularly, in my view..." Camellia's voice trailed off as she gazed at the flickering candlelight like a distant star. Then she shook off the memory and met his eyes. "The following spring, when my friends could talk of nothing but come-outs and finding husbands, I was of course deemed perfectly ineligible for any desirable match, spared from all but a few pitying glances. I decided to embrace my fate—my *freedom*. I did not need a man. With five younger siblings, I had had my fill of raising children. All my life, I had been jotting down stories, but now that I was to be a spinster, I began to write in earnest." Behind her spectacles, her green eyes sparked with familiar energy. "And if by chance the gossip about my indiscretion did not immediately deter a gentleman, I would simply say or do something rather outlandish to prove to him I would not suit."

Recalling their first meeting, he had no difficulty at all imagining what those outlandish things might have been.

"Will you tell me what happens to Granville?" he asked after a moment, nodding toward the unread pages.

Her fingers tightened around them. "Nothing."

"Nothing?" Surely Róisín's seducer would be subject to a more fitting reckoning than Camellia's had been.

"That is, I do not—I do not know anymore," she said, rising. "Originally, I intended for Róisín to return to Belfast the following year, carrying her broken harp as if it were a child, playing the song of a woman scorned by her lover, who died when she pushed him off a cliff."

It was a chilling image, both for what it revealed about the characters and what it foretold about the future of Anglo-Irish relations. But he took some comfort in Camellia's hesitation. At least she was having some small bout of conscience about killing him off.

Gabriel, too, got to his feet, and in the small room they stood for a moment, toe to toe, separated by little more than the half dozen sheets of paper she held, close enough that he could feel her tremble. How he longed to take her in his arms, to prove he was something more than a convenient villain. Was any part of her hoping he would?

He leaned his body away from the possibility. "About last night..."

Her eyes darted nervously around the room, looking anywhere but at him. "Oh, please do not."

"Do not what? Speak of it?"

One hand released the papers and fluttered in search of a word. "Apologize. Scold. I—I had done with all that nonsense years ago. A woman of my age and situation may, I trust, be permitted to indulge her curiosity from time to time, and I merely wanted to know if certain rumors about...Lord Ash were true."

He dared to catch her chin in his hand and bring her gaze to his. "And were they?"

Rebelliousness sparkled behind her spectacles. "No."

He recognized the challenge in that word. The invitation. The lie he did not dare to correct. As he lowered his mouth to within an inch of hers, her eyelids fluttered down obligingly. "Then I'll wish you a good night, my dear," he whispered. "So sorry to disappoint."

Five minutes later, when he stopped at the stable door and looked back, he could still see her at the window, backed by the candles' flickering light.

* * * *

Cami made certain to rise early enough that she was dressed and waiting downstairs when Gabriel came to fetch her. No more intimate moments behind closed doors. No more courting disaster. *The Wild Irish Rose* was not a romance. She knew how the story had to end, and she must not try to rewrite history, neither his nor her own. He was an English nobleman, unmoved either by Ireland's past glory or its present plight, and—

In her mind, she heard him ask for another chapter of Róisín's sad story. Heard the quiet fury in his voice as he reacted to her own tale of woe. No, not unmoved. Whatever his reputation for heartlessness, she knew at least a portion of it to be false.

Oh, that had been the worst of it from the beginning, the discovery that "Lord Ash" was a creation, a fabrication, no more real than her pen and ink one, but crafted with a far more malicious intent, and not by Gabriel alone, either. How, in all these years, had no one managed to catch a glimpse of the pain-filled eyes behind that mask? Or why, among all the women he had purportedly known, had he chosen to reveal himself to her?

But perhaps he didn't have a choice in the matter, any more than she seemed to have.

Her fingers tightened on the handles of her valise. All her bravery had deserted her. She found herself wishing he would not ask to hear more.

"Good morning," he called to her as he approached, looking infuriatingly better rested and less rumpled that she, although she had been the one to enjoy the benefits of a proper bed. Dare she hope that with all that energy he would elect to continue on horseback and leave the carriage to her?

But after he handed her into the coach, he followed and settled in across from her like a sultan awaiting his entertainment. "What adventure now befalls poor Róisín?" he asked as soon as the driver had chirruped to the horses.

Masking a sigh, she dug the manuscript from her bag. After she had delayed as long as she could, shuffling through the stack of paper twice as she pretended to look for her place, she began.

"The next morning dawned cool and bright, and Róisín's harp was tuned and ready with the sun. With every bard that played and sang, the trembling of her fingers increased. How could she presume to play before them?

"When her turn came, she tilted her instrument against her breast and plucked the first notes of the keening melody she had written, weaving together the stories of Deirdre and Meadhbh and all the strong women who had made Ireland proud.

"She did not win the competition, of course. She was, as Cathal had said, only a woman, and the only woman who competed, at that. But she won the hearts of many of those who heard her, a prize more valuable to her than gold.

"She also won the attentions of Lord Granville, which value I shall leave it to the reader to determine."

From that point on in the story, myriad scratches and scribblings made her own hand more difficult to decipher. More slowly, she read of how Granville showed an interest in Róisín's song and the history that lay behind it. Her friends whispered that his interest was pretended. The women of her village shook their heads and declared that even though St. Patrick had long ago driven all the serpents from the green isle, Róisín still ought to be able to recognize one when it slithered across her path.

Meanwhile, in her innocence, Róisín imagined she might turn a stranger to Ireland into a friend.

"Where in God's name are Cathal and Fergus while this preening dandy attempts to have his way with their sister?" Gabriel demanded, dashing Cami's hope that he had begun to doze.

"Do you know what had happened just a few months earlier in Belfast?"

He waved the question away in obvious annoyance.

"Several young men, men who spoke with great admiration for the revolution in France, met and formed a society they hoped would bring together both Protestant and Catholic in the cause of an independent Ireland. After the festival, they took the harp as their symbol." Between the sentences she left a little prompting pause, willing him to put together the pieces.

"The United Irishmen, you mean. So this festival was a real event? And they were there, recruiting members to their cause?"

"Yes."

The answer did not seem to satisfy him. "So the Maguire brothers are off raising a glass to freedom while their sister—"

"Their goals are the same, Gabriel," she said, holding up one hand to settle him. "To make English eyes see Ireland in a new light. And besides…" It was her turn to study the landscape as it slipped past the window. "It's only a story."

"Well, go on with it, then," he grumbled, folding his arms across his chest.

Reluctantly, she took up her pages once more. To earn Róisín's sympathy and trust, Granville plied her with stories of his troubled childhood and misspent youth. It was here where the character had ceased to be based on a man from Cami's past and had become a version of the man before her now. A man whose father had died under mysterious circumstances, who had been raised by a cruel uncle, and whose skill at hazard had led him to commit more than a few cruelties himself.

"Hazard?" Gabriel's mouth was twisted slightly to the side as if he had ground the word between his teeth before spitting it out. "I thought you intended to craft the image of a clever rake, Miss Burke, not a boy shooting marbles with his chums."

Had she really once quibbled with Felicity's description of him as dark? A thundercloud was building across his brow. Of all the things she had expected him to find objectionable, a villain who diced had been the least of her worries.

He had let her read without interruption, without even much change in his expression, until that moment. Before she could think of a suitable reply to his critique, the carriage gave a lurch, drawing their eyes to the window. She had not noticed that the scenery beyond it had been growing increasingly rugged, while the road had narrowed until it was barely wide enough for the coach.

Gabriel swore under his breath.

"What is it?" she demanded. "Is one of the horses injured? Have we damaged a wheel?"

"We should be so fortunate." He shoved himself back into his seat, folded his arms across his chest, and shook his head. "No, it would seem we're nearly to Stoke."

Chapter 17

Gabriel felt her eyes upon him and wondered precisely when, over the course of the last fortnight or so, he had lost the ability to look at the hand he'd been dealt without reacting—or at least, without revealing his reaction.

The driver was meant to have turned north at Shrewsbury and taken them toward Holyhead. Gabriel thought he had been explicit in his instructions. Instead, they would be at Stoke in a matter of moments, almost as if the old coach had known its way home and driven them there of its own volition. The road here was too narrow to attempt to turn around; branches scraped the sides of the carriage as they passed. There was nothing for it, now, but to go on.

Without meaning to, he sent another hard look across the coach at Camellia, and she too slid back in her seat, notching her slight frame into the corner farthest from him, eyeing him as she would a mad dog.

Desperate for something to busy himself, he began to collect the scattered pages of her book, sorting and stacking them until they were neat, a ritual he had enacted countless times with a pack of cards. The paper fluttered in his shaking hands.

Never hold your cards during the game.

"I suppose the estate has been in your family for generations?" She was holding out the last few sheets in one hand and the silk ribbon in the other.

The ribbon slipped through her fingers as he pulled it toward him, a bright thread of connection across the chasm of the coach. "Stoke Abbey was a gift to my ancestor more than two hundred years ago, following the dissolution of the monasteries."

"Ah, yes." Her sigh was world weary. "Henry VIII. Ever so fond of claiming what wasn't his."

"I suppose you would include Ireland on his list of improper acquisitions." History had never been Gabriel's favorite subject, but his memory was impeccable—a blessing at the card tables, if a curse at other times. "Though strictly speaking, his predecessors had already acquired the land. He simply—"

"Named himself its king." She accepted the bundle he had assembled and held it on her lap. "I'd say it still fits the pattern."

Gabriel forced himself to look out the coach window. He had visited just twice since moving away, once on the anniversary of his father's death, at his guardian's insistence, and once to take official charge of the property when he had achieved his majority, at which point he had promptly put the estate's management into the very capable hands of his steward.

Would this third return prove to be the final leave-taking? Or, with Camellia at his side, could it somehow be a homecoming?

"In half a mile, the abbey should be visible to the west," he said. Without asking her permission, he shifted to sit beside her so they could keep watch together, though it was less a matter of wanting her to see his birthplace than of his being unwilling—unable—to face it alone.

The coach struggled to climb a rise, but when they reached its peak, the valley spread below them, undulating waves of green that would carry them to the splendid island at its center: Stoke Abbey. He heard Camellia draw in her breath before the carriage rattled on through a copse, along a stream. Seamlessly, the wilderness gave way to formal gardens and graveled drives. Generations of renovations and improvements had transformed a medieval monastery into a modern dwelling place, though it still retained much of its gothic character, with narrow leaded windows and flying buttresses supporting the long roof of the Great Hall.

In short order, they were rolling beneath a massive, ivy-covered arch into the courtyard. Had he announced his arrival—had he known of it himself—no doubt uniformed servants would have been turned out in two neat rows to flank the master as he entered, even if they would have to have been hired from the village for the occasion. No need to keep a full staff on hand; after all, three-quarters of Stoke had been unoccupied for twenty years. Only the east wing had a regular tenant, the steward having taken up residence there some time ago.

As if the thought had conjured the man into being, Gabriel spied John Hawthorne, a tanned, wiry, pewter-haired man of fifty, striding across the flagstones. With more eagerness than he had anticipated feeling, he reached past Camellia to open the carriage door.

She cringed, but not at his touch. "What—good God, what *is* that thing?" Her voice was a harsh whisper; all her breath seemed to be held captive in her lungs.

At Hawthorne's heels plodded his mastiff. "A dog," Gabriel said, hoping that, despite her fears, the answer might provide some reassurance, as the creature indeed looked like the sort of beast one's imagination dredged up during a nightmare, with its loose jowls and massive build. "It's a gentle breed. He wouldn't harm a flea."

"It's not really the fleas I'm worried about."

When the door swung open, he expected her to refuse to exit the coach, but she nodded once and stiffened her spine as if arming herself with his promise. Ducking through the door, he made certain to position himself between her and the dog as he helped her down, then extended a hand to the other man. "Hawthorne," he exclaimed. "Well met! Miss Burke, may I introduce John Hawthorne, my steward?"

"This is certainly unexpected," Hawthorne said. Dark eyes darted in Camellia's direction before returning to Gabriel's face. "But no matter, no matter. Glad to have you back at last. Miss Burke?" Hawthorne bowed and the dog sat, or rather sagged beneath the weight of its frame and its years.

"That cannot be Titan?" Gabriel marveled. At hearing his name, the dog tilted its enormous, graying head. The last time he had been at Stoke, Titan had been a pup. Not quite ten years had passed, but, like Finch men, mastiffs were not an especially long-lived breed.

"It is, it is," Hawthorne insisted. "He's got more life left in him than he lets on. Why, he did his lad's duty by Squire Talbot's bitch just this winter. We've a fine litter of whelps in the stable." He slapped Gabriel on one shoulder and sent Camellia another quick glance. "Just what the old place needs, eh? Young ones running about to liven things up."

The insinuation did not escape Gabriel's notice. He mustered a smile and reached out to pat the dog's head. "A rascal to the end, eh, old boy? That's my motto." Turning to Camellia, he offered his arm. "Miss Burke is on her way to Ireland; I was pleased to be able to offer her my escort this far." He did not delude himself into imagining that the explanation would prevent further speculation about her otherwise unchaperoned presence.

Together, the three of them approached the house, where the housekeeper now waited. She sank into a deep curtsy. "Welcome home, my lord," she said. "I did not know if I'd live to see the day. And Miss Burke, is it? Welcome. I am Mrs. Neville. I've already sent Mary to see to your rooms."

He heard Camellia thank her, felt her arm slip from his as Mrs. Neville offered to show her up. As Hawthorne walked away, he called over his shoulder, saying he'd be ready to meet with Gabriel in an hour.

Finding himself suddenly alone on the threshold, Gabriel hesitated. But the ghosts of the house whispered to him, reached out their icy fingers, and pulled him in.

* * * *

After she had bathed and changed her dress, Cami followed a maid to the dining room, marveling along the way at the abbey's splendor. When the maid deposited her before a pair of tall, gilt-trimmed doors, a footman ushered her through into a regal drawing room.

Mr. Hawthorne rose from a nearby chair and bowed. Thankfully, his giant dog was nowhere in sight. "Ah, Miss Burke, good evening. I was just on my way out," he said with a glance toward Gabriel at the sideboard. An obvious untruth, since the two men had been deep in conversation when the door opened to admit her.

"No, please," she said. "I did not mean to interrupt."

"You did nothing of the kind, ma'am. Now that Ashborough has returned, we can talk farming at our leisure."

Farming? Perhaps that had been the subject of their discussion, though she doubted it. She glanced at Gabriel, who looked as unruffled as ever. Even if he and his steward had been arguing about something, as she suspected, was it still a relief to him to be away from those who insisted on calling him *Ash?*

Mr. Hawthorne excused himself, leaving the two of them alone in the cavernous room. At least, it seemed cavernous to her, until the footman opened a different set of doors to announce that supper was served and she caught a glimpse of the dining room. She gasped. It was a room fit for kings to dine in—and they probably had.

"Bit much, isn't it?" Gabriel spoke near her elbow, then stepped past her and said something in a low voice to the footman, who promptly went through into the dining room and closed the doors behind him. "Come." With a light touch at the small of her back, he guided her to the chair Mr. Hawthorne had vacated. "Mrs. Neville is anxious to entertain me in state, I believe, but I never was accustomed to it. When I was a boy here, I mostly ate in the schoolroom, of course, and my father—well." He sank into the chair opposite, leaving the sentence unfinished. "I've asked them to bring us our supper in here."

She looked about at the ornate furnishings, swags of cut velvet drapery, and more than a few Old Masters and supposed this was what passed for a cozy, comfortable room in such a house.

While a pair of footmen moved a round, curved-leg table between their chairs, a maid brought in china, silver, and glasses. Over plates of leek soup and savory roast duck, she rolled a pair of questions around in her mind.

"You're quiet this evening, Camellia," he said when they were nearly finished.

She let herself study his face. How quickly those features had become familiar to her. Dear to her. "I've been trying to decide which of your behaviors is more confounding," she said. "Staying away from Stoke, or deciding to return now."

His lips curved upward as he reached for his wine. "Ever the forthright Miss Burke. Come," he said. After draining his glass, he pushed away from the table and held out one hand to help her rise. "May I show you a bit of the abbey?"

Thinking he meant to ignore what she'd said, she nodded and laid her hand in his. But rather than releasing her hand once she stood, he threaded his fingers between hers, so their hands were clasped, palm to palm. His touch was a kiss, soft and warm. "The reasons for my behavior, like the questions themselves, are tangled together," he said, raising their joined hands and pressing his lips to her knuckles. "As you were reading this afternoon, it became clear that you knew just enough of my story to craft an explanation for Granville's villainy. I wonder if you will think the whole story an explanation for mine."

Still gripping her hand, he led her into the corridor, nodding at the impassive footman who held the door for them. Flickering sconces cast their light over bronze and marble statues and gave their features an eerie sort of life, but no warmth. Cami struggled to imagine growing up in such a place. She could sense Gabriel's unease too, and wondered again what had called him home.

When they came to a curving staircase, they climbed it. The next corridor that opened before them led to her bedchamber, she thought, but he turned and went the other way, into another wing of the house. "The portrait gallery," he announced. Candles had been lit here too. Were they lit every night, although the house was empty? Or had Mrs. Neville anticipated where the master would wander after dark?

He made no objection when she stopped from time to time to study a painting, picking out the features that had become his, a strong nose here, thin lips there, a Scottish ancestor with ginger hair that had likely lent Gabriel's that hint of copper when the light touched it.

He made no comment, either, until they came to a large portrait that looked, from the subjects' clothing, to have been completed sometime near the middle of the current century. A man in a powdered wig, a woman with a powdered face, and two somber-eyed boys in short pants, who looked to be about five years old. "My father and my uncle were twins, as you see, born just a few minutes apart. Identical, though by the time they were grown men, even a brief acquaintance would have enabled you to tell them apart."

"I suspect it would have been more difficult when they were young," Cami said, looking from one face to the other. Even the artist had struggled, falling back on the traditional symbolism—the heir standing beside his father, the other brother kneeling at his mother's feet—to differentiate them.

"Impossible," Gabriel agreed. "At least, according to my uncle, who claims to this day that he was in fact the elder, stripped of what was rightfully his by a careless nursemaid."

She sucked in a breath. "Could he have been right?"

"No one else ever thought it likely." His fingers tightened around hers. "But he let it drive him mad."

She had met the man and knew it was not an idle remark. Now she searched for signs of that madness in the haunting eyes that bored through her from the canvas. "They both look...forgive me...rather unwell."

"They were not expected to survive their infancy. Born too soon, as sometimes happens with twins. Both of them suffered from chest complaints. My uncle still has weak lungs. And this," he said, gazing down the shadowy gallery, "is not the sort of house that invites boys to run and play and outgrow their childhood ailments."

With a tug on her hand, he urged her away from the family portrait. "Now, as for your story. I do indeed have a cruel uncle, and had I been entrusted to his care—well, I would probably be dead." A chill shuddered through her, and he released her long enough to shrug out of his coat and lay it over her shoulders before taking her hand again, almost as if he expected at some point to have to keep her from running away from what he had to tell. "When my father died, Uncle Finch was desperate to find some way of disinheriting me and restoring what he saw as *his* title and lands. Whether my father believed him capable of murder, I do not know, but he made explicit provision for my guardianship in his will. I was immediately sent to live with Sir William Hicks, my mother's brother, a man of some property in Lancashire. Unlike your Granville, I was in fact raised by the soul of kindness and generosity. After my father's funeral, I saw little of my Uncle Finch until I was a grown man, though his son and I were at school together. So I do not think a cruel uncle an adequate excuse for your villain's scurrilous behavior. At least, my uncles bear no responsibility for what I am."

Cami was tempted to protest. Of course a child's experiences shaped his character. So far as she could see, he had been influenced by both his uncles. He was kinder and more generous than he would admit, but he had also been affected by the threats from his father's brother. How could he not?

He paused now before a portrait of a young woman, whose dark blond hair and light eyes gave no hint at her relationship to Gabriel. Cami would have called it an ordinary picture, but for the dusty black crape draped around the frame, which made a haunting impression. Their movement had stirred the air, making the crape sway slightly, like something out of a horrid novel. The effect was complete when he spoke in his deep voice. "My first victim."

"Your mother?" Cami whispered, not daring to look at him.

"She died in childbirth. My birth."

"A tragedy," she said, tightening her grip on his hand. "But not your fault."

He reached up with his free hand and tugged down the ancient black fabric, which disintegrated in his fingers. "Tell that to my father."

They left the gallery through the doors on the opposite end and descended another curved stair, two flights this time, and into what she thought must be the east wing of the abbey. She knew she would never find her way back to her room on her own, knew also that she must not hope he would accompany her there. Gabriel, however, strode down the corridor with the confidence of a man who walked these halls daily, rather than someone who had not set foot in them in years.

At the midpoint, he stopped before a door on their left. "My father's study," he said, and opened the door to show her in. Gabriel lit a few candles, revealing a large room, but not overlarge, without either the dining room's soaring ceilings or the drawing room's ornate furniture. Comfortable. He knelt at the hearth to set fire to the kindling and logs that had already been laid.

Perhaps someone had guessed he would come to this room, after all.

The room bore no signs of disuse; no dust marred the tabletops and the air was not stale. During the day, it would probably be quite a cheery space, with tall windows overlooking the valley in which the abbey was nestled, just visible in the dusky twilight.

"Sit," he said, motioning her to a chair near the hearth while he seated himself in the center of a small sofa, facing the fireplace rather than her. For a time, the only sound was the popping and crackling of the fire. When he spoke again, she felt as if he had been telling a story in his head and only thought to speak it aloud halfway through. "People said it was a mercenary match, but he loved her more than life itself." Another pause. "A curious phrase, is it not? 'More than life itself.' But true in his case, at least. When she died, he simply…stopped living. Of course, I had no way of knowing what he'd been like before, but people were always happy to oblige me with tales of the man he'd once been. Before I came along and blighted his happiness."

"I'm sure he—" Cami bit her lip to stop herself from offering the platitude. Perhaps his father *had* felt that way about his son, and perhaps he'd made his misery known, cut himself off from the child whose birth had changed his life so dramatically. She recalled a detail from earlier in the evening. "Before supper, when you said you used to eat in the schoolroom, you were going to say something about your father and stopped yourself. Did you never even dine together?"

Gabriel shook his head. "He didn't eat. Sometimes not for days at a time. He didn't bathe, either. He slept, he moaned her name, and when his physician gave him laudanum to dull his senses, he slept some more. Once in a while, he would rouse himself, promise to shake off his doldrums. And he would, for a few days, a week or two at most." The memory roused him to his feet, and he paced across the hearth rug as he spoke. "Then, he would dress, read, take an interest in Stoke. In me. I would fall asleep, letting myself dream of the next day, but inevitably when I woke, it would be as if a window had shut, or a light had gone out." He threw himself once more onto the sofa, leaning forward with his elbows on his knees. "I knew I had done this to him, and I could never be enough to make up for what I had taken from him."

Her heart threw itself against her ribs, as if it were trying to break free and go to him. "Gabriel—"

"Don't." The fire painted his expression with streaks of light and shadow. She wished she could see his eyes. "I know now that it was a sickness. Of the heart. Of the mind. But I couldn't understand it then. The week before my tenth birthday was one of his good weeks. We read *Robinson Crusoe* and declared this Stoke Island and tromped through the woods on the lookout for cannibals. For my birthday, he promised to take me out and teach me how to shoot a stag. I imagined making a suit of its hide, patterned after poor Crusoe's, though his was made from goatskin, of course."

He paused, and she leaned forward too, apprehensive of what was to come. "I was up and dressed before dawn," he continued. "I'd even slept with my gun at the ready beside my bedroom door, just like Robinson in his cave. As soon as there was light to see by, I picked it up and went downstairs to my father's room. All was dark, quiet. When he didn't answer my knock, I went in and—and found him. He'd taken his gun to bed too. Don't," he said again, though she'd been careful not to make a sound. Tears glimmered on his cheeks, but he warned off her sympathy with the wave of his hand. "He had no manservant. No one had heard the shot. And all I could think—" A rattling, rasping breath shook his shoulders. "All I could think was that he'd go to hell if anyone found out what he'd done, and he'd never see my mother again. So I—I opened the window, and I fired my gun into the air. Then I called for help, and when help came, I told them I'd done it. That I'd killed my father."

Camellia dug her fingers into the arm of the chair to keep herself still. "And they believed you? You were a child...."

"I thought it was my fault he'd done what he did. I wanted them to believe me. I *made* them believe me. And when my Uncle Finch arrived, he was only too happy to think it was true. He seemed sure I'd be hanged for my crime. But there wasn't even an inquest. The magistrate declared the shooting had been an accident, I went to live with my Uncle Will, and that was that. It wasn't until I went away to school that I learned everyone seemed to know my history—and they were only too willing to believe the worst of me, thanks to Uncle Finch. I couldn't deny having done it, of course, or I'd tarnish my father's name. Even Fox does not know the truth."

She wanted to contradict him, certain Mr. Fox knew more than Gabriel realized. But she didn't, conscious as she was of the enormous trust he had placed in her. Stories were powerful things, whether told or untold, and to hold such a story inside, for twenty years...

"I buried myself in my schoolwork," he went on, his voice calmer, more distant. "But there were no books, no lessons, deep enough in which to drown my guilty secret, or to hide me from the taunts of my peers."

"But—but you weren't really guilty of anything," she protested.

The familiar, cynical smile crept across his lips. "If that's true, I've made up for it since. I discovered I had a certain knack for cards. As well as what dear Foxy calls 'a way with women.' I ceased to be Gabriel and became 'Lord Ash.' Blackening reputations and charring hopes, remember?" he said wryly, repeating what he'd told her the night of the Montlake ball. "One year, I was to spend Christmas with Fox's family in Sussex, probably the last respectable household in Britain in which I was grudgingly welcome. I fixed that by indulging in a flirtation with his sister Victoria, which nearly cost her Dalrymple's more serious affections. The old earl had had enough and tossed me out on Christmas Eve. Uncle Will had died the year before. I was utterly alone."

A small noise of pity escaped her throat, but he seemed not to hear it. Certainly, he had made it clear he did not want it.

"I had cut myself off from polite society," he continued. "The only place I felt at home was at the card table, and when my peers sneered and called me 'Lord Ash,' I decided to drag them down to hell with me. Like your Granville, I was ruthless. And I made more enemies along the way. Fortunately Fox was, well, dogged in his affections—he refuses to let my soul go without a fight. He ignored his father's dictates and dug me out of the pit time and again. But in the end, I found a way to ruin him too."

"No," she breathed.

"Oh, yes. He's more than half in love with Lady Felicity, and I would not be surprised to learn she returns his affections." He glanced at her. "I would have married her in spite of it."

And in spite of your feelings for me, she wanted to add, though she was neither brave nor foolish enough to speak the words. She rather feared he might say he would have married her cousin *because* of them.

"I don't—I don't understand," she said instead. "What made you decide to marry to begin with?"

A faraway look settled in his eyes. "My cousin Julian, my Uncle Finch's only son, has been raised with the expectation of one day becoming Marquess of Ashborough. I've always known it, though for most of my life it had been easy enough to ignore. Then one night, I overheard him gambling against what everyone believed to be his future inheritance." One hand lifted to gesture at the room, at Stoke. "I realized I couldn't let my uncle win that bet...." A sharp shake of his head, as if clearing it of the memory. "I decided to spite him. I would take a wife, get an heir on her, and cut him off."

Her gut churned. How lightly men sported with women's lives. And one another's. "What made you choose Felicity?"

He lifted one shoulder in a guilty-looking shrug. "Her brother's note happened to be at hand. Though she seemed a perfectly pleasant young woman, I felt no particular attraction to her when we met—which was exactly as I'd hoped." Cami's surprise must have shown on her face. "As my history would suggest, my...affection can lead to no good end. I did not want a wife for whom I felt...anything," he explained. "I meant what I said: she would have been perfectly safe from me."

You, on the other hand...

Even the memory of those words against her lips had the power to send a secret thrill of longing through her. If the attraction between them was dangerous, Cami didn't want to be safe. Hadn't been safe for some time.

"What happened to change your plans?" she asked.

"Uncle Finch was not willing to concede defeat. Some weeks back, I made the mistake of trying to help a young Frenchwoman." A bitter laugh barked from his lungs. Vaguely, she recalled the gossip column's quip about the Frogs he had been said to kiss. "He learned of it and spun yet another tale. Now she's in the Tower, suspected of involvement in the assassination attempt on the king—wrongly, I might add. And I am very shortly to be accused of treason as her associate."

She popped to her feet, and his coat slithered off her shoulders and onto the chair. Unable to contain herself any longer, she took two unsteady steps toward him. "But—that's—that's preposterous. Treason? Why—why on earth did you leave London? Why not stay and fight? Did you come here thinking to—to—?" A horrible suspicion had begun to form in her mind.

"To take my father's way out?" He looked up at her with another grim smile. "You needn't worry. I haven't his courage."

Warily, she moved closer to him, as one would approach an injured animal. When he did not object, she perched on the edge of the cushion in the narrow space between the rolled arm of the sofa and his body, not touching him. Just there. "I'm sorry," she whispered, watching the flames lick along a stout log. "Sorry for what you suffered as a child. And for being the cause of your having to relive it tonight. But what you've told me only increases my certainty: Your uncle must be stopped. You must go back. You must defend yourself."

"Lord Ash has done too many indefensible things."

"Lord Ash? Are you speaking of the same man who tried to help a poor émigré? Who spared Felicity's feelings? Who kept her brother from debtors' prison? And all of it to their benefit, not your own. You're not a villain, Gabriel." Two hot tears rolled down her cheeks, but she did not try to check them, not wanting to draw his attention. "Oh, I thought myself so clever when I began Mr. Dawkins's revisions. I n-never th-thought..." The tears came thicker, faster, clouding her spectacles.

Suddenly, she felt his hands on her shoulders, gently turning her to face him. His face too was streaked with tears. Carefully, he unhooked her spectacles from behind her ears and set them on the table beside the sofa. Then he wrapped his arms around her, and she laid her cheek against his chest, as she had done that day in the carriage. Her fingertips played in the knot of his cravat, stirring up the warm scent of his cologne, and she nestled closer to draw it in, draw him in.

They fit together, two sharp edges locked tight and smooth, and she knew then that she would fight his demons bare-handed if she must, but they could not, would not have him. He was hers.

"Oh, Gabriel. I never thought I might be adding to your pain." His heartbeat muffled her whisper. "I never thought to fall in love with you, either. But I have."

Chapter 18

Still trembling from the release of his confession, weak from laying down the burdens of his past, Gabriel tried very hard not to hear her.

No, no, no. The denial scrubbed through his brain with the pounding of his pulse.

But her words were more insidious still, slipping past his hard shell, his thick mask, to wend their way into his bloodstream. Heat bloomed in his belly and spread to his limbs in a tingling rush. His arms tightened around her.

Yes, yes, yes.

Malevolent forces had been at work in his life from the beginning. In time he'd even come to court them. But surely, surely, their appetite had been sated. They had taken so much. Mightn't they let him have this? Just for now? Just tonight?

Because, of course, he dared promise her nothing more. He'd spent a decade or more making enemies of the very men who would decide his fate. He'd likely be convicted—if he hadn't been already.

Cold terror came rushing back, creeping through his veins the way frost spreads across a stream and turns its merry babbling inexorably to ice. He forced himself to set her away from him before they both froze solid.

"I think, my dear, you cannot have been paying attention," he said, looking at her with what he hoped was his customary mocking expression. "Did you not hear me explain what has happened to the people who care for me, or for whom I have dared to care? I'm damned, Camellia. I ruin everything I touch."

As he spoke, he watched an unexpected sternness settle over her features, the face of a woman who had scolded and cajoled five younger siblings out of their childish fears. When she parted her lips to speak, he spoke first.

"Please." He certainly was not a child, in some ways had never been a child, but he was not above begging. "Please don't let me ruin you too."

If anything, his plea only served to etch the expression deeper. "It seems I am not the only one who hasn't been listening," she said. Shifting, she settled on her knees facing him, palms flat against his chest. "I do believe I told you I cannot be ruined."

"Camellia." It was his turn to be stern. "I'm quite serious."

"As am I," she said, laying a string of whisper-soft kisses across his cheeks, tracing the path of his tears. "I am used to being in control of a plot's twists and turns. But every encounter with you has been something unexpected. You sent all my careful planning out the window. From this point forward, however, I'm taking back the pen. This is my story too." Her lips were at his ear. "And I'm not going to leave you tonight, no matter what you say."

His tears kept flowing, melting away the mask he'd worn for so long—it had only ever been papier-mâché—but he let them come, let her see the grief he'd been hiding. Her fingertips whisked the moisture away, but she did not tell him not to weep. Instead, she held him, murmuring words against his hair, in a language no one had ever spoken to him before. Beneath her gentle ministrations, the shudders of anguish became tremors of need.

After a time, those fingers moved to slip loose the buttons of his waistcoat and slide the knot from his cravat. Though he knew he should stop her, he did not. The heat of her touch on his chest was a brand, and he could not resist her claiming. They were here, together, at Stoke, and she *knew* and still wanted him. Still...*loved* him. *Ah, God.*

Laying his arms across the back of the sofa, he opened himself to her, let her have her way with him. What her lips lacked in experience, they made up for in eagerness. As she traveled from his earlobe, along his jaw, down his throat, he could feel her little hums of pleasure vibrating against his skin. Her hair smelled of wood smoke and spring rain and every simple comfort he'd never known. Her fingers tickled through the hair on his chest, then traced his collarbone, before gripping his shoulder for balance as she lifted herself higher and settled astride him.

Then, with one hand on either side of his head, fingers tangling in his hair, she parted her mouth over his. He dropped his hands to her hips, circling first, then kneading, sliding lower, over her thighs, down her legs, to slip beneath her skirts and petticoats and shift on an illicit quest. When his fingers at last found her bare skin, she whimpered, and his self-control began to fray. Using her slight frame to steady himself, he shifted higher on the seat. She was still above him now, but only just, and he met the searching strokes of her tongue with more demanding ones of his own. The silken skin of her thighs invited his touch.

No sooner had he dared to slide his fingers between them, grazing her crisp curls and wet heat, when she moved again, wobbling to balance on her knees as her hands scrambled down his shirt front to the buttons of his fall.

This would not be the leisurely pleasure-seeking of two nights past. Just raw, unvarnished need—a feeling he doubted she had ever let herself own. Something he had never let another see.

At first she did not even break the kiss. Her eyes were closed, her fingers determined as they worked the buttons loose. But when the task was done, she pulled away just enough to see what she'd wrought. One hand dropped to shove his shirttails away and his cock stood between them, hard and eager. Her bright eyes darted back to his—seeking permission, he thought, as she reached out one daring fingertip to sweep up his heated length. But then she snagged her lower lip between her teeth and did it again, her eyes roaming to take in every grimace of pleasure that streaked across his face as she stroked him.

"Taking more notes for your book, my dear?" he managed to tease, before her increasingly sure touch turned the possibility of speech into nothing more than a gurgle of lust at the back of his throat.

"No need. I'm quite sure Granville is not—ah!—anything like this," she said with a breathless laugh as his own fingers slipped over her damp, swollen flesh. Raising her skirts higher, he pulled her closer, lower, until her wet heat brushed his groin. "Yes-s-s-s."

He captured that hiss of sound with his mouth as he entered her, relishing the feel of their joining. In this position, he was utterly surrounded by her—her arms, her legs, her sex. Utterly hers. She moved experimentally at first, a trifle unsteady. But with his hands on her hips to guide her, she soon mastered the rhythm, and was well on the way to mastering him. Her hair tumbled loose, and he reached up one hand to tug her bodice down to free her breasts. Releasing her mouth, he caught one pink bud between his lips and sucked as she arched against him.

When the tremors of her climax began, he knew his own could not be far behind. Darkness edged his vision, and he was on the point of surrendering to it when a voice niggled at him. The memory of her voice. The voice of reason.

"Ah, love," he gasped, digging his fingers into her hip bones to slow her, to free himself. "We can't—I've got to—for your sake—" He could not leave her with child.

"No. Don't." Her thighs gripped him tighter, like a rider urging a wary mount over a jump. "I want you—all of you," she pleaded, sensing his weakening resolve. "Together...please."

It was not a particularly well-reasoned argument, but he found it surprisingly persuasive. And after another stroke, it was a moot point. He hadn't the strength to deny her, to do more than meet her downward thrust with an upward one of his own, and he was coming...with her, in her. Beyond reckless. Beyond ecstasy.

Afterward, with her body slumped against his, he let sleep claim him, refusing for once to let his mind go to work calculating odds.

* * * *

Cami wasn't initially sure what had woken her. A noise? Without opening her eyes, she took stock of her surroundings. The late marquess' study. Birdsong. Sunlight pressed on her eyelids. Gabriel was warm, relaxed, asleep beneath her. They lay chest to chest, his head tipped back, her arms flung around his neck, one hand dangling off the back of the sofa, her cheek resting against the top of his shoulder. She was—oh, dear—still sitting astride him, and that cool draft suggested her skirts were still hiked to her waist. Between her thighs, she felt heat and stickiness, and she recalled what she'd urged him to do last night. A risk, yes. One of many.

And she would not be sorry for taking any of them. No matter what happened.

She shifted slightly and realized she also felt...*him*, hard and eager, even in sleep. Before she could decide what, if anything, to do about that, she heard again a strange snuffling sound and something wet swiped across her hand. Licking her. She cracked open one eye and drew in a sharp breath. Titan was standing behind the sofa, his broad head tilted to the side, studying her with sad brown eyes. When she didn't move, he nudged her hand again, clearly trying to decide whether she was edible, or...perhaps, asking to be petted?

Did she dare?

As if sensing her hesitation, Titan dipped his head, nuzzling under her fingers to make it impossible for her to refuse. His coat was short and tan; the darker mask about his eyes and muzzle was flecked with gray. But silky soft, she discovered as she rubbed her thumb over his forehead, smoothing out the wrinkles there before reaching back to scratch behind his ears. When she paused, he nudged again. Gently. Just as Gabriel had promised.

"Good boy," she whispered, and his tongue lolled out. "What are you doing here?"

Her brain put together the answer to that question just as her ears told her the truth.

"Ashborough?" The steward's voice. "Are you down here?"

Cami scrambled to her feet, reaching for her spectacles, jostling Gabriel awake. "Mr. Hawthorne is coming. Get up!"

Thankfully, it took but a moment to shake her skirts down to their proper places and to tuck her less than ample bosom back where it belonged. When she looked up again, Gabriel had paused in his own flurry of tucking and buttoning to give her an appreciative ogle.

"For goodness' sake, you're meant to be a notorious rake," she whispered furiously. "You've seen my—oh, just hurry!"

Mr. Hawthorne's boots could be heard thumping ever closer. "Mrs. Neville said you never made it to your bed last night, and I feared—"

Her hair was a wild tangle she was trying to tame with one hand while digging between the couch cushions for hairpins with the other. Wordlessly, Gabriel held out his wrinkled cravat.

"What are you suggesting?" she hissed. "That we blindfold Mr. Hawthorne?"

His lips twitched, trying to contain a laugh. "For your hair," he mouthed, gesturing with a swirling motion toward her head.

A few seconds later, the steward crossed the threshold and his dog plodded obligingly toward him. "Why, Titan, here you are."

Grateful for that brief distraction, Cami wound the cravat around her hair, turban-style, and threw herself into the chair by the now cold hearth, hoping desperately she'd achieved something approaching eccentric fashion statement, studied nonchalance, or both.

"Ah, good morning, Ashborough. What, did you fall asleep down here? And...why, Miss Burke. You're up early. I, er, didn't—oh." He'd been looking from one to the other of them as he spoke, oblivious to what he'd stumbled upon. Until Gabriel stifled another laugh. "Oh, forgive me." Color flared in the older man's cheeks as he dropped his gaze and busied himself with rubbing Titan's ears. "But I did say I'd fetch those account books first thing." Without looking up, he gestured with the folded newspaper in his hand toward the desk on the far side of the room. "I'll just come back in a bit, shall I?"

"No need, John. I'd merely forgotten you've been using this room as your office. We'll discuss them now. Miss Burke, would you be so kind as to ring for coffee?"

She did not hesitate to accept the opportunity for escape. As she hurried toward the bellpull near the door, Mr. Hawthorne asked Gabriel in a low but firm voice, "I know it's none of my business, Ashborough, but when may we except an announcement of your betrothal to—?"

She turned back and spoke over him, pretending not to have heard the steward's question. "What time can the coach be ready, my lord? I really must get to Holyhead in time to make the last packet. I'm bound for Dublin today, Mr. Hawthorne," she explained, meeting his eyes with her firmest gaze. "My family is expecting me."

"Dublin?" His brows rose. "Well, now, Miss Burke, I suspect this"—with one hand, he snapped open his newspaper and laid it on the desktop—"may change your plans."

Reluctantly, she drew closer. At first her mind could do no more than take in snatches of print: *rebels—armed insurrection—spread to the countryside—crushed.*

Gabriel spun the paper to face him and leaned over the desk to read more carefully. "It seems a group of United Irishmen seized the mail coaches as they left Dublin, possibly as some sort of signal," he said after a moment, then paused to read more. "The plot was foiled, however. The militia have put down the rebels in the area surrounding Dublin."

Cami felt herself sinking; Mr. Hawthorne caught her by the elbow and helped her to a chair. *The militia have put down the rebels....* She knew what that meant. Her brothers. Their friends. Likely dead at the hands of the loyalists.

"Well, Hawthorne is right. This rather changes things." With one hand Gabriel folded the newspaper and returned it to his steward, ignoring her outstretched hand. What did it contain that he did not want her to see?

"Changes what, my lord?" She struggled to her feet. "I have to know that my family is safe. I must go to them."

His gaze raked over her. "Not alone."

Was it her imagination, or was that a flicker of suspicion in his dark eyes? Was he remembering what she'd told him about Paris and Galen? Did he imagine she had known something of this plot?

"I'll make arrangements for the coach to be ready as soon as possible," he said, stepping away from them both. "Clearly, Miss Burke still requires my escort."

"No. You mustn't get wrapped up in this," she argued. Surely he realized that a trip to Dublin under such circumstances, any association at all with the United Irishmen, would only add fuel to the flames his uncle had been fanning.

But her protest fell on deaf ears. "That other matter will have to wait, John," he added as he bowed sharply and strode from the room.

Instead of following, she sank back into the chair. Nothing was going to plan. "No. He must not—Mr. Hawthorne, you must help me. I really have no fear for my own safety. Dublin is my home. But Lord Ashborough must return to London as soon as possible."

The steward gave a gruff noise of agreement. "He ought never to have left."

"Well, why did he?" she demanded. "Did you not call him here? Some urgent matter of business, he said…." But, no. That had been *her* supposition. Mr. Hawthorne frowned, and understanding washed over her. "He did it for me, did he not?"

"I believe he wanted to see you safely home, yes."

She thought of Mr. Hawthorne's and Mrs. Neville's evident surprise at their arrival. "He never meant to come to Stoke, did he?" Mr. Hawthorne said nothing in reply, but his expression told her she had guessed right. She would have refused Gabriel's help if he'd offered it outright. So he had found a way to make it difficult for her to say no, by goading her into his carriage, then claiming to be traveling this way already. And in the process, he had compromised his future and put himself through hell.

"But if you know that he ought to have stayed in London," she said after a moment, "you must also know…"

"About the mischief his uncle has planned? Aye." Disgust made his voice rough. "Sebastian Finch was always one for wild talk, and folks will likely know this treason charge is no different. I cannot think it will come to aught."

"Unfortunately, Lord Ashborough has made other enemies."

Mr. Hawthorne looked taken aback at her announcement; even Titan had a quizzical tilt to his head.

Indecision prickled along her spine. This man had known the Marquess of Ashborough from a boy. Who was she to reveal to him the man Gabriel had become, the scoundrel known as Lord Ash? She drew a steadying breath. "I'm sorry to have to tell you this, Mr. Hawthorne, but your employer is an inveterate gambler. And the very men he's ruined likely will be only too happy to return the favor."

An odd smile creased the steward's face. "His lordship's fancy for a game of cards is no secret, Miss Burke. Why, for a time, it was how he kept this place afloat. His father loved this place, after his fashion. But he could not care for it. When he died, things were in a shambles. The tenants were desperate. Young Ashborough did what he had to do to turn things around. Oh, I don't doubt but what he's taught a few wastrels a lesson over the years, but he never was a bad lad."

"I believe you're right, sir. Unfortunately, he's taken his enemies' words to heart for so long, he's come to believe the worst of himself." She did not try to explain her own role in the process. "I fear he's lost his will to fight back."

Mr. Hawthorne shook his head. "Then others must fight for him. If it comes to that, I've got proof aplenty he's not the man they believe him to be."

"What sort of proof?"

"Why, the estate records alone will show he's a good master, a responsible landowner—better, I'd wager, than many of them." He turned and plucked up one of the ledgers from his desk. "Take a look."

Warily, Cami accepted the baize-covered book. At first, she was not certain of the significance of what she was seeing. Estate records, of course. Investments. Improvements. Eventually, the orderly columns of figures revealed to her the extraordinary care that had been taken of a place many said had been abandoned.

"And then there's this." He stabbed at the facing page with a stumpy finger.

Her eyes flicked up and down over a tally of donations. Sizable donations. To foundling hospitals, orphanages, charity schools. And one particularly large sum to St. Luke's Hospital in London, a reform-minded institution that had been established in recent decades to counter the infamous exploitation of the poor inmates at Bethlehem Hospital—Bedlam, as it was commonly known.

"Orphans and madmen, he wanted to help. Said he knew something o' that." Wordlessly, she returned the book to him, and he set it on the desk with the others. "If good works count for aught, he's done his bit and then some. Why, he told me last night that so long as he was here, he wanted me to help him find a way to go on getting money to them, just in case something happened to him."

It seemed Gabriel's gambling had put something on the positive side of the ledger, after all. But would it be enough to change people's minds about him? It did not explicitly counter his uncle's claim.

"Will you help me, Mr. Hawthorne? Help me persuade him to go back and speak in his own defense?"

"And leave you to go haring off to Dublin by yourself?" He shook his head. "Sorry, ma'am. It won't work. Ashborough's always been one to protect what's his. Since he was a lad."

His.

Always before, she had recoiled at such notions of possession. But now, the word lit a spark inside her. If she was his, then he was equally hers. This time, she would rescue him.

And she would do it the way she did anything. With her pen.

"Very well, Mr. Hawthorne," she said, rising. "Will I find paper and ink in that desk? I've a letter to write, and I'll trust you to get it into the proper hands."

Chapter 19

Gabriel gripped the ship's rail more tightly. "Is the Irish Sea always this rough?" he asked, looking out over the churning gray water as dusk fell.

"No," she said, her eyes scanning the horizon for the first glimpse of the Bay of Dublin. "Sometimes it's worse."

Once more, he was headed in the opposite direction from that in which he should have been traveling. But…no. Not really. In the process of telling his story, he'd realized he still wanted—needed—to fight his uncle. To fight for Stoke and claim what was his, the good he'd done, along with the bad.

None of it would matter, however, if he could not find some way to share it with Camellia.

She had said very little about his insistence on accompanying her to Ireland. Had said very little at all, in fact. When the coach had rolled into the courtyard at Stoke Abbey, horses fresh and prancing, she had stepped out neatly dressed and freshly combed, no sign of the passionate woman who'd ridden him to exhaustion the night before. After thanking Mrs. Neville, she'd shaken John Hawthorne's hand, then, to Gabriel's astonishment, patted placid Titan on his broad head before accepting his help, though the merest brush of hands, as she climbed into the carriage.

They'd arrived in Holyhead in time to catch the last packet, just as she'd hoped. All the berths had been taken, but she had insisted that the stifling air of a cabin would make her seasick anyway. As the ship battled through the waves for hours and darkness fell, he'd been content to stand quietly with her, facing down the spray, wondering what they would find at journey's end. "We're lucky the packet wasn't delayed," he said, breaking a long silence. "I overheard some passengers telling of another crossing, when they were forced to wait several days for a favorable wind."

"On any map I've seen, the Irish Sea looks to be an insignificant body of water. Especially, I suppose, to people who have built great empires across oceans," she added, her words almost lost to the noise of wind and waves. "Certainly England has never seemed to regard it as much of a barrier to their desires, despite its hazards."

"Ireland's ties with France cannot help but make Britons nervous, especially in a time of war. The island are too close, with too much shared history," he added, thinking of her disdain for Henry VIII, "for them to be completely separate."

"Proximity is not propinquity," she countered. "The countries—their languages, cultures, religions—are too different to be successfully joined."

"Hence the tragedy of Granville and Róisín." For a long moment, he said nothing more, weighing her argument. "But if Granville were different... What was it you said? If he could be transformed from a stranger to a friend..."

In the light of a rising moon, the silvery rims of Camellia's spectacles seemed to send out sparks as she shook her head. "It would not be enough. Róisín has learned the value of her independence. And she is determined to keep it."

When they reached the harbor, Gabriel was at some pains to find a hackney willing to carry them into the center of the city. Though he had never been to Dublin before, he felt certain the streets were not usually so quiet, especially in the hours past dawn. An uneasy, unsettling sort of calm, as after an explosion. Here and there he saw redcoats milling about in groups of two or three, looking watchful.

The hack rolled to a stop along a quiet street lined with neat brownstones; then the coach creaked and tilted as the coachman leaped down to open the door and put down the steps. After he handed Camellia down to the street, Gabriel saw a flare of something like panic in her eyes.

As he had done after supper at Stoke, he tangled her fingers with his and squeezed. "You're home now, Camellia," he whispered as she squeezed back. "It will be all right."

Before she could reach for the knocker, the door opened just a crack, and a young woman's face peered out. "Who's there? What's your business? Och, can it be Miss Burke?" The door swung wide as the maid curtsied to usher them in. As soon as the coachman had deposited the bags, she shut the door tight again, but not before peering up and down the empty street.

"Miss Erica did say she'd written to you, but not one of us believed you'd come. So dangerous, Miss Burke. I don't see how—"

"I had an escort, Molly," Camellia replied, turning the maid's eyes on Gabriel. "Don't fret. Where's—?"

Her question was lost in a screech as another young woman came thundering down the stairs. It was easy to guess her appearance had inspired Róisín's. Red hair streamed down her back, and the bridge of her nose was sprinkled with freckles. "Oh, thank God," she said, throwing her arms around Camellia. Her hands, he saw, were as rough and ragged as a scullery maid's, and nearly as ink stained as her sister's.

"Erica, may I present Lord Ashborough?" Camellia was holding herself back from the embrace, an effort to maintain some semblance of decorum in front of a guest, he guessed. "Lord Ashborough, my sister, Miss Erica Burke."

Gabriel bowed. "Ma'am." Erica managed a distracted curtsy in reply.

"Now," Camellia said, in a voice he had never heard her use before, "where are my parents?"

"At the Nugents' country house near Enniscorthy. For two weeks. They were reluctant to go without you here to watch over us, but Paris persuaded them to leave him in charge here."

"And where is Paris?"

She scowled. "Gone, God knows where. Molly told me that Galen left before dawn the day we—the day the mail coaches were seized," she corrected, with a glance at Gabriel. "Paris left soon after, and a few hours later, he brought Galen back. Then he left again straightaway, and I haven't heard from him since. Galen is—oh, come and see," she cried, dragging her sister up the stairs. The maid disappeared after them, leaving Gabriel alone in the entryway.

"Psst!" A girl's face peered out from behind the back of the staircase. "You can sit in here with us, if you'd like."

Intrigued, he accepted the invitation. The room at the back of the house was a large family parlor filled with comfortable, not quite shabby furniture, most of which had been rearranged to create a maze of table legs and chair backs, over which a damasked tablecloth had been thrown to make a hideaway of sorts. The far end of the room contained a large desk and several packed bookcases: a gentleman's study, which could be closed off from the rest by a pair of doors, though by the look of things, they were rarely shut. On all the walls hung framed sketches of plants and flowers, some taken from books, others the work of more amateur hands.

While he had been examining the room, a second child, younger than the first, had crawled from between two chairs and now stood before him, a familiar expression of curiosity and defiance on her face. He guessed she was perhaps six or seven years old.

"I'm Daphne," said the older girl, the one who had spoken first. "And that's Bellis—Bell for short." Both of them had light brown hair and blue eyes; he could see something of the Trenton features in their faces, and he supposed they must take after their mother. "How do you know Cami?"

Cami. Given his own experience, he wondered how Camellia felt about having her name clipped. But perhaps she preferred it. Perhaps with those who were privileged to call her Cami, she was another person entirely.

"I am an acquaintance of your uncle, the Earl of Merrick," he explained, careful not to claim anything that wasn't the truth. Children could always tell when an adult was lying—at least, he had always been able to tell.

"You're English," Daphne pointed out.

"I am."

She took in his admission with an expression of interest. "Well, go on."

"When Miss Burke received Miss Erica Burke's letter—"

"Oooh, Paris is in trouble, isn't he?" Bellis exclaimed, somewhat gleefully.

"I—I don't know," Gabriel replied. "In any case, your sister wished to return to Dublin immediately, of course. But it would not do to have her travel all this way alone, so I offered my assistance and the use of my coach."

The answer seemed to satisfy them. "Maybe now," Bell opined solemnly, "Erica will stop shrieking at us like a banshee. Would you like tea?"

"Yes, thank you." He looked about for the tea table and found that the girls had already put it to other uses in their building project. With care, he slipped one chair from beneath the tablecloth and seated himself near the desk. "What happened to your brother Galen?"

"Dunno," Daphne said, handing him an impossibly tiny cup and saucer, then filling it with airy nothing from an equally tiny teapot.

Biting his lip to keep from laughing, he raised the cup to his mouth and pretended to take a noisy sip. "Mmm. Just how I like it."

After a while, when it became clear he was too big to fit into their fortress made of chairs, he ceased to be an object of interest, and the girls returned to their play. He rose and went to the window, but it afforded no view of the street.

"Gabriel?" Camellia's voice was high and brittle.

He turned to find her in the doorway, white lipped and wide eyed.

"Cami, you're home!" Knocking over a chair, Bellis flew to wrap her arms around her eldest sister, followed quickly by Daphne. Camellia hugged them and kissed them, running her hands over their heads as she exclaimed at how they'd grown and expressed her hope that they'd been good.

Tangled in her skirts, clinging to her, the girls seemed to drag her already weary frame lower with the weight of their affection. Gabriel stepped forward. "How is your brother?"

Camellia quickly shook her head and darted her gaze at her young sisters, refusing to answer in front of them.

"Daphne, I think your sister could use a cup of tea too. A real one," he added, lest there be any confusion. "Is there anyone in the kitchen who could—?"

"Cook left," Bell piped up. "The same day Paris did. Won't Papa be angry?"

"I can do it myself," Daphne declared.

"Thank you, dear," Camellia said. "I'll send Molly down to help. In the meantime, Lord Ashborough, if I could trouble you for a piece of advice?" She turned, indicating he was to follow her upstairs. "Galen has sustained an injury to his leg. Erica has been doing her best to treat him, but…well, I remembered how neatly you were able to bandage my ankle, and I thought, perhaps…"

He thought of infection, gangrene, or worse. Injuries no one could treat. "Of course," he said, with more confidence than he felt.

Two flights up, they entered a bedchamber. Erica bent over a young man of perhaps fifteen or sixteen, with red-brown hair a few shades darker than her own and a face nearly as pale as the linen against which it lay. His eyes were closed, but his grimace of pain indicated he was not sleeping.

When Camellia laid her hand on her sister's shoulder, Erica readily conceded her place to him. "Galen," he said, and the boy's eyelids fluttered. "I'm Ashborough. I'm going to have a look at your leg."

Taking his groan for assent, Gabriel lifted the quilt to find the young man still wearing his boots. "He was in too much pain for me to pull them off, and he wouldn't let me cut them," Erica defended herself. Muffling a curse, Gabriel ran one hand along the supple leather and felt what was almost certainly a protrusion of bone, immobilized by the shaft of the boot. Above the cuff, the leg was swollen. Good God. Had the boy's concern for his tight-fitting, fashionable footwear cost him his leg, or saved it?

"He needs a physician," Gabriel declared, straightening.

"I know it," Erica said. "But I didn't dare fetch one."

"Why not? The streets are quiet."

"They are quiet today, your lordship. Was I to leave my brother and sisters here alone and go out and perhaps not—?" With every word, her voice rose.

"Erica." Camellia spoke firmly, but quietly. "Lord Ashborough understands. I understand. Sir Owen Sydney lives just on the opposite side of the square. I'll go now, and—"

"And abandon me again?" Erica looked stricken. "Not on your life."

"I'll go," Gabriel said, leaving no room for argument. "While I'm gone, cut up strips of linen for bandages, rummage up something firm and straight to use for a splint, and find whatever you can to dull your brother's pain. Laudanum, if you've got it. Spirits. Anything. He's going to need it."

* * * *

Sometime after she had managed to get Daphne and Bell into bed, and hopefully to sleep, Cami found Gabriel in the sitting room, restoring to their proper places the chairs that the girls had apparently turned into some sort of fairy cave or...or fortification. She shuddered at the word. Even inside the house, they were not safe from the rebellion.

When had darkness fallen? Earlier, she had felt nearly overwhelmed by her own exhaustion, but she had denied it so ruthlessly for so long, she knew it was useless to try to sleep now. Sir Owen had left some time ago, his expression grim, but hopeful. They'd eaten, although Cami, who'd lost track of the hour, was at a loss to know what to call the meal the girls had scrounged from the larder and proudly set before them. Erica had dozed over it, propping up her head with her elbow on the table. Afterward, Cami had helped her to bed too.

While she watched from the doorway, Gabriel finished with the chairs, folded Mama's best damask tablecloth, which the girls must have filched from the linen press while Molly was distracted, and found her father's decanter of Irish whiskey, still open on his desktop, now half-empty. A good deal of it had been poured down Galen's throat, to blunt the pain of having his boot removed and the broken leg set. Eventually, he'd fainted, for which small mercy Cami had offered up a whispered prayer of thankfulness. Still, the house seemed to echo with the memory of his screams.

When Gabriel poured a tumbler-full with trembling hands, tossed it back, and poured another, she could guess he still heard them too.

Stepping toward him, she spoke into the dimness. "Does it help?"

He twisted sharply in surprise, then offered her a grim smile. "Not enough."

In half a dozen steps, she was before him. Wordlessly, she plucked the glass from his fingers, gave its contents a little swirl, and took a searing gulp. "You're right," she agreed, returning the glass to the desktop.

"Come," he said, taking her hand. "Sit."

She waited, though, until he had settled into a chair, then nestled into his lap and let herself sag against the breadth of his chest. Idly, she straightened the knot of his cravat. Was it really only a week ago that she had weighed whether or not to kiss him? The events of the past few days had woven them together like the warp and weft of the finest Irish linen. Not just physically, either, although the mere memory of their joining made her body thrum with pleasure, despite her exhaustion. He might believe his heart to be broken, capable of nothing more than breaking other hearts in turn. But she knew acts of love when she saw them. Without Gabriel's strength, the elderly physician would never have been able to set Galen's leg. Without his playfulness, the little girls might have succumbed to fear. Without his support, she would surely have collapsed hours ago. "Thank you," she murmured against his neck.

When he said nothing in reply, she decided he too must have fallen asleep.

Sometime later, whether hours or minutes she could not say, she heard the rattle of a door. Before she had time to decide what to do, footsteps bounded up the back stairs and a figure loomed in the doorway.

"Cami? Is that you?" Paris's voice. Then, "What in the hell are you about?"

She scrambled to her feet, and behind her, Gabriel rose, his motions so swift and smooth and silent, she wondered if he had really been awake all this time. "My lord, may I introduce my brother, Mr. Burke?" she managed to say. "Paris, this is the Marquess of Ashborough. He has been kind enough to bring me all the way from London."

"Burke," Gabriel said in his deep voice, stepping forward, hand extended, as to an equal.

Paris, however, did not accept his hand. "You're English." Even in the darkened room, she could see the glitter of hatred in his eyes.

"So is our mother," she reminded him.

"How dare you touch my sister?" Paris demanded, ignoring her.

"That's enough, Paris," she snapped, stepping between them. "How dare you leave Erica to manage alone? And Galen—"

The question softened him slightly. "Is he all right?"

"Of course not. It's a miracle he didn't lose his leg. Sir Owen Sydney came this afternoon. He'll never walk without a limp, if he walks at all. And you left him—"

"If I'd *left* him," Paris countered, jerking his chin a notch higher, "he be dead in a ditch outside Rathmines where the horse threw him. And if I'd stayed here with him, you might soon have had the militia breaking down your door."

"My God," she breathed. "What have you—?"

Paris held up a hand to stop her. Behind them, she heard Gabriel rattle a tinderbox; then a light flared to life, casting shadows across her brother's face and its hard lines of dirt and grief and hate. "Not another word. Not in front of him."

Gabriel calmly continued to light candles until the room's darkness had been driven back. "I'll excuse myself," he said, coming to stand beside her. "Unless Camellia wants me to stay."

She had never wanted anything more. But Paris's fierce expression belonged to a man she hardly knew. "Go on," she choked past the sudden knot in her throat. "I'll be fine."

Gabriel searched her face, then nodded and was gone. Hardly had he crossed the threshold before her brother bit out, "Ashborough? Not the man who was going to marry our cousin?"

"No," Cami said without thinking. "I mean, yes. But he's not marrying her now. And he's not marrying me either, lest you get any ideas."

"I should say not, Cam," he declared. "I'd have thought you'd learned your lesson there."

Her hand itched to slap him, as she would've done when they were young. But though he stood just half a head taller than she, the man before her now, darkly handsome and coldly arrogant, was clearly beyond her reach.

"Tell me what's happened," she said instead, leading him to a chair.

"Everything's botched," he declared, polishing off the tumbler of whiskey still sitting on their father's desk. "I knew of the plans, of course. The idea was to seize the mail coaches as a sign for the rest of the country to rise. Then someone else swore it was off. Do you think I'd have let our parents leave town if I'd thought the rebellion was about to begin? I'd have been asleep in my bed if I hadn't got word that Galen had sneaked off to join the fray." He shook his head, his expression a mixture of pride and disapproval. "Well, it was pretty much chaos. Dublin went out like a damp squib. But it seems the embers are still burning in the surrounding counties. I've just got word from Wexford—"

"Wexford?" The Nugents' estate lay in that county to the south of Dublin. "Where Mama and Papa are?"

He nodded soberly. "The people there fought back and cut the militia down. It might be just the spark we need to set the whole country ablaze," he added, his face animated with a grim sort of energy. "Dublin Castle is scared."

"So am I." She got to her feet and began to pace. What might become of her parents, trapped in the center of the fighting? What might become of them all? "If it's known you're involved, you shouldn't have come home," she told him. "You'll bring this war right to our doorstep."

"I had to come," he insisted, catching her hand as she passed. "Henry Edgeworth was shot. He's...he's gone, Cam."

Tears stung in her eyes, but she refused to close them. Still, her mind conjured the image of Erica's face when she learned of her intended's fate. "Oh, Paris."

"Thank God you're here," he said, squeezing her fingers.

And then she did allow her eyelids to drop, for she understood he meant for her to deliver the news to their sister. After blinking back her tears, she searched his dark eyes. "Is this really what you wanted?"

"It means freedom," he reminded her. "For us. For Ireland."

One of Róisín's brothers would have said as much. Oh, how had she ever imagined that a mere book could change the stubborn hearts of men?

Cami shook her head and released his hand. "It means death."

Chapter 20

Gabriel made his way upstairs, but not before overhearing Camellia's sharp retort to her brother: *He's not marrying me, either.*

Was it the truth? There'd been no discussion of marriage between them, certainly, beyond his own insistence that he couldn't marry anyone. He knew the source of his own hesitation, but now he saw more fully what lay at the root of hers. With marriage came children, the management of a household, and as she'd told him, she'd had her fill of those things already. From the moment of her arrival, her family had been only too eager to lay their burdens at her feet, and he had watched her siblings drain what strength and energy she had, then demand more. To be sure, today had been an extraordinary day, but he suspected that even an ordinary one left her very little time to follow her own passions, nor the peace to dream her own dreams, just as this house, filled to overflowing with the people she loved, left little space for the work she also loved. He understood, suddenly, the appeal spinsterhood held out to her, even if it meant serving as a lady's companion.

An undeniable passion had flared between them. She'd spoken words of love that he longed, even now, to return. But there was truth in what she'd said aboard the ship as they crossed the Irish Sea. England and Ireland were too close to be fully independent of one another, but too different to be successfully joined. Couldn't the same thing be said of an Irish patriot and an English rake? If Granville and Róisín could not find happiness, even in the pages of fiction, how could he and Camellia hope to find it in this world?

Outside the door to Galen's room, he paused, then went in. The boy was sleeping fitfully. Soon, he would wake and call for his sister. This, at least, was a burden he could lift from her shoulders. After checking to see that Galen was not feverish, Gabriel settled himself into the chair in the corner of the room to keep watch.

Twice during that short night, he soothed the boy back to sleep, the second time administering a dose of the laudanum the physician had left. Sometime after that, he dozed and was awoken by the patter of rain on the window. By the gray light of dawn, he could just make out a dark-haired figure kneeling beside the bed. Paris gripped his younger brother's hand and appeared to utter a silent prayer.

Despite the dissimilarities of their circumstances, Gabriel could recognize in the man something of his own brashness, a confidence that a combination of good looks and brains would carry him over any rough patches, even those of his own making.

He also knew guilt when he saw it.

After a few minutes Paris rose and left the room, giving no sign he had noticed Gabriel. Galen slept soundly now, and some of the color had returned to his face. Satisfied that the boy would rest quietly for some time, Gabriel ventured downstairs.

His better nature, such as it was, hoped Camellia was asleep somewhere. The rest of him was selfish enough to be glad at finding her in the cozy kitchen, though she was not alone. Paris sat, head in hand, poring over papers spread before him on a scarred table.

"Camellia," Gabriel said quietly as he crossed the threshold. She looked up at him with red-rimmed eyes.

Paris turned with a scowl, covering his papers with one arm. "Still here, Ashborough?"

"His presence is not a danger to this family, Paris."

"I'm not so sure." He shared his sister's black hair and slender build, but his eyes were dark and they cast a disapproving glare between him and Camellia before returning to his reading.

"It's you who's the danger, Paris." Erica brushed Gabriel's shoulder as she passed into the room. Like her sister, she was red eyed and haggard. "Look what you've already done to your brother," she demanded shrilly. "And to me."

"Shh." Camellia stepped between them. "You'll wake the girls. And Galen—"

"Was resting comfortably when I left his room a few minutes ago," Gabriel said.

Her eyes flared with a mixture of gratitude and surprise. "Thank you for checking on him."

Paris's expression was more wary. "I shouldn't have let Galen get involved in all this," he admitted, rising. "But Henry was his own man."

In a quieter voice, Erica said, "I think we both know that wasn't the case."

Camellia stepped closer to Gabriel. "Henry Edgeworth was Paris's dear friend and Erica's betrothed," she explained in a low voice. "He was killed last night."

"What are those?" Erica asked, leaning over her brother's shoulder.

The question earned Gabriel another wary look.

"I'm not here on behalf of the Crown, Burke," he said. "I'm here for your sister's sake." In the harsh light from the lamp above the table, Camellia looked to be on the verge of splintering into a thousand pieces, holding herself together with her arms wrapped around her body. How he wished he could be the one to keep her whole, but in truth, he feared his touch might instead be the breaking point. "And as I told you last night, I'll stay until she says otherwise."

"Dispatches from Dublin Castle," Paris said at last. "Edgeworth overtook the runner and managed to hand them off before he…well." With a shudder, he broke off the explanation. "We're hopeful this will tell us what they know about our plans, prevent another massacre. But—"

As he eased back in his chair, Camellia peered forward to see what was written on the papers. "That's nothing more than gibberish."

"It's some kind of code." Paris ran a shaking hand through his hair, disordering its dark waves. "I've studied it forwards, backwards, and sideways. The leaders of the Society are counting on me to figure it out, but I'll be damned if I can break it."

"Encryption is mathematics, plain and simple," Gabriel said. "Well, perhaps not simple, but…"

"Lord Ashborough is something of a mathematician," Camellia explained, then shook her head. "But you can't do this," she said to him in a voice that was intended to brook no argument. "You're English."

It was the third time in less than a day that a member of the Burke family had made the observation. It was the first time the words had stung. She'd given him her body, told him she loved him. But in the end, did she still see him as nothing more than Granville, an enemy to the cause she held dear?

Gabriel stepped toward the table

Burke drew back, still suspicious. Moving closer, Camellia whispered, "Don't. It would—it would be treason."

He understood, then, the source of her concern. It was a gamble, certainly. Enough to condemn him—if he were not already condemned. Thinking again of the smattering of scars on her leg, the risks she'd taken for others, he thrust out his hand. Wasn't it time someone took a gamble for her?

"I'll try to break the code for you, Burke, on two conditions. First, you must swear to use whatever information the documents contain to disengage, not to take more lives. And second, after you deliver the message to your leaders, you must return to your family and keep them safe. For you, this war is over."

Still, Paris hesitated. Camellia laid her fingertips on Gabriel's outstretched arm.

"If no one finds out what's in those papers," Erica reminded her brother in a brittle voice, "Henry will have died in vain."

Slowly, Paris gathered the papers and handed them to Gabriel.

Camellia's fingers fell away. Without looking at him, at any of them, she turned and walked from the room.

* * * *

Upstairs, she entered the room she shared with Erica and threw herself down on her bed. Gabriel had already put himself in danger for her. But this...? She should stop him, of course. Except that if he succeeded, he'd made Paris swear to leave the rebellion. A tremor passed through her, and unshed tears burned in her throat and eyes. If she let Gabriel risk his neck, Paris's might be saved.

She had not intended to fall asleep, but she must've, for she jerked awake when Erica entered the room. The gray light at the window told her nothing about how much time had passed.

"What—? How long—?" She scrambled upright, shoving hair away from her face.

Erica caught her hand, laid it on the coverlet, and began to smooth Cami's wayward locks with gentle fingers. "It's afternoon. Lord Ashborough insisted you be allowed to sleep. But I thought you would want to know that Galen is propped up in bed, drinking a bit of broth. The swelling has gone down. His toes are warm."

"Oh, thank God." The physician's most dire prediction had been loss of circulation in the limb. Without proper blood flow, Galen might have lost his leg. "I should—I must go to him." Erica moved aside so she could rise. Hand on the door, Cami stopped, remembering. "And—and Paris?"

"Gone to deliver a message to the Society. He vowed to be back by nightfall. Back to stay."

"Lord Ashborough did it, then? He cracked the code?"

Erica nodded. "He did. It was—it was really quite amazing to watch him. His mind doesn't work like other people's. He sees patterns—like a man playing chess who knows every move his opponent will make before the game even begins." Her voice fairly glowed with undisguised admiration. "It's a remarkable gift—"

"Yes, well, it's a gift he uses to gamble at cards, Erica," she snapped uncharitably. "He sees others' weaknesses and turns them to his advantage."

Erica tipped her head as she searched Cami's face. "Ah, I see. And you never did want anyone to see your weaknesses."

She recoiled. Was her sister right? Was she acting out of fear not for Gabriel, but for herself? Certainly she'd made herself uncharacteristically vulnerable where he was concerned.

Setting her jaw, she marched to Galen's room and found him just as Erica had said. Molly was with him, trying to spoon broth into his mouth, while Galen protested he could feed himself. Stubborn. Just like a Burke. Cami scolded him, dismissed the maid, and took over the task herself.

Though he was clearly improved from the day before, the effort of eating, combined with his pain, drained him, and in half an hour he was settling in to sleep again. As she was leaving the room, she spied Gabriel's bag in the corner and carried it out with her. Whatever the perils to her own heart, it was dangerous for him to dally here, amid the chaos of the rebellion. If she loved him, and she did, she was going to have to find a way to say good-bye.

Back in her own room, she rummaged among her things until she found the tattered pages of *The Wild Irish Rose*, bound with the red silk ribbon. Róisín's tale was still incomplete—not because she did not know how it ended, she realized suddenly, but because she had not been able to make herself write the words. Now, though, it was time to face what came next. Carefully, she tucked the manuscript into Gabriel's bag. Would he destroy it, and the scandalous portrayal of him contained in its pages? Or would he cherish it as a memento of their days together?

Either way, it was now his story, as much as hers.

On the landing, she paused to listen to the sounds of a tea party coming from the sitting room, Daphne, Bellis, and...Gabriel. If only the world could see the man she knew. This man.

She stepped to the doorway, keeping the valise out of sight. "May I have a word?"

Gabriel rose from the floor, careful not to overturn the tiny tea table. "Is everything all right, Camellia?"

In this house, she had always only been Cami. It was how she'd come to think of herself. Until Gabriel had reminded her how beautiful her name could be.

She backed into the corridor without answering, and he followed. She knew the exact moment his eyes spied the bag she carried. "What's this?"

"You said you'd stay until I asked you to go."

As he looked from the bag to her face, she watched his features harden. "And you're asking."

"Gabriel, please." She held up one hand, not quite laying it against his chest. "It was dangerous for you even to come to Dublin. In English eyes, the United Irishmen are not patriots, but traitors. If anyone were to discover what you did this morning, how you helped Paris, it would... It would give your uncle all the ammunition he needs. No storytelling required."

His posture shifted as he took in her words, but he did not speak.

"You have to go back to London. Mr. Hawthorne told me—he told me how many people you've helped. As long as you're free, you can go on helping them. You're not a villain, Gabriel," she said again. "Don't let your uncle convince the world—convince *you*—that you're really Lord Ash."

"And how do you propose I stop him?" Stepping back, he folded his arms across his chest and regarded her with that familiar sardonic expression. "Shall I reconsider my plan to force Merrick to give me his support by marrying his daughter?"

She flinched when the words struck her. "I...I do not know." Despite the sudden weakness in her arms, she held out the bag. "I only know there's nothing—" Her eyes darted to his face, then flicked to the door and finally settled on her own hands, clenched so tightly before her that her knuckles were white. She had to do this; the longer he stayed, the more danger they were both in. "There's nothing for you here."

The lie hovered over them. "Well," he muttered after a moment, lifting the bag from her grasp, "I suppose it's better than getting pushed off a cliff. But not by much."

When he brushed past her and out the door, her heart went with him.

Chapter 21

Though they really should have been unpacking, the warmth of the July afternoon called Erica outside to explore Hampstead Heath, and Cami dutifully followed. A month ago, when her sister had proposed this scheme, Cami had been dubious. But after six weeks of caring for Galen, amusing her little sisters, and telling her parents about her time in the Trenton household while managing to reveal very little of substance, she had once more grown impatient with her lot. It was not that she didn't love her family, of course. It was the realization that they would go on believing and behaving as if they needed her, even when they didn't.

Tens of thousands had been killed in the rebellion, and though Ireland's future was uncertain, it seemed unlikely that the United Irishmen's dream of independence would be realized. Paris had been crushed by the defeat. Still, life went on. Galen was up and walking again and talking of going to university when the new term began. Mama could certainly manage Daphne and Bell without help, and Papa had his work and his flowers to occupy him. So when Erica had come to her—dressed in half mourning for Henry, because their mother had proclaimed widows' weeds unseemly for a woman who had never been married—and suggested a way that she and Cami might proclaim their independence, Cami had agreed to seize the chance.

It had taken some doing, convincing Papa to give them the money he had set aside for their dowries, persuading Mama that two sisters living on their own would not be courting scandal. Even Cami had balked when Erica had suggested a house on the outskirts of London. "Dublin is full of painful memories. And the Irish countryside is too unsettled," Erica had insisted. "London has museums and lectures and the Royal Academy...."

Whether those institutions would welcome a young woman and her dreams of becoming a botanist, Cami was skeptical. But she let herself be persuaded, because...well...

The slightest breeze rippled her skirts and the ribbons of her bonnet as she turned and looked down from the heath. From here, she could see the house they shared with Mrs. Drake, a widow, and two of her young sons. Their elder brother had gone off just that spring to join the navy. The youngest had related the news to Erica, breathless with the thrill of it, while his mother looked on, eyes shadowed with worry.

Next door was the sweetest rose-covered cottage, occupied by two middle-aged men, both former sailors. The portly, bespectacled one was a surgeon, at work on experiments having to do with a cure for yellow fever; he had already invited Erica for tea. The other man, considerably more grizzled and gruff, could be seen even now at work in his garden. Cami found it hard to imagine that he was indeed responsible for filling boys' heads with tales of sea adventures, as Mrs. Drake had claimed.

Cami's room overlooked Mr. Bewick's rose garden, and when she had set her new desk on the table by the window, she had felt certain it would be a pleasant place to write. At last, she had the peace and quiet she required for her work. But would her broken heart let her take it up again? Standing here on the heath, with the hazy suggestion of London in the distance, she was only too conscious of the fact that Mayfair was not five miles away.

News of anything other than the rebellion had been scarce in Dublin. If there had been word of the fate of a certain treasonous English nobleman at the hands of his peers, the papers had not wasted ink or space on reporting it. She had written more than one letter to Felicity, but recalling Gabriel's parting threat to resurrect his marriage scheme, she had never worked up the courage to send any of them. They sat in her writing desk, beside a lengthy explanation and apology to Mr. Dawkins, along with a few other sheets, tear-stained stops and starts that bore no name, no direction, only the words and worries of her heart. Those unsent letters were all the writing she had managed to do in six weeks. In the pit of her stomach, she carried the fear that they were all the writing she would ever do, now.

On the outskirts of London, though, news of Gabriel's fate would not be hard to come by. Mrs. Drake took the *Times*; Cami had seen it lying on the table in the entryway beside the post. Dread of its contents, more than Erica's pleas or the summer heat or the drudgery of unpacking, had driven her outside. With a sigh, she turned her back on the panorama spread before her and scanned the heath for her sister.

When she spotted a floppy-eared pointer loping toward her, she froze out of habit. But as the dog came closer, she realized she was not filled with her usual terror. Oh, her heart still raced, and she was muttering a silent prayer that the beast would simply pass her by, but the buzz of fear no longer filled her ears, and when the dog skidded to an inelegant stop before her and sat, looking expectant, it took her only three tries to work up the nerve to hold out her hand to be sniffed.

"Lelantos!"

Not only the dog's name was familiar, but also the voice in which it was spoken, a halfhearted scold that made her smile. She looked up to find Mr. Fox striding across the open field, two more dogs on leads and a broken leash in his other hand.

"Why…why, Miss Burke? Is it really you?" he said, when he reached her side. Lelantos looked from one to the other, eager for praise, which came in the form of a scratch behind his ears from his astonished master. "What luck, old boy. That's some quarry you sighted. We'll make a hunter of you yet."

"It's a pleasure to see you again, Mr. Fox," Cami said with a curtsy, although she could not quite keep her eyes from looking past him, wondering whether he was alone.

"And you, Miss Burke." He bowed. "I had not heard you were back in town."

"I've only just arrived. You are—you are well? Your family is well?"

"Oh, yes, yes. All splendid. Even the dogs," he said, looking down at them.

Gathering her courage, she reached out to pet all three of them in their turn. "Where's the fourth?"

"Medea?" A flush crept across his cheekbones, unrelated to the warm summer day. "At home. She's…she's another litter on the way, and I have every hope that this time—"

He was as nervous as an expectant father. "I'm sure motherhood will agree with her, Mr. Fox," she said, wishing she could forget who had given the poor dog her unfortunate name.

"You have called on your aunt and uncle, I'm sure? And…and your cousin, of course?"

She could not decide what to call the note in his voice. Something more than polite curiosity. "Not yet. Has she—?"

Her question was forestalled by the arrival of her sister, clutching a spray of flowers—specimens, as Erica would say—in her ungloved hands. "May I introduce my sister, Miss Erica Burke? This is Mr. Fox." She paused, uncertain what description of their relationship to add. But it mattered very little, as Erica was too taken by the dogs to pay much attention to their master. Social situations had never been her strength.

Cami glanced at the horizon to discover she was facing south again, toward town, like a broken compass drawn to a false point. "I wonder, Mr. Fox, if you would tell me—"

"You've heard the news, I'm sure—"

They spoke over one another. Cami snapped her gaze to Mr. Fox's face. His eyes were scanning her with interest, but she fared no better at reading the expression in their gray depths than she had with his voice. "No, I can see you haven't," he said. "Well, Lady Felicity should be the one to explain it all."

"Please, Mr. Fox."

But he was not to be persuaded. "I'll take you to Trenton House now, if you like. My curricle is just in the lane. But the dogs—" He looked suddenly worried, remembering, she supposed, her fear of them.

"I—I don't mind them so much," she said. And it was the truth. "But Erica—"

"I've promised to take tea with Mr. Beals, remember?" her sister said.

It would be a shocking lapse of both duty and propriety to leave her sister to the company of two gentlemen they hardly knew, even if, as Mrs. Drake had whispered, they weren't exactly the sort to threaten a girl's virtue. "I couldn't possibly..."

"Oh, Cami. Go on," Erica insisted, dusting off her hands one at a time on her skirt. "Maybe someone in our uncle's household will know what became of Lord Ashborough after he left Dublin. It would be a relief to have you stop fretting over him."

A shudder of shock passed through her. Had she really been so transparent? She jerked her gaze to Mr. Fox, but he was busy tying a knot in the broken leash and appeared not to have heard.

Together, they descended the rise, Mr. Fox apologizing for not being able to offer both of them his arm. When they had taken their leave of Erica, they walked on to his curricle. Only blind Tiresias was allowed to ride; the other two dogs happily trotted beside them on the short drive into town. In less than half an hour—time spent in discussion of the weather and various other summer topics that felt to Cami like a deliberate attempt at diversion, rather than Mr. Fox's customary pleasantries—they arrived on Brook Street. He helped her down but declined to accompany her inside, saying he had better be off with his menagerie.

Although she told herself she had imagined it, Wafford seemed to smile as he showed her in. Hardly had she crossed the threshold when Felicity approached, arms outstretched. "Cousin Camellia, oh, thank goodness. I've been so worried. Did you make it to Dublin safely?" Cami nodded. "And your family—?"

"We were fortunate, compared to many."

"When did you return to town?" As she reached Cami, she hesitated. Her brow furrowed, as if she had just remembered something unpleasant. "It was really very heartless of you not to have written."

"I'm sorry," Cami said, scrambling for an excuse. "I—I feared my aunt would take a dim view of my letters."

"Oh, well, you needn't have worried about that." Ready and willing to forgive, Felicity linked their arms and led Cami up the stairs. "Mama is in Derbyshire with Stephen. Since shortly after Papa returned. He is busy with the House of Lords most every day, of course, and—"

They were passing Uncle Merrick's study at that very moment, and Cami could not help but catch the sound of voices. A familiar voice. Not raised, but clearly angry.

"I would have succeeded, you know, if not for your interference." The speaker hesitated between phrases, as if his lungs were too weak to draw a full breath.

"I would not call it success, sir, if threats were needed to get the votes." Her uncle's voice, considerably calmer.

"But it was you, was it not, who put it about to the papers? His—his *philanthropy?*" He spat out the word. "Well, it doesn't mean he's not a rat. A rat with a guilty conscience."

Felicity tried to urge her to continue down the corridor, but Cami's feet felt glued in place.

"Five thousand pounds to St. Luke's," the rough voice continued, "with the promise they'd never reveal his name. Now, what I'd like to know is how you found out about it."

"I had a letter."

Cami's heart leaped. She knew her uncle must be referring to her letter, in which she'd told him what Mr. Hawthorne had said. From the sounds of things, it had helped to sway opinion in Gabriel's favor and thwart his uncle's plot.

"Hmph. Anonymous, I suppose." Before she and Felicity could move, the door flew open and Lord Sebastian Finch stomped through, leaning heavily on his cane. "Out of the way, girl. *You?*" He caught sight of Cami as he passed, and now paused to look her up and down. "This is your niece, isn't it, Merrick? Your Irish niece?"

Her uncle now stepped into the doorway, and a smile warmed his blue eyes, so like his daughter's. "Why, Camellia. This is a pleasant surprise. Welcome back."

"So you're the one my nephew took to Dublin, eh?"

Cami snagged her lip between her teeth, while her uncle's eyes widened at this revelation and Felicity looked down at her hands.

"Didn't think I'd know, did you?" Lord Sebastian sneered. "But the coach came from Finch House, and there are those who remain loyal to me."

Oh, that ill-fated journey. Why, why had Gabriel ever undertaken it?

But she knew the answer to that question now. The terrible, wonderful answer.

He had done it for her.

Lord Sebastian crossed his hands over his cane. "Strange place for an Englishman to be, on the eve of a rebellion."

"What are you insinuating, Finch?" Uncle Merrick demanded.

Cami, however, had already begun to put together the scattered pieces of the man's puzzling words. It sounded as if he hoped to find a way to associate Gabriel with the rebellion, to implicate him in something illegal, as he had, thank God, apparently failed to do with the assassination attempt on the king.

Only this time, as she well knew, his talk of treason would be true.

"And then there's that story everyone's blathering on about," Lord Sebastian continued, "*The Irish Something*—"

"*The Wild Irish Rose*?" Felicity chimed in. Only sheer force of will kept the gasp of shock from passing Cami's lips. "Oh, isn't it thrilling?"

"It's dreck, girl," he declared, thumping his cane against the floor for emphasis. "But there's a character in it who seems more than a little familiar. Almost as if the author had a close, personal acquaintance with such a villain..." He sized Cami up once more. "An Irish writer, of course. Has to be. And likely a woman..."

"Enough, Finch. Surely you're not suggesting my niece is acquainted with the person who penned a popular work of fiction, merely because they are both Irish?" Her uncle glanced her way, and with the eye farthest from Lord Sebastian, out of that man's line of vision, he gave a slow wink. Again, she fought to keep her reaction from showing on her face. "Or that your nephew is somehow involved with the United Irishmen? Have done with your tiresome theories about Ashborough. They grow wilder than *The*

Wild Irish Rose." Lord Sebastian scowled, but Uncle Merrick's expression remained remarkably pleasant. "Won't you let me walk you out?"

With another smile of welcome for Cami, he motioned her and Felicity down the corridor while ushering his unwelcome guest in the opposite direction.

In another moment, she found herself in Aunt Merrick's sitting room. "Well," Felicity said as she seated herself, "that was an odd encounter."

"Yes," Cami agreed, taking a chair. Her head whirled with the strange and surprising things she'd heard, along with a few new questions. She decided to begin at the beginning. "I gather you knew that Lord Ashborough took me to Dublin?"

"Of course. I sent him after you. I could not let you travel alone."

Cami parted her lips to reply, though she could not think what to say. The cousin who had worried over her reputation on the public stage had thought her safer in the hands of a notorious rake?

"Oh, Camellia," Felicity said with a laugh, "I suppose you thought you were keeping a great secret, but if you could have seen your eyes every time the man spoke to you." She shook her head in a mock scold, and her golden curls caught the room's primrose-tinted light. "He was relieved, I think, not to have to make me an offer. But you could have knocked me over with a feather when he wrote a letter for Papa and in it—why, what do you suppose?" Cami shook her head. "He agreed to waive Stephen's debt and restore my dowry."

She had known of the former provision, of course, but not the latter, even more generous, one. "On condition of your father's assistance with the treason charge, I suppose," she said, thinking of Lord Sebastian's complaint.

Felicity's lips lifted in a small smile. "Papa was grateful, to be sure. But no. He asked only that my father be willing to consider an honorable suitor for my hand: Mr. Fox." From the sparkle in her cousin's eyes, Cami could guess his suit had been successful. "We are engaged! And we shall be married as soon as he is ordained. Lord Ash has gifted him the living on his estate."

"How shall you like being married to a clergyman?"

That question, Felicity did not need to answer. "Oh, but Mama was furious. When I told her I saw very little use in being trotted around to garden parties and balls and soirees after that, she took King and went into the country."

Cami leaned forward and took her cousin's hands in hers. "I envy you your happiness. You were truly named, Felicity."

Felicity accepted the compliment with a blush. "Now, let's see," she said, tapping her lips with one finger. "What else have you missed while you were away?"

"Lord Sebastian said something about a scandalous book…?" she prompted, feeling certain her eagerness was once more plainly to be read on her face.

"Oh, yes. *The Wild Irish Rose*. Every tongue is wagging about it. What with the uprising, people are intrigued by anything to do with Ireland. One of the papers called it…what was the phrase? Oh, yes: 'a prescient allegory for the present troubles.' But it's not a book. At least, not yet."

"I beg your pardon?" Cami said, although she had heard every word.

"The story is being published in parts in some gossip sheet called *The Quizzing Glass*."

Cami knit her brow. "In parts?"

"A section at a time," Felicity explained. "They began appearing a month ago. Papa says it's really quite innovative—far more people can afford a penny for *The Quizzing Glass* than can afford a guinea for a novel. The idea is that each installment builds up interest for the next."

Cami's mind flooded with more questions. Had Mr. Dawkins changed his mind? Gone to print with what she'd first sent him? Decided the story was too timely to wait, the appetite for scandal too great, to risk forgoing the potential profits? But she asked only, "Have you read it?"

"Everyone has, Cousin." Felicity rose from her chair to search through the papers on her mother's escritoire. "Ah, here it is. The latest installment. See for yourself."

Hesitantly, Cami took the periodical from her cousin's hand. Her words. Róisín's story. In print. And in the hands of half of London, according to Felicity.

She had expected to feel joy at having realized her dream. Instead, it felt a great deal more like she'd swallowed a lump of lead. "Is the author known?"

"'A lady.' That is all the printer will say. One of your countrywomen, evidently, as Lord Sebastian said. And something of a radical."

Remembering her uncle's wink, she tried to detect any hint of slyness in her cousin's voice or face. Did she, too, suspect?

To hide her own expression, Cami dropped her eyes to the page Felicity had put before her, some early bantering exchange between Lord Granville and Róisín. The villain's similarity to Gabriel struck her afresh. No wonder Lord Sebastian seemed sure he could use the story against his nephew.

"Why, Cousin Camellia, are you ill?" Felicity rose and hurried to her side. "I should have realized the story might upset you. It has made you think of things you would doubtless rather forget."

Cami looked down and realized she was crumpling the pages of the magazine. With trembling fingers, she tried to smooth them out.

She'd given Gabriel the story for safekeeping. Oh, what had he done?

Chapter 22

"I would not wish to complain, my lord." From the doorway, Arthur Remington spoke in his starchiest voice. "But that...*creature* would seem to have found another of my shoes."

The rumbling, gnawing sound of a beast worrying its prey drew Gabriel's attention from what he had been reading to the carpet that stretched between the doorway and his customary chair near the window. Nearly half of what had been a fine Turkish rug was covered by the sprawling form of a large tan dog whose enormous feet indicated it still had a great deal of growing to do.

"Has she?" He dropped onto one knee to scratch the dog's ears with his left hand, while the right snatched away her plaything. "Now, Elf, my girl. We both know Remy has decidedly poor taste in footwear, but you mustn't keep tormenting him about it." As Gabriel held up what remained of the shoe, now dripping with slobber, Remington regarded both master and dog with an uncharacteristically fastidious shudder. "Remember, he only agreed to let me bring you here after I gave him his ticket to leave, and if we are too bad, he might just decide to use it." He dropped his voice lower, as if taking the dog in confidence. "I confess I did not write him a glowing character, for I did not wish it to go to his head, but I suspect he's more than capable of forging a better one."

Remington only arched one brow. "If you are quite through, my lord? You have a visitor."

"In broad afternoon? Surely Foxy has better things to occupy—"

"It is not Mr. Fox, my lord. I've taken the liberty of letting her in."

Her?

With the slightest tip of his head, Remy stepped to the side, and the doorway now framed a slender, bespectacled woman with raven hair.

"*Camellia.*"

He was quite certain he must be hallucinating, until Elf lumbered to her feet and began to snuffle around the apparition's hems. Camellia did not flinch—more proof she was a product of his wayward imagination. He reached out one hand to catch the dog's collar, discovered he was still holding the battered, slobber-coated shoe, and dropped it. Delighted at the unexpected return of her plaything, Elf snatched it up and resumed her prior occupation.

So many times in the weeks since he'd left Dublin, he'd been on the point of throwing caution to the wind and going back to her. Then he would remember: She had made her choice. *A wise woman*, as he'd once said. Too wise to plan a future with him.

Still kneeling, hand outstretched, Gabriel held his breath when Camellia reached out and laid her fingers in his.

She was warm. Flesh and blood. Real.

"Gabriel?" As usual her green eyes were scouring him from head to toe.

At the questioning note in her voice, he gave a self-deprecating laugh, rose to his feet, and led her around the dog and into the room. "When did you return to town?"

"Only yesterday." She was clad in one of her plain, loose-fitting dresses. Remy must already have relieved her of her pelisse and gloves and bonnet.

"Alone?"

To his relief, she shook her head. "Erica is with me. She was eager to leave Dublin."

"Understandably so." He gestured her to a chair and returned to his own. "Is she otherwise well?"

The question required more reflection than he had expected. "I—I am not entirely certain. Erica is my sister, and dear to me, but she and I have never..." She paused again. "I am not in her confidence."

"I see." It was Gabriel's turn to hesitate. "And you? Are you well?"

"I hardly know that, either." Her voice acquired a sharper edge. "Over the past six weeks, I have been torturing myself, thinking what might have become of you." He'd been torturing himself, too, trying *not* to think of her and certain she had not been thinking of him. "I made myself picture you with my cousin," she said, and he could tell by the uncomfortable set of her jaw precisely what that picture had entailed. "I even told myself you must be dead. I thought I had imagined every conceivable scenario. I did not, however, picture you cozy at home with a dog."

Hawthorne had foisted the mastiff pup on him when he'd passed by Stoke on his way back to London, insisting Gabriel would benefit from the responsibility of caring for her, as well as from the canine devotion he would receive in return. Whether the steward had been right was a secret Gabriel intended to carry to his grave.

Realizing she was the topic of conversation, Elf paused in her destruction of the shoe, looked from one to the other of them, then heaved herself to her overlarge feet and came to lay her head on Camellia's knee. Gabriel reacted swiftly to spare her, leaning forward to pull the dog away, but to his shock, Camellia laid her palm on Elf's head and smoothed the wrinkled skin there.

"I met Mr. Fox today," she continued, and her voice seemed to him to have lost some of its sharp edge. "He was walking his dogs on Hampstead Heath, near where Erica and I have taken a house."

"Was it he who brought you here?" Gabriel asked in genuine surprise. Fox could be a stickler for propriety, and it was most improper for a lady to call on a gentleman—to say nothing of bearding a rogue in his den.

"No. He took me to Trenton House to see Felicity. I came away with a great deal of information." That, Gabriel suspected, was a bit of an understatement. "From there I walked to Grosvenor Square, but the butler at Finch House insisted you were not at home. I had not yet decided what step I should take next, when your downstairs parlor maid—a French girl by the name of Adele—whispered to me I might find you here." She paused. "Is she the one? Did you manage to help her once more?"

"Remy did it, actually. By the time I returned to London, he'd rounded up proof she could not have been involved in the assassination attempt. After that, it was no great matter to secure her release."

"And to clear your name as well."

"Yes." Though the resolution to his uncle's threat had been rather anticlimactic, the thought of what might have happened still had the power to make him wake in a cold sweat. Or perhaps that was simply a consequence of waking alone. "Of course, that was not all I had to do in town. You had given me a commission to execute."

"You refer, I suppose, to taking *The Wild Irish Rose* to Mr. Dawkins. But I had not considered it a commission."

Without conscious thought, he reached into his coat pocket and rubbed his fingertips over the length of silk ribbon he had secreted there. "Perhaps not. Still, Dawkins was glad to have it." It had required all Gabriel's strength to part from the pages over which she had labored, however. "He told me he considered it an ideal test for his new publishing method."

Her eyes were fixed on the motion of her own thumb, stroking the dog's short fur along the line where the black mask of her face met the tan of her body. Elf gave a blissful groan, and a damp spot began to form on Camellia's knee beneath the dog's drooping jowls. After a moment, Camellia said, "What if the story provides society with fresh proof that what your uncle says about you is true?"

"Because of Granville, you mean?" He made a scoffing sound in his throat. "People see what they wish to see. And in any case, it's only a story, as someone once told me. It's hardly proof of a crime. A solicitor's daughter ought to know that."

"Your uncle knows you were in Dublin, however. What if it's also discovered you were aiding and abetting the United Irishmen? Oh, Gabriel." Her whole body sagged. "Why did you do it? The trip, the code, the book..."

"Why did you send me away?" he countered.

"Because I was afraid," she said, her voice raw in its honesty. "Because I could not bear to have you take more risks and make more sacrifices." Briefly, her hand stopped its motion. "Because I love you."

His breath caught in his chest. "Ah. Then you understand." Withdrawing his hand from his pocket, he echoed her movement, fingering a seam in the leather of the chair's rolled arm. "And because I love you, I could not bear it if your story were never told."

"Róisín's story," she corrected swiftly. "Ireland's story."

"*Your* story." He pushed himself forward in his chair, drawing her eyes with the movement. "The words of your heart and your mind and your pen."

"Those words may yet add to your troubles," she pointed out.

He shook his head. "If you will persist in claiming that they have anything to do with me, say only that they've added to my legend." Surely that was a flicker of amusement that crossed her expression? "I had to do something," he continued, letting some of the old mockery creep back into his voice. "All this talk about my good deeds was quite ruining my reputation. As it is, I suspect no one will ever look at Lord Ash the same way again."

Quickly, she rose—to hide a smile, he thought. Unhappy at being disturbed, Elf gave a little groan of displeasure and turned to Gabriel. But he too had got to his feet. Resigned, the dog flopped onto the carpet and went back to chewing on Remy's shoe.

"Mr. Dawkins's new scheme of printing books in parts seems promising," Camellia said, drawing one fingertip along the spines lining the bookshelf. "But what does he mean to do about the ending? The manuscript you gave him was unfinished."

"I'm not sure." Gabriel felt hopeful but hesitant, a gambler with a promising hand, waiting for the deal of the final card to decide his fate. "Have you changed your mind about the outcome of the story?"

She paused, evidently puzzling over the title of some thick volume. The ink stains on her hand had faded. Not surprising if the circumstances of recent weeks had curtailed her writing, he supposed, but those marks of her literary labors were as much a part of her as her emerald eyes and her quick tongue, and he missed them now as he had been missing all the rest of her for weeks.

"I confess it's been troubling me for some time," she said at last. "I had hoped to show my readers that Ireland was more than capable of being independent."

He dared to take a step closer. "And you have."

"But Papa says the outcome of the rebellion will almost certainly mean more English control, not less."

His heart sank a little as he imagined how she and her brothers must feel about such a result. "I fear he's probably right. Not exactly a happy ending for Róisín, to be under the thumb of a man who's proven himself unworthy of her."

Turning, she fixed him with that familiar defiant spark in her eye. "Róisín, under a man's thumb?" Her nose wrinkled slightly and her head wagged in disbelief. "She has far too much spirit for that."

"True," he agreed, and hope dared to swell once more. "But what then?"

She steepled her fingertips before her and looked thoughtful. "I had in mind a match made on more even ground, in which each complemented what the other lacked. A true union, in which the whole is stronger than the parts."

"In other words," he said, coming forward to cover her hands with his, "you imagine a resolution in which the arrogant, dissolute Englishman is reformed by the love of an independent-minded Irishwoman?"

Her eyes remained focused on their joined hands for a moment before rising to his face. "I do."

He dipped his head and brushed his lips across hers. "An inspired revision, my love."

"Well," she said, freeing her hands to step more fully into his embrace, "I've recently been reminded that happy endings need not be limited to the pages of fiction." Her cheek rested against his chest and her arms came around his waist. "You've made Felicity and Mr. Fox very happy."

"They make one another happy," he said, laying his cheek against the top of her head. "I had only to get out of their way."

"'Get out of their way'?" When her head tipped back, he looked down into her incredulous eyes. "Is that what you call it? Enabling them to marry by presenting Mr. Fox with a very lucrative living on a certain estate in Shropshire?"

That piece of raillery earned her another kiss, more thorough than the last. "Your readers may be disappointed, you know," he said, when he was at leisure to speak. "I believe the current fashion is for villains to suffer a grisly end."

The wicked gleam in her eyes was matched by the sly upturn of her lips. "Fear not. Granville's uncle will get his just deserts for trying to tarnish the reputation of our hero."

His bark of laughter made Elf pause in her noisy labors. "Well, it seems you've tied up all the loose ends," he said when the sound of chewing filled the room again. "You have only to put your name to the tale and you shall be the toast of the town."

"Ah," she said, reaching up to trace his jaw with her fingertip. "But a lady must be ever mindful of the impropriety of setting herself before the public. So which name shall I use?"

A little flutter of panic rose in his chest, born on the wings of his long-standing conviction that what he had to offer, no sensible woman should want. Holding her in his arms left very little room for fear, however. "How would you feel about signing your work 'Lady Ashborough'?"

She tipped her head, considering. "Society would be scandalized. Poor Mr. Dawkins would have to print more copies to keep up with demand."

"Camellia…" Another time, she might tease him to distraction. But just now, he could not bear it.

With a trembling smile, she relented. "Yes, my dear." Tears glimmered in her eyes. "Yes, I'll marry you."

Bending, he lifted her into his arms—oh, she really was too thin—and carried her to his favorite chair. He'd always thought it comfortable, but the addition of her slight curves made it perfectly snug. As he pressed his lips to her forehead, he wished it were possible for them to stay ensconced in that spot forever.

Which, of course, it was not.

Some part of his thoughts must have been visible on his face. Worry flitted across her eyes, the shadow of a cloud on a grassy knoll. "Gabriel?"

"I was recalling a long-ago conversation with Fox," he said. "I will miss this place, but bachelor rooms are not suitable for a bride."

Camellia lifted her head to look around the sun-dappled, book-filled space. "I like it. It's cozy. And I am used to small houses, as you know. Though it must be a trial for poor Elf."

At the sound of her name, the dog scrambled once more to her feet and came to join them, wedging her head into the already overstuffed chair. Camellia shifted slightly to make room for her but did not recoil.

"When did you cease to be afraid of dogs?" he asked.

"Who says I'm not?"

"Elf." As if to lend support to his case, the dog, who would have sensed fear if there had been any, instead gave a blissful sigh.

Camellia reached out tentatively to touch one velvety ear. "I'm not *over* my fear, exactly. But when I told you the story of the dog in the park, I realized what I feared most was a memory. Not even *my* memory. One that had been created for me, built up over years and years, until I mistook it for my own."

Gabriel weighed her words. Hadn't he done the same? He had been hiding from his birthright, from his future, from love because he'd heard the story of his villainy so often, he'd come to believe it was true.

"I wonder what you would think of living at Stoke after we are married?" he asked after some time had passed.

Her hand reached up to cup his cheek. "I know now what that place is to you. Are you certain you want to do that?"

He met her steady, searching gaze, the eyes of the woman he loved. With Camellia at his side, he could take back his name, his life, his home. He recognized at last his father's determination to protect his son's inheritance. He understood at last the value of that gift.

But this decision was not only about him.

"It would be closer to your family," he pointed out. "And if one is willing to side with Henry VIII, it's where the Marquess—and Marchioness—of Ashborough belong. But most important, I can give you something there that I cannot give you here: a room of your own in which to write."

She drew back in surprise, though he didn't let her go far. "You want me to go on—?"

"Writing? Yes. If it makes you happy, *yes*."

"But the household responsibilities... And—and—"

"Children? A distinct possibility," he admitted, snugging their bodies closer together. When her lips pursed in a scolding frown, he kissed them. "I know you left Ireland in search of a quiet place to do your work," he said, more seriously. "I also know something about the seclusion you believe you want. I've been alone—and lonely—all my life."

A little knot of uncertainty formed between her brows, not quite hidden by her spectacles. Perhaps it was mirroring a similar expression on his own. Lifting her hand from his cheek, she smoothed her fingertips over his brow, just as she had done with Elf. He understood, suddenly, why the dog had groaned when she stopped.

"What you called independence, I thought of as isolation," he explained. "But why must it be one or the other? Stoke Abbey's an enormous place, my love. Surely we can create an island of peace for you amid the loving chaos of family."

She gave him a rather skeptical look. But there was something else in her eyes, something he'd glimpsed there once before.

She was intrigued.

"We'll create a private sanctuary, a writer's retreat," he promised. "Shall I write to Mr. Hawthorne and tell him he must give up my father's study? It's quite the nicest room in the house."

Shifting slightly, she took his face between her hands and kissed him back. "Thank you," she whispered. And went right on kissing him.

"Well," Gabriel murmured teasingly against her lips, "you did seem to find the space...inspirational."

A few moments later, with a rumbling canine sigh of resignation, Elf returned to the floor to finish off Remy's shoe.

Author's Note

The 1798 Rebellion in Ireland has been called "probably the most concentrated episode of violence in Irish history" (R.F. Foster, *Modern Ireland: 1600–1972*). Though most of the fighting was over in a matter of months, as many as 50,000 people are estimated to have died. At war with France, Britain was determined to prevent another uprising and brought Ireland more firmly under its control. The 1800 Act of Union abolished the Irish Parliament and created a new political entity: the United Kingdom of Great Britain and Ireland.

In cartoons and elsewhere in the popular press, contemporaries caricatured the union as a "marriage." Like most marriages of the time, it was an unequal match in terms of economics, rights, and power. Nevertheless, some writers saw potential in the metaphor, most notably Sydney Owenson (1781?–1859), the daughter of an Irish actor and an Englishwoman. Owenson saw herself as a cultural go-between, a hybrid of English and Irish identities; she even claimed to have been born while her mother was crossing the Irish Sea.

Owenson (after 1812, Lady Morgan) was a prolific writer and an outspoken advocate of many causes, but if she is known today, it is likely for *The Wild Irish Girl: A National Tale*, published in 1806. Owenson's tale was so popular that in certain circles she was known by the name of its heroine, Glorvina. The book initiated an openly political subgenre of the novel of manners (a foremother of the modern romance novel). Typically in a "national tale," an English hero travels through Ireland and learns to love the country and its people, as personified by the Irish heroine. It is to that little-known literary tradition that I pay homage with my creation of Camellia Burke and her novel, *The Wild Irish Rose*.

Keep reading for a sneak peek at

The Duke's Suspicion

The next in the

Rogues & Rebels series

Coming soon from

Susanna Craig

and

Lyrical Press

Chapter 1

As dark clouds rolled over the Cumbrian sky and thunder rumbled in the distance, Erica Burke realized she had made a serious error in judgment. Several errors, in fact.

The most serious error, obviously, had been leaving her journal at the inn where they had stopped for dinner. She was often forgetful. *Careless*, other people called it. But in truth she cared a great deal. Losing her journal would have meant losing months of work, losing the record of every botanical observation she had made since coming to England.

It would have meant losing a piece of herself.

To be fair, though, she would never have left her journal at a posting inn if she hadn't been traveling. So hadn't the real error in judgment been agreeing to accompany her sister on her wedding trip to begin with? Ladies often took a female companion on such a trip, a custom grounded in the assumption that the activities and interests of ladies and gentlemen, even newly married ones, were entirely separate. But Cami's insistence on Erica's joining her had had very little to do with convention. And as far as Erica could see, her brother-in-law, Lord Ashborough, had only one interest: his new bride. The only activities in which he wanted to indulge were... *Well*.

With a wary eye toward the sky, Erica hopped from the coach and hurried back across the filthy inn yard, blaming the sudden wave of heat that washed over her on the exertion. She had been promised the chance to explore the plants and flowers of the Lake District, and she was determined not be put off by the occasional moment of embarrassment, or by the knowledge that her presence was entirely extraneous. Her only concession had been to ride in the baggage coach on occasion, with Mr. Remington, Lord Ashborough's manservant, and Adele. Try as she might, Erica could not bring herself to think of the French girl as "Lady Ashborough's maid." It would have required her to concede that Cami was now a lady, and not simply her overbearing elder sister.

On the threshold of the inn's dining parlor, she was forced to reevaluate her assessment once more. A group of rowdy young men now filled the table at which she and her party had been seated only a few moments ago. Avoiding as best she could the men's eyes, hands, and voices, Erica pressed forward to retrieve what was hers. Perhaps the most serious error had been leaving Lord Ashborough's mastiff, Elf, in Shropshire with the new vicar and his wife. Elf was neither fierce nor especially brave, but even half-grown, she was enormous, and Erica had no doubt that her mere presence would have sufficed to forge a path through the room.

On the bench closest to the window sat a man with greasy dark hair. If the sight of him thumbing idly through the pages of her journal had not blanketed her vision in a red haze of anger, she might have noticed his red coat. His militia uniform.

"Kindly unhand my journal." Though she spoke quietly, she thrust out her hand, palm upward, so forcefully that the muscles of her arm quivered.

He did not rise, and a lazy smile revealed rather mossy teeth. "What have we here? An Irish rebel—?"

The words sharpened her senses, brought the moment into vivid relief. The coat of his uniform was grimy from travel and frayed around the collar and cuffs. On one shoulder a darker stripe of fabric curved downward into a frown. Something had once been sewn there and had either fallen off or been removed. Perhaps he had recently been stripped of his rank.

As if observing her own actions from a great distance, she watched her hand sweep the journal from his grasp and then swing back. The sturdy leather binding—no delicate lady's commonplace book, this—struck along his jaw, effectively wiping the grin from his face. One of his fellow soldiers guffawed, and suddenly the noises and odors of the room rushed back to full force, threatening to overwhelm her. Her narrow pinpoint of focus expanded into a swath of chaos. Clutching her journal in one hand and her skirts in the other, she ran from the room.

Hitting him had been yet another mistake. She could not even say what had prompted her to do it. Her distrust of soldiers? His disdain for Ireland? Perhaps a bit of both. Oh, why could she never seem to control her temper, her impulses? Was he following?

Outside once more, she paused only to scan the inn yard for Lord Ashborough's coaches. But the yard was empty. Perhaps around the corner? No? Well, surely that was his carriage, standing by the church....

Oh, no. *Now* she understood her most serious error. When she'd discovered her journal missing, she'd hopped from the baggage coach without telling Mr. Remington to wait. He must have assumed she was riding the rest of the way with her sister. Erica's absence would likely not be noticed for hours.

She was stranded.

She could almost hear Cami's voice telling her to wait right where she was. But Erica's hasty reaction to the soldier's sneer had rendered this village's only lodging less than hospitable.

Regrettably, she had a great deal of experience with crises. Most, like this, of her own making. And sitting still had never been her preferred method of coping with any of them.

She furrowed her brow, trying to recall the map in the guidebook. People came from all over Britain to visit the Lake District. There would be signposts to Windermere. Surely even she, with her notoriously poor sense of direction, could find it. With another glance at the threatening sky, she began to walk.

What was a little rain?

For the first mile or so, she watched the clouds tumble toward her, listened to the peals of thunder as they swelled and grew, seemingly born of the earth as much as the air. Mud from an earlier rain dragged at her hems and sucked at the soles of her walking boots. At the second mile, she gave up the roadway in favor of the grassy verge. Cold, thick drops began to fall, speckling her dress and face. Almost before she could stuff her journal into her pelisse, the sky opened and water poured down in sheets, whipped by the wind like clothing on the line, blinding her.

Something sharp snagged at her skirts, jabbed at the chilled flesh of her thigh beneath. The hedgerow. A flash of lightning showed her a gap in its tangled branches, barely wide enough for her to pass through. And a little way beyond it, an abandoned stone cottage. Would its thatched roof provide shelter? She could not tell until she reached it.

Head down, she pushed onward. The wind snatched at her sodden bonnet. Nearly strangled by its ties at her throat, she scrabbled with numb fingers to loosen them. Once free, the bonnet whirled into the storm and was gone.

The twenty yards standing between her and her goal seemed to take almost as long to travel as the two miles she had already come. At last, its stout slab door stood before her. Here, in the shadow of the low building, the wind still lashed, but it no longer threatened to carry her away. As she leaned her head against the door to fumble with the latch, she felt a movement. Not of her own making. Not the rumble of the storm, either.

The door swung inward and she collapsed onto the dirt floor at the booted feet of a stranger.

The cottage was not abandoned, after all.

Even a cursory glance told her these were not the sort of boots generally worn by cottagers, however. The supple leather was not muddy or scuffed as it would have been if the man was a laborer or had recently trudged across the open field. Perhaps he had been traveling on horseback. Or perhaps he simply had been wise enough to take shelter before the rain began.

Without speaking, he stepped around her to shut the door, muffling the storm's noise and closing out its murky light, casting the single room into near darkness.

Oh, God. This was it—her most serious error in judgment. *Ever.* Erica scrambled to her feet and whirled about to face him, feeling her rain-sodden skirts slap against her legs. But he was already moving past her again.

"Wait there." His voice was pitched low, barely audible beneath the storm.

Gradually, her eyes were able to pick out his shape, now on the far side of the small room. A narrow seam of light formed a square on the wall behind him—a window, blocked by wooden shutters. She heard a rattle, a scrape, a hiss. Flame sparked to life in his hands then became the warm, flickering glow of a candle.

"That blast of wind blew it out," he explained with a glance past her at the door. Was it her imagination, or was there an accusatory note in his voice?

The candle lit his features from below, giving them a sardonic cast. Impossible to tell whether he was handsome or plain, dark or fair, young or…well, his voice, his ease of movement certainly did not suggest an old man. And he was tall—taller than Papa. Than either of her brothers or her brother-in-law. Taller even than Henry…

Oh, why, in this moment, had she thought of Henry? But so it always went, her mind flitting from one idea to the next, fixing on precisely the things she ought to forget, and forgetting the things she ought to—

My journal!

With a shudder of alarm, she slithered a hand between the wet, clinging layers of her pelisse and her dress and pulled the book from its hiding place. As she hurried toward the light, the man drew back a step. With the candle between her and her journal, so the stranger could see nothing but its binding, she turned the book over in her hands, then thumbed through its pages to assess the damage. The leather cover was damp; rain had wetted the edges of the paper here and there. It would look worn and wrinkled when it was dry, but so far as she could tell, the journal's contents were miraculously unharmed. A sigh of relief eased from her.

When she laid her journal on the tabletop, the candlelight once more threw itself freely around the room. The stranger was looking her up and down, his expression both incredulous and stern. A familiar expression. Cami wore it often in Erica's presence.

Of *course* she looked a mess. Who wouldn't, under these circumstances? Icy rivulets ran from her hair down her face, and beneath the howl of the wind, she could hear the steady patter of her skirts dripping onto the floor. If this were a scene in one of those novels her sister denied reading, the hero would probably invite her to strip off her drenched clothing and dry herself before the fire. Something shocking would likely follow.

But there was no fire. And this man showed no intention of acting the part of a hero.

As if to confirm her thoughts, he shook his head and folded his arms across his chest. "What in God's name are you doing out in a storm like this?"

* * * *

When Major Lord Tristan Laurens asked a question, he expected an answer. He certainly did not expect the subject of his interrogation to bristle, fling a lock of wet hair over her shoulder—spraying him with rainwater, almost dousing the candle—and reply, "I might ask you the same."

Unblinking, she faced him across the table, communicating quite clearly that if he was waiting for her to bend first, he might wait forever. He had some experience coaxing information from unwilling sources, and he knew better than to begin by barking at them. But her arrival had caught him off guard. He had never liked surprises.

The silence that stretched between them was eventually broken by her fingers drumming against the cover of the book she'd unearthed from her bodice. She radiated a kind of nervous energy that refused to be contained. When another moment had passed, she plucked up the book, tucked it against her breast, and began to move around the room. Its narrow compass, crowded with ramshackle furniture, prevented her from pacing.

Or perhaps the predictable, orderly, back and forth motion of pacing was anathema to this woman.

She put him in mind of a bedraggled spaniel, with her slight build, rapid movements, and curling hair hanging limply on either side of her face. Though, admittedly, far more attractive than any spaniel he had ever seen. The precise shade of her red hair was difficult to determine under such dim and damp conditions. He tried to imagine what she might look light bathed in the warmth of a shaft of sunlight, but gave it up as a bad job. Sunlight was unlikely to be granted them anytime soon.

When her wandering feet brought her within arm's length of him, he held up one hand in hopes she might cease. Her jerk of surprise made him wonder if she had forgotten his presence entirely.

"The storm doesn't show any signs of abating. Perhaps we ought to begin again." He made a crisp bow. "Tristan Laurens."

Her gaze raked over him, and for a moment, he thought she meant not to respond. "Mr. Laurens," she said after a moment and curtsied.

Ought he to correct her? At the very least, he might have introduced himself as "Major Laurens," as he'd not yet resigned his commission. "Lord Tristan" was entirely incorrect now, of course. Both Father and Percy were gone, had been gone for some time. Still, it felt strange to think of himself as a duke, stranger still to call himself Raynham. Men of seven and twenty did not usually acquire new identities in quite so abrupt a fashion.

In the end, he let her assumption stand. After the weather cleared, they would go their separate ways, and his rank would be irrelevant.

Her fingertips danced over the book she was holding. "I am Erica Burke."

"Erica?" It was not a name he had heard before.

"*Erica* is the Latin word denoting the genus to which several common species of flowering shrubs belong." His surprise at the explanation must have been evident on his face, for she continued, with a little grimace of resignation, "Heather. It means heather. My father named his children using Linnaeus's *Species Plantarum* as his guide."

Her Irish accent was distinct but not unpleasant. From Dublin, if he had to guess. And though he suspected her of having given a variation of that explanation many times, it did not have the air of a rehearsed speech. So she knew at least a bit of Latin and a little botany. An educated woman, then. A bluestocking? A pedant?

Or something more unusual, and more interesting, than either?

Though mildly curious about her siblings' names, he focused his concern on the fact that her family had let one of their number out of their sight. A young woman wandering about alone faced dangers far greater than a little rain, especially in a time of war, when so many were desperate.

Having learned his lesson about speaking sternly, however, he dipped his head in a nod of greeting. "It is a pleasure, Miss Burke, to meet someone else who has known the travails of having been named by an eccentric father. Mine was a student of the Arthurian legends."

That confession brought the twitch of a smile to her lips, quickly wiped away by a crack of thunder that shook the tiny cottage. "Oh, will this storm never end?" She began once more to move about the room, like a caged bird flitting from perch to perch.

"It will, of course." He tried to speak in a soothing tone, though it was not something he'd often had occasion to use in the army. "But I think we must resign ourselves to the fact that darkness may fall before it does."

"You mean, we must spend the night? Here?" A panicky sigh whooshed from her lungs as she sank onto a wooden chair. "Oh, when my sister discovers I'm missing, she'll be furious."

Furious? Not worried?

Seizing the opportunity, he righted her chair's partner—though they matched only in being equally rickety—and seated himself near her. "You are traveling with your sister? How did you come to be separated?"

"We—my sister, her husband, and I—are bound for Windermere. Their wedding trip. There are two coaches in our party, and I believe the occupants of each must have thought me safely aboard the other. But I had—" She leaped up again, fingering the leather-bound book.

Dutifully, he got to his feet, as good manners dictated. He had not been away from polite society long enough to forget everything he'd learned. "I'm sure she will be too relieved to discover you are safe to upbraid you."

The candle's flickering light painted her face with shadow. Was she amused? Skeptical? "It's quite clear, sir, that you do not know my sister."

"No. I do not believe I have that pleasure."

She laughed, a rather wry sound, and sat down again. So did he. A moment later, she was up, trying to peer through the narrow crack around the shutters. "How long will it take for them to reach Windermere?"

"They were driving into the storm," he answered as he rose. "Several hours, perhaps, for although it's not a great distance, fifteen miles or so, the roads in that direction are prone to flooding." She turned from the window and a wrinkle of concern darted across her brow. "I expect they stopped somewhere along the way to wait out the rain," he added, trying to reassure her.

"Oh." Once more, she sank onto a chair. This time, he remained on his feet—wisely, it turned out, for she soon resumed her erratic wandering. "But then, mightn't they have returned to that village a few miles back, expecting to find me? I have to go."

"Absolutely not."

The commanding note brought her to an abrupt halt. Her mouth popped open, preparing to issue an argument.

"I will personally see you safely reunited with your sister as soon as possible, Miss Burke." Already, he feared he would regret making such a promise. "In turn, you will not put yourself at unnecessary risk."

Her parted lips pressed themselves into a thin line, and she sat, nearly toppling the chair with the force of her frustration.

This time, she stayed seated long enough that he began to think of returning to his own chair. Hardly had his knees bent, however, when she uncrossed her arms and laid one hand on the edge of her seat to rise. His awkward position—caught between sitting and standing—must have caught her attention, for she waved him down with her free hand, the one not clutching her book.

"I know it's the custom for a gentleman to stand when a lady does, but you'll do yourself an injury if you try to keep up with me." Three of her quick steps put the breadth of the deal table between them. The candle lit her face, revealing a scattering of freckles. "I've never been noted for my ladylike behavior, if you hadn't already guessed. So why should you worry about acting the gentleman? Not that I doubt you *are* a gentleman, Mr. Laurens," she added hastily, looking him up and down where he stood. Color infused her cheeks. "And I certainly hope you will not take my thoughtless remark as a license to—well—"

"Miss Burke." He stepped into the river of words, hoping to divert their course. "You may rest assured, I *am* a gentleman. You're far safer in here than you would be on the other side of that door."

Her nod of acknowledgment was quick, a trifle jerky, and he realized she was trembling. Now that the heat of the blush had left her face, he could see more clearly the bluish cast of her lips. "Come," he said, moving both chairs closer to the table, closer to the meager warmth offered by the candle. "Take off that soaked pelisse."

That order sent another flare of uncertainty through her eyes. But after a moment, she laid her book on the table and attempted to comply, though her fingers shook. The dress beneath was nearly as wet and clung provocatively to her curves. He took the sodden pelisse from her hands and quickly turned away. On a rusty hook near the door hung his greatcoat. After making a simple exchange of wet garment for dry, he returned to her side.

Once enveloped by his greatcoat's length and breadth, she allowed herself to be guided to a chair. "I'm afraid I dare not build a fire," he explained as he took the place across from her. "The chimney looks on the verge of collapse." Indeed, some of its uppermost stones had tumbled down through the flue into the firebox. They lay glistening in the candlelight as rain trickled over them and damp air seeped into the room.

The candle gave at least the illusion of heat, though he knew, and she must too, that it would not last until dawn. It was only September. They were in no danger of freezing to death. But it promised to be a miserable night.

"You should try to get some rest," he urged.

For once, she did not argue. Laying one arm on the tabletop, she used it to pillow her head. With one finger of the other hand, she traced the tooled leather binding of her book. "Thank y-y-you," she stuttered through another shiver masked as a yawn. "It has been a tiring day."

"Yes," he agreed automatically.

Except he wasn't tired. He'd ridden a good distance since morning, it was true, but today's exertion was nothing to what he had known in recent years. But if it wasn't fatigue that had prompted him to take shelter when the storm clouds rose, then what was it? Major Lord Tristan Laurens would have spurred his horse to a gallop, outrun those clouds, and made it home before nightfall, no matter how tired.

Raynham, on the other hand, was not so eager to reach Hawesdale Chase.

Crossing his legs at the ankle, he leaned back in his chair and prepared to pass an uncomfortable few hours. Rain continued to fall steadily, though the thunder now rolled farther off. Erica's restive hand at last fell still, but even in her sleep, she still guarded her book. It made him wonder what was inside. Already the candle's heat had begun to dry her hair, transforming its tangled waves from rusty brown to polished copper. He had no notion of what had become of her bonnet, or even if she had been wearing one at all. She had no gloves, either, and her nails were short and ragged. *I've never been noted for my ladylike behavior,* she had told him, with only the merest hint of chagrin. He did not envy the sister who had been charged with her keeping.

Yet he could not truthfully say he was sorry for an excuse to stay put a few hours more.

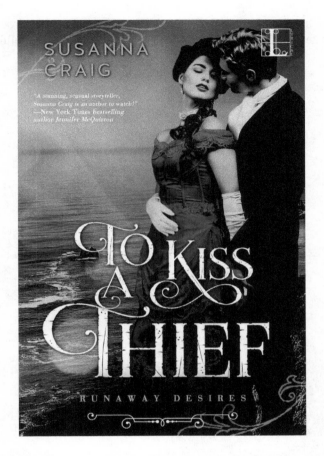

In this captivating new series set in Georgian England, a disgraced woman hides from her marriage—for better or worse...

Sarah Pevensey had hoped her arranged marriage to St. John Sutliffe, Viscount Fairfax, could become something more. But almost before it began, it ended in a scandal that shocked London society. Accused of being a jewel thief, Sarah fled to a small fishing village to rebuild her life.

The last time St. John saw his new wife, she was nestled in the lap of a soldier, disheveled, and no longer in possession of his family's heirloom sapphire necklace. Now, three years later, he has located Sarah and is determined she pay for her crimes. But the woman he finds is far from what he expected. Humble and hardworking, Sarah has nothing to hide from her husband—or so it appears. Yet as he attempts to woo her to uncover her secrets, St. John soon realizes that if he's not careful, she'll steal his heart...

Susanna Craig's dazzling series set in Georgian England sails to the Caribbean—where a willful young woman and a worldly man do their best to run every which way but towards each other...

After her beloved father dies, Tempest Holderin wants nothing more than to fulfill his wish to free the slaves on their Antiguan sugar plantation. But the now wealthy woman finds herself pursued by a pack of unsavory suitors with other plans for her inheritance. To keep her from danger, her dearest friend arranges a most unconventional solution: have Tempest kidnapped and taken to safety.

Captain Andrew Corrvan has an unseemly reputation as a ruthless, money-hungry blackguard—but those on his ship know differently. He is driven by only one thing: the quest to avenge his father's death on the high seas. Until he agrees to abduct a headstrong heiress...

If traveling for weeks—without a chaperone—isn't enough to ruin Tempest, the desire she feels for her dark and dangerously attractive captor will do the rest. The storm brewing between them will only gather strength when they reach England, where past and present perils threaten to tear them apart—even more so than their own stubborn hearts...

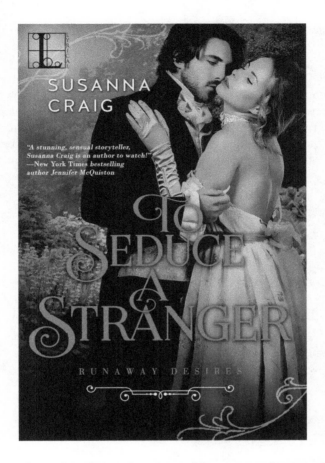

Desire waylays the plans of a man with a mysterious past and a woman with an uncertain future, in Susanna Craig's unforgettable series set in Georgian England.

After her much older husband dies—leaving her his fortune—Charlotte Blakemore finds herself at the mercy of her stepson, who vows to contest the will and destroy her life. With nowhere to turn and no one to help her, she embarks on an elaborate ruse—only to find herself stranded on the way to London…

More than twenty years in the West Indies have hardened Edward Cary, but not enough to abandon a helpless woman at a roadside inn—especially one as disarmingly beautiful as Charlotte. He takes her with him to the

Gloucestershire estate he is determined to restore, though he is suspicious of every word that falls from her distractingly lush lips.

As far as Charlotte knows, Edward is nothing more than a steward, and there's no reason to reveal his noble birth until he can right his father's wrongs. Acting as husband and wife will keep people in the village from asking questions that neither Charlotte nor Edward are willing to answer. But the game they're each determined to play has rules that beg to be broken, when the passion between them threatens to uncover the truth— for better or worse...

About the Author

A love affair with historical romances led **SUSANNA CRAIG** to a degree (okay, three degrees) in literature and a career as an English professor. When she's not teaching or writing academic essays about Jane Austen and her contemporaries, she enjoys putting her fascination with words and knowledge of the period to better use: writing Regency-era romances she hopes readers will find both smart and sexy. She makes her home among the rolling hills of Kentucky horse country, along with her historian husband, their unstoppable little girl, and a genuinely grumpy cat. Visit her at www.susannacraig.com.